undying thirst

CRIMSON COVEN
BOOK 2

ALLIE SANTOS

*To my readers, I appreciate every single one of you . . . and thank
you for being as vampire-obsessed as I am.*

a note from allie

I know you might hate me a little by the end of this book, but the finale will be worth it, I swear! Catalina will reach her vampily ever after and have tons of sex while she's at it.

Love,
Allie 🖤

content warnings

Murder Attempts on MFC, Arson, Violence, Mention of Past Rape, Murder (on page), Descriptive Sex, Foul Language, Descriptive Murder Scenes, Forceful Sex Scenes, Exhibitionism, Voyeurism

Please be advised that the following trigger and content warnings contain spoilers for the story and plot of the novel.

UNDYING THIRST is a Why-Choose Paranormal Romance. Please be advised that Undying Thirst contains adult content. The main characters partake in rough, bloody sex. Including period sex. There are no romantic male-male relationships, but there are instances during sexual situations where males will touch. They only love/crave their heroine.

Disclaimer: Vampires in this world do not think like humans, although some may try. They are instinctual, possessive, and lustful. The main male characters will own the female main character through whatever means possible.

Undying Thirst is set in a mythical world and all contents are purely fiction.

ONE

ren

JAX POUNDED his fist into the door frame. Over and over again until the wall ruptured, his shoulders moving up and down in hard bursts.

I tilted my head, watching him. He wasn't emotional. Usually he said some dramatic bitter-infused comments and stalked off to steep in his own discontent.

This new rage-filled version of him would have impressed me more if the wobbling of Catalina's lip would leave my thoughts. The image caused an uncomfortable pinch in my chest that I attributed to sharing my blood with her.

Asher stared blankly down at the urn that'd been set on the ground, his expression tight. Surprisingly, he wasn't running his mouth as usual.

The front door creaked as it swung open. Asher's attention lifted, eyes wide and hopeful until he saw Tobias enter with his brows furrowed.

"What's happened?"

His attention dropped to the urn and his lips tightened.

"Why is that out here?" Tobias's gaze thinned. Not only

were Imogen's ashes in there, but it also contained a jewel many vampires had literally killed for. An ancient artifact we'd never let out of our sight.

"Catalina tried leaving with it and Jax stopped her." Asher's voice was hollow. It was silent other than the ticking from the grandfather clock at the base of the stairs.

"Did Calliope threaten her?"

Asher studied Tobias. I'd been gone for what felt like only a blink of an eye, and yet my Coven mates had changed. My lips thinned—the reason was somewhat clear. She had a sweetly rounded ass, too tempting for her own human good.

"Asher kicked her out," I offered since I was helpful that way. Not at all because I wanted Tobias's tight restraint to rupture. The madness was there, right below the surface. As the oldest, he needed to exert the strictest restraint when it came to our baser instincts, and it was fun watching him lose it. He was closer in age to me than the other two. The smug bastard irritated me, thinking he did something by avoiding "sin."

"How could you do that?" Tobias said sharply. Such anger. A smile played along my lips.

Tobias behaved . . . as if he cared. What had happened in the month I was gone?

"I told her to leave so I could figure out what happened. Jax was scaring her," Asher snapped, fangs flashing. His irises turned red for a split second.

"There's nothing to figure out," Jax hissed. "Calliope must have sent her. She's been a plant this entire time."

"There must be an explanation."

Jax whirled and backhanded his twin.

"Snap out of the hold her pussy has on you, Asher."

Asher calmly spat blood on the floor, rolling his jaw with a smirk. In a sudden burst of motion, he kicked his foot out, slamming it into Jax's stomach.

I burst into laughter—they never fought. That little human had created the chaos I delighted in.

"Calliope wanted us to give her the ring in exchange for Ren." This was news to me. I clenched my teeth. Sneaky bitch would answer to me later. She took my patience with her too far.

Asher stiffened, turning to Tobias at his declaration. "Figure yourselves out. I will check on her," he added.

"You're not going near the human," I said, pushing off the wall.

There was only one option: she had to die. If there were an option to turn her, I would have considered it, if only to watch her create more havoc between the twins. But only about twenty percent of females survived the transition, and with the vampire illness, all that would become of turning her—if she didn't die—was a blood-mad vampire.

Tobias watched me, still and ready to strike.

I raised an eyebrow.

There was something wrong with that human, and I would find out what it was before snuffing her life out. She belonged to me since she had my blood in her, and the fucking priest wasn't taking her from me. I would have offered him the scraps, but there would be nothing left once I was done with her.

Tobias started for the door—ignoring me. That had never happened. Tobias was levelheaded and willing to listen and discuss; he'd never turned his back to me. I hissed. He wasn't getting near her.

I rammed into him, sending him into the wall opposite from the living room entrance. He caused a Tobias-shaped hole.

He pushed off the wall and calmly dusted the plaster bits from the front of his shirt. In a burst of motion, he charged, slamming his shoulder into my midsection. I slid across the rug, crashing into the settee. Wood cracked, and the sound echoed off the walls. I grinned through the pain, letting it course through me.

If the mere mention of the human wrought this havoc, keeping her around a little longer would be fun.

After she'd sunk her blunt teeth into my neck, I shouldn't have been surprised she had little tricks she'd used to draw in the others . . .

"Come back to our conversation, Ren," Tobias spat, braced against the wall with the large hole.

"Her taste . . ." I hummed. "She was made for being drained." Her blood reached through the foggy veil coating my human memories and brought forth the taste of sweets from my childhood. Flavors I'd forgotten about. Her taste coated my tongue, and her blood satisfied my cravings and calmed the violent hunger that had dogged my entire existence as a vampire.

She was so fucking delicious my mouth watered at the thought of her.

I refused to be bound to a woman again, but I wanted to play with her and bleed her until I was satisfied.

My cock stirred. Very interesting. I'd never once been remotely tempted to fuck a human.

"You will not harm her."

I slowly nodded.

"Yet." I grinned, stretching my neck side to side. "The human is mine to find," I repeated.

"Hubris is a sin, Ren." Tobias sneered, his usually unruffled appearance a disarray.

"Shove your self-righteousness up your ass, Tobias."

He ran his tongue over his bleeding lip. "I won't go easy on you." His irises flickered red.

We were fighting for the long haul. Long overdue.

A smirk lifted my lips, and I met him mid-run. We crashed together with a resounding thud.

TWO

catalina

INCESSANT, rhythmic beeping infiltrated my ears and burrowed into my mind.

I clawed back to consciousness and sucked in labored breaths. Something tugged at my philtrum. I scrunched my nose, triggering a coughing fit, and my eyes watered. I couldn't breathe, but this time it wasn't because of my lungs—a mask covered my nose and mouth. I smacked at the plastic and yanked it off. The band popped off from behind my ear.

A stabbing pain struck through my side and raced down my leg to my knee. I whimpered, struggling to catch my breath. Everything burned. But on the bright side, I wasn't dead if it hurt this bad.

The flip book of the last few moments before I blacked out poured into my thoughts. The vampire coming at me, the car hitting me—it whirled in my brain and a sour taste coated my tongue. I attempted to scoot higher on the uncomfortable mattress, but sharp pin pricks of agony coursed down my spine.

I swallowed hard. That evil bastard that held me captive,

feeding on me until I couldn't even move . . . I shivered, nausea rising.

Had it been him? Had he found me?

Death should have swallowed me whole.

I slumped, panting and weak. An empty bed sat a few feet from mine, the white bed sheets neatly wrapped around the thin mattress. Linoleum floors, pale walls, and the television mounted on the wall across from me all pointed to a basic hospital room. The scent of antiseptic filled my nostrils.

My legs rested at an incline; the left one wrapped up in a cast all the way to my knee. The small of my back pinched uncomfortably. I needed to stretch out, but every twitch sent pain to my ankle and my right wrist, which was also in a cast and lay in a sling close to my chest. Using my good hand, I braced myself and attempted to scoot higher on the bed. I didn't budge.

Wait, there had to be a button to adjust the bed. Just needed to find where it—

The door creaked. The nurse was just in time . . .

"Cat." Ren's voice sent chills up my spine. Then he was in my face, grinning down at me as he bared his teeth.

I screamed and jerked back. Ignoring the agony spiking to my injuries, I dragged myself back, cringing away from him. His palm settled over my mouth, cutting me off. Ren lowered his head—long, smokey eyelashes rimming chocolate-colored eyes. His eyes held no emotion of any kind, akin to a serial killer. A ball of fear jammed my esophagus, making it difficult to breathe.

"You say or try anything, I will kill her in front of you. And it will not be a peaceful death."

I whimpered, nodding frantically with his hand over my

mouth. The door creaked and he let me go in a smooth motion, crossing his bulging arms.

"Hi hun, glad to see you're awake." She strode over to the side of the bed and checked the monitors.

"How long have I been out?" I croaked with my abused voice. Probably from the screaming.

"You slept for roughly eighteen hours." She clicked her tongue as she studied the screen. "Your husband showed up a few hours ago. Just in the nick of time before visiting hours ended. He hasn't left your side since." Husband. Ha. Ha.

"Oh," I mumbled, eyeing Ren. He looked much too calm for my peace of mind—like a snake before it struck. "How long will I be here for?"

"You best prepare to hang out with us for a while," she said, sympathy coating her voice. "The cops wanted to talk with you about whether you saw the person involved in the hit and run." She clicked her tongue disapprovingly. "If a passerby hadn't called for help, you could have bled out in the middle of the intersection."

I heard the words and I understood them, but I still felt like I was floating outside of my body. The bright lights . . . the impact . . . excruciating pain, then nothing.

"I'll let them know you're awake when they—"

Ren straightened, arms dropping to his side.

"No."

I stiffened, my stomach dropping.

The nurse frowned and looked up from her computer to Ren standing before her. He'd moved impossibly fast. She visibly startled, but quickly collected herself.

"She will be discharged tonight," Ren announced.

"It's the middle of the night—" His finger went up and I shut up.

Lovely. Bitterness spread through my chest, mingling with defeat.

"Do whatever you have to, but destroy the record of Catalina Herrera," he continued, his tone remaining simultaneously soft and demanding. I gritted my teeth; there was nothing I could do. Helplessness gnawed on my insides. "Now."

The nurse stiffly strode toward the door like a puppet. I dropped my head forward. I could feel his gaze on me.

"Up, human, we have to get back before sunrise."

Why was he so cheerful? I gritted my teeth, wanting nothing more than to cuss at him, but I had a feeling he'd just get off on it. Gingerly scooching to the edge of the bed, I slipped my good hand under my thigh and braced to lift it off the mattress. My leg hung off the edge, the weight of the cast shooting agony into my bones. I hissed out a breath to hide the whimper.

The room spun so I focused on my surroundings to ground myself. I sat on an abrasive bed sheet, the nightstand held a large plastic container with water, and . . . my phone rested on the side stand, the screen shattered.

"If you don't keep up, I'll get bored, and when I get bored, I start killing," Ren announced matter-of-factly with a slight shrug.

After sliding the broken phone into my pajama pocket, I plucked the single crutch leaning against the wall and dragged myself after Ren. Nausea twisted my stomach. Everything hurt so badly, and the pain increased with each beat of my heart. Whatever drugs I'd been given were likely leaving my system and now I felt like nails were being hammered into every inch of my body. The crutch creaked with my quick step and hop. The smooth material of my pjs rubbed between my thighs.

Ren's stride was much too long. Was he doing it on purpose? A woman rounded the corner, attention fastening on him. His rumbling voice echoed to me, but it was too low for me to make out the words. The woman straightened and continued walking past me, a stiff expression fixed on her features. Her appearance offered me a reprieve in the sense that I'd managed to catch up, or to at least not be fifteen feet behind him.

"Please, just let me leave. I won't tell anyone about your existence." I huffed between words, gritting my teeth at the creak of my limb's protesting movement. He suddenly stopped and my forehead smacked right into the middle of his back. I hissed out a breath, wincing from the impact.

His neck bent and the full weight of his dark, almost black eyes seemed to spear into my chest. With my next breath, he was in my face.

I gasped, jerking back.

His finger hooked into the collar of my shirt, stopping my tip backwards.

"The stupidity of humanity will never cease to amaze me." I audibly swallowed. The corner of his lips slowly lifted like the Cheshire cat. "I would have already killed you if you had not . . . intrigued me. So instead of whining, you should be thanking me."

He let my clothes go, and fortunately, I'd already caught my balance. I reigned in my flight instinct, since it was bound to trigger my asthma. I inhaled sharply, taking as much oxygen into my chest as possible. Even if I did run, I wouldn't get far.

The dull clicking of my crutch hitting the tile mingled with my puffing breaths.

Ren moved with such ease; it looked like he was almost floating. The top of his head almost reached the high ceilings. I had been so foolish; what had I been thinking trusting fucking vampires? I ground my teeth, sucking in the wracking sob urging to break free. Affection wasn't something I even thought I wanted. I just wanted to survive, but the possibility of experiencing the sweet gestures—of relaxing in someone's presence—had been too tempting, and I'd lowered my guard.

But not having to worry about anything wasn't a privilege I could afford.

"Are you going to kill me? Will you?" I sucked in a lungful of oxygen, and it sent jagged agony into my ribs.

"Not yet."

His stride didn't shift. He hooked his arms behind his head and stretched. Such a laid-back air to him while he'd talked about my death.

If this was the end of me, everything was settled for Peter in my will. I'd prepared for my death since I'd escaped the vampire that almost murdered me. My lawyer had a string of instructions to keep him in boarding school abroad and then provide him all the information to my accounts.

The only other person who would reach out to me was my agent because she expected my draft submission.

Other than that, no one would question my disappearance or death. Peter was all I had.

Another thrum of hurt travelled through my chest. I really meant nothing to Asher and Jax. I'd thought it was different between us. Jax had softened toward me—I could have sworn it, but he proved me wrong.

A silent sob wracked my shoulders, and I pressed my lips together to stifle it, keeping my head down as I struggled to keep up with Ren's wide stride. He stayed a few feet in front of me, compelling any human we crossed.

The low hum of music swelled.

Each step I took not only throbbed through my entire body, but it also enhanced the agony pulsing through my heart.

I'd been such an idiot.

Caring about vampires turned out to be my downfall, and I hated myself for being so weak.

I was nowhere near special to Jax. My eyes dropped to my clenched hand. The vampires next door shouldn't have this hold on me.

They'd shown their true colors.

Calliope had done me a favor by forcing me to steal the urn. Even though I wasn't going to go through with it—God, I hadn't even known what it was, I'd just been lashed with accusations and hateful looks. They didn't bother hearing me out.

I clenched and unclenched my teeth. The shard of pain that traveled up my arm reached my elbow and I winced. This was a lesson I never should have had to learn, because I never should have allowed myself to weaken to the vampires.

A sad, heart-breaking lesson. They would never have valued a weak, pathetic, useless human. I exhaled slowly.

Jax was right. Who was I kidding?

Finally, the glass panes framing the front door came into view. A few more steps and I'd be exiting my last semblance of safety, but even that was an illusion. Humans could do nothing to them and just as Ren had threatened me with the nurse, he'd kill any other person that tried to get involved. I couldn't have that on my conscience, so I would meekly follow.

A cool breeze billowed in and flittered my hair around my face.

Ren gripped the back of my neck and guided me toward the vehicle parked along the curb. I hobbled toward it as fast as humanly possible, unwilling to trigger Ren into lashing out.

"In," Ren ordered, taking the crutch from my hand.

Grunting, I opened the back door and dropped on the edge of the cushion then awkwardly dragged my leg cast in after me. Ren handed me my crutch and slammed the door shut, cutting off the chirping crickets.

THREE

catalina

REN MADE it back to Crimson Manor just before sunset. I tapped my fingers on the leather seats, giving it a few more seconds. I wanted as much distance between us as possible, but I also couldn't wait too long.

He was so sure I'd wait like a good human.

After tossing his order at me, he'd slipped out of the car and loped up the long cement stairs. From this vantage, I could see nothing more than the vines weaving through the wrought iron gates. Crows perched atop the metal bars embedded into the brick columns, twisting and turning their necks eerily.

As quietly as possible, I popped the door open. The light came on in the luxury vehicle. I needed to get inside my house before he caught me. With my heart in my throat, I swung my legs onto the embankment and hoisted myself up with the crutch.

Hobbling up my drive, I swept my gaze over the expanse of the vampire's manor. A faint orange light reflected from the highest window. I counted. It was the floor I hadn't been on yet.

I wouldn't invite them in. I would wait them out until the

sun rose, then I'd make my escape. After all, they had to go for cover soon. I peered at the sky. The stars were already beginning to disappear.

Could I make it? I hastened up the porch, huffing and puffing through the pain. God, I was so close. Each time the heavy cast scraped against the cement; my shoulders hiked. Almost on my porch. For the first time tonight, I allowed hope to take hold of my throat.

I'd give myself a half hour to pack everything I could. The boards of my porch creaked under my weight and the quick thump, thump, thump of the crutch pounded into the wood. Living next to vampires offered me security to the point that I never locked my door. And for a split second, I was grateful for my naïve trust. My hand slipped off the doorknob from how severely I shook, but I managed to get the door open and slammed shut behind me.

I did it.

A breathless laugh escaped my lips. I was inside, safe. Now to wait them out.

Packing was the only goal, because I was out of here as soon as the blessed sun rose. I'd crawl to the bus station if I had to. I gathered one large rolling luggage from the closet beside the front door where I left all the boxes and other packing bags. I didn't have the luxury of taking more with me.

I squeezed the crutch under my armpit to keep it in place as I rolled the luggage closer. Wrapping my palm around the hand grip of the crutch, I stretched two fingers from the same hand to cling to the rolling bag's handle. I awkwardly inched my way down the hall to my bedroom and set it up on the bed. My heart thundered in my chest with the speed of a hummingbird's wing. My laptop was absolutely vital. If I lost that, months of hard work on the manuscript would be down the trash, at least for the drafts I hadn't backed up. As soon as I could, I'd email Peter to let him know he wouldn't hear from me for a while, back up my projects to the cloud, then I'd smash it.

I made my way to the closet and swept my gaze over my collection of clothing. I plucked my favored pieces and placed them on the bed before grabbing a pile of less pricey clothing. I'd roll everything up so I could fit everything possible.

As frivolous as it seemed, I needed my skin care routine to go with me. In the bathroom, I stuffed everything into a little makeup bag. Plucking them from my counter and dropping them in the bag unceremoniously. I didn't have the luxury to wipe them all down and space them out. At the top, I set my microfiber towel and zipped it up. On my way back to the luggage, I grabbed my medication. Especially my inhalers. I hadn't needed to use anything recently because feeding me their blood had offered me some healing perks. I froze with my good arm extended. They gave me their blood, and according to them, that meant they could track me down . . . but the Pale One never found me. And they couldn't compel me. Whatever oddity made me different was likely protecting me from that too.

I would run with that because freezing up wasn't going to do me any good.

I plopped the medicines into the little pouch imbedded in the luggage, then grabbed a long-sleeved shirt to wrap up my computer so it wouldn't bang around inside.

A dull thud vibrated the front door. I gasped, my hands numbing.

Even if it was a vampire, they couldn't come in without invitation. The only one I'd stupidly invited in was Asher . . .

and Jax had somehow gotten in because of some weird twin thing.

But they wouldn't be knocking if it was them. I dragged my bum leg behind me until I reached the door. I pressed my palm to the door's surface and peeked into the peep hole. Wide shoulders and a massive stature. I had to look up, even through the hole, to see Ren's face.

A knot swelled in my throat, and I backed up as slowly as possible.

"I hear you." I froze. "Allow me in," he ordered.

I sank my teeth into my bottom lip. I would wait him out, he was bound to go inside when the sun rose.

"I'll burn you out if I have to," a faint taunting entered his tone. My chest inflated. I hadn't considered that option being a possibility. Stupid. Stupid of me.

The door vibrated again and again until a jagged line appeared in the middle of the wood. I flinched until my back was flush against the wall. "I told you to wait in the car, little human. You're really fucking testing me."

"Leave me alone," I shouted, the words bursting from my soul.

Silence. I drooped against the wall, panting.

"Suit yourself."

I should have run sooner. I should have—enough. I couldn't turn back time or change things. Screwing my head on straight now was vital if I wanted to survive.

A tickle entered my nose and I sneezed. Flames suddenly exploded to life from my kitchen and my shoulder slammed into the door. I couldn't tear my eyes away from the flickering fire crawling up the walls. None of this made sense. I shook my head in disbelief. Why was this happening?

Smoke formed in the direction of my bedroom.

My things! I limped down the hall, the rug I'd placed to hide the hole flipping in my haste. I couldn't lose everything I worked so hard to collect. I gritted my teeth through the sharp pain in my limbs. Even the sway of my torso caused my arm to tighten uncomfortably. Tears welled in my eyes and upon my next inhale, I sucked in thick smoke which sent me into a coughing fit.

I froze at the threshold of my bedroom. Wood creaked, and a beam splintered on the floor. Embers erupted from the rupture.

"Catalina," a muffled shout reached through the fog in my brain. I took another step forward, gaze fastened on the opened luggage scattered across the ground. "Stop." The order didn't sway me from stepping into the room flickering with red flames. Smoke crawled up the walls, coating the ceiling as it snaked its way up in tendrils.

Fingers dug into my arm, and I fought against the stiff hold. My back slammed into a chest and arms banded around my waist.

"No," I screamed. "Let me go."

"Stop fighting me, Pet," Asher grunted in my ear.

A vampire. My breath choked up in my lungs and my fight turned up a notch. Flames coated the ceiling and crept much too close.

Binx might be under my bed! He liked to hide . . .

"My cat!" I cried out and dug my good hand into the door frame.

"Let go, Catalina," he hissed.

"No. You let me go," I croaked, gripping on for dear life even though the tug flared pain throughout every inch on my body. Spots danced in my sight and my chest became excruciatingly tight.

If I passed out, it was over—my cat would go up in flames. My things. Everything I'd collected through the years would be incinerated. His arms banded around my stomach and I lost my grip on the door frame. A cry took the last of my oxygen and the world blurred into nothing.

FOUR

catalina

A BURNT SCENT seared the insides of my nose. Everything was on fire!

Flames licked my arm . . . Gasping, I shot up. A nail hammered into my ankle and I screamed. Panting, I palmed my broken leg. Moving was agonizing. A drilling agony, deep and relentless.

The pain medication was for sure out of my system.

"Take care, little human," a sinister voice echoed off the walls.

A chill traveled up my spine. I picked up and held a pillow to my chest with my good arm. Poor defense against vampires, but clutching it brought me comfort.

A lamp lit up the bedroom. Red silk bed sheets bunched under me, and gold glinted off the fixtures embedded into the wall. No, no, I couldn't be back—a chestnut wardrobe loomed against the furthest wall near the door, confirming that it was Asher's bedroom.

"Tell me about your dealings with Calliope." Ren's crossed arms bulged. His cool gaze flickered with avarice, and he pushed his shoulder off the wall. This creature walking toward me had burned my house to force me out.

Yet, all I wanted to do was rub my nose against his skin to breathe him in. He reached the end of the bed, and I helplessly looked around. The metal shutters were raised to expose the night. Before the fire, it'd been close to morning, so I clearly slept through the day.

He suddenly appeared next to the bed, looming over me with the corners of his mouth tilted up and his teeth showing. It was less a grin and more a baring of his teeth.

I flinched.

My gaze bounced to the door—to freedom.

"Running will land you another injury."

I tore my gaze away from the exit. I could only see the corner of the doorframe since his wide, massive shoulders blocked most of it.

My heartbeat drummed in my ears. I was too high up and unless I wanted to snap my neck upon landing, I could see no way out—alive. I struggled to swallow, my rib cage aching with each inhale. Ren wobbled in my vision, his broad, strong features blurring. I gritted my teeth and focused. On his strong nose with a shorter bridge, the stiff set of his lips, and the tan hue of his skin, a shade lighter than mine—attractive and wild eyes. I fisted the silk sheets with my good hand, focusing on relaxing the tension wracking my limbs. It made everything feel worse than it was.

Unlike when I first arrived to this God forsaken town, I'd managed not to have an asthmatic attack from merely being in the presence of a vampire.

Some would say that was a positive that came out of all of it, but I was not 'some'. I bit the inside of my cheek hard enough that I tasted blood.

My heartbeat calmed a notch. Enough so my chest didn't burn.

"What is it about you?" Ren loomed closer, too close, his face hovering inches from mine.

I jerked back and the movement agonizingly tugged at my injuries. I gasped.

"You've caused quite the stir. Is it just because of your," he paused and his tongue flicked out to swipe across his lower lip, "succulent taste?"

"I don't know what you're talking about," I croaked.

He gripped my chin, stealing the precious control I'd managed to wrangle on my heart.

"You're not too bad on the eyes. You have nice, perky breasts that'd look delightful painted with my cum." I felt like a horse being sized up. "If I were into fucking humans, you would make the list." His white fangs flashed. "That is, of course, before draining you dry."

Tears welled in my eyes. He stared at the single one that escaped and rolled down my face and his pupils dilated.

"Yes," he breathed against my cheek. "Cry, weak human. That's all you can do."

I gritted my teeth, trying to control my rampant emotions. Not crying in front of them was non-negotiable. Nor would I beg. I wouldn't be brought down before my death; I would keep that part of myself from their evil grip. With everything in me, I suppressed the urge to sob and glared at him.

His eyes narrowed. Since his dark eyelashes slanted down, it created a divot between them. His skin was so smooth, it seemed pore-less. Unfair vampire perks.

I had multiple skin care routines to attain skin like that and had never achieved that level of flawlessness without make-up.

He released my chin with a harsh shove.

The back of my head smacked into the headboard. I cried out as a dull thud radiated down to my arm.

The door crashed open and Tobias stormed inside, his coat fluttering behind him. Soot stained his clothes.

"What did you do to her?" he hissed.

Ren lifted his hands and backed up.

Then Tobias was in my space. Moving too fast. They all moved much too fast.

I sucked in a breath.

"I've been searching for you," Tobias breathed as he clasped my face with such care—opposite to Ren's grip.

Tobias searched for me? Why? I didn't understand any of this.

A knot swelled in my throat with so much emotion it became lodged. I dropped my eyes, not wanting to face his piercing gray ones. His sweet breath was tinged with orange. His voice, his scent, his touch reached inside me and prodded me to soften.

Seams of his frayed collar split in two. Brown splatters stained the white shirt. Dried blood.

"Catalina?" he murmured, his voice lilting with hints of his English accent.

A slight chuckle dragged my attention to Ren.

What did he find so funny?

I gritted my teeth.

Tobias and Ren were opposites. The flip of a coin. One was coldly evil and the other attempted a semblance of morals.

Or so I thought, until he lied to me. I shouldn't let my

guard down. He'd fooled me. No, I fooled myself. They were vampires, I let myself get carried away from the start. I had no one to blame but myself.

Locking my jaw, I glared at Tobias.

"You lied to me about blood-whores." It was a non-issue, since I knew I couldn't be one if the Pale One never made me one, but I'd trusted the lies he told.

The time frame to become a blood-whore was significantly shorter than the reality. Asher planned for me to be his blood-whore all along, and Tobias went along with it. They never saw me as a person, I was just a play thing.

Something to manipulate.

And Tobias was the one they all believed to have a 'moral compass'. The fact remained that even if they were born human, vampires became twisted and inhuman.

Nothing but their pleasure mattered to them.

Asher practically told me his intentions. He'd had such an apt name for me: Pet.

Well, I should have fucking read the signs.

Tobias's hand slipped off my face, his fingertips gently grazing down my cheeks before lowering to the mattress. He propped his fist on my other side, corralling me within his arms, while not touching me. I backed as flat as I could against the headboard, avoiding even his coat grazing me.

His eyebrows furrowed and if I were being fanciful, I would have said guilt flickered across his features.

"I did lie." He cleared his throat.

He hadn't needed to confirm it, I knew.

"I want to leave." My voice held a huskiness, and it was difficult to swallow. But it was the taste coating my tongue that drove in what caused me to be in this state: smoke from Ren burning my rental down. I didn't want to think about the ramifications. Now I was homeless, I didn't know where my car was, and what would my landlord demand?

I bit the inside of my lip again to snap myself out of it.

I'd stress about that later, if I even had a later.

Tobias's angled jawline flexed and the tips of his mussed brown hair kissed the top of his eyebrows. Enough staring at his confusing, yet perfect features.

"Just get it over with," I croaked. I dragged my glare to Ren hovering behind him like an intimidating wall. He had no right to be that large. None of them did. They towered over me and any other person I'd ever encountered. "Kill me."

Tobias straightened as if his spine was pulled by a string.

"What have you said to her?"

Ren's gaze burned a hole in my forehead.

"Don't get your panties in a twist, Priest. I won't kill the human just yet."

"You will not kill her at all. We agreed."

Ren was suddenly in Tobias's face.

I cringed back and stifled my whimper, clutching my arm close to my chest.

"We tied," Ren hissed. "It was an impasse."

"Enough." Asher entered, carrying a tray. "She does not die."

"You should have no say, Youngling," Ren snapped.

"Jaxon is my age," Asher said. "His vote would not count either, and by your logic, Tobias is the oldest, so his vote holds more weight than yours."

Ren stilled eerily. Red flashed in his pupils briefly, but it quickly disappeared.

"The discussion isn't over," he intoned eerily and

disappeared from where he stood. My throat closed up—I would not see him coming when he killed me.

Asher placed the tray on the bedside nightstand. Faint redness smudged beneath his eyes and was easy to see because of his pale skin. His Viking-like stature should have intimidated me, but my body remembered the way he touched me. Stupid, fucking idiotic body.

I clenched my teeth so hard they might break.

His lack of belief in me hurt the most.

Out of all of them . . . I'd weakened for him the most. I believed in him and everything he promised.

My nose burned and I gritted my teeth harder, keeping those tears inside even though it hurt.

"What happened to you?" Asher loomed beside the end of the bed, gaze roving over my body.

I focused on my clenched hand. I'd been clasping it so tight my nails created little dents on my palm.

"Fetch Jax to check her wounds," Tobias ordered.

"She is mine, I will tend to her." Asher set the tray on the nightstand.

"She is not only yours," Tobias hissed.

"I've fucked and fed from her."

Tobias's nostrils flared, his shoulders rising and falling.

"Do not speak of her as if she were a whore."

"Do me a favor and shove your sanctimonious morals up your ass." Asher brushed his hands across his chest as he straightened, smearing some red substance across the silk fabric.

Tobias flashed to Asher. I startled, struggling to make sense of Tobias wrapping his hands around Asher's throat. I couldn't tear my attention off the train wreck happening a few feet away from me. Even though the English vampire was a few inches shorter, and slighter than the Viking, menace emanated from him.

"Do it," Asher smirked.

Tobias's eyes flashed red, but he finally dropped Asher. "Get Jax to heal her." With that he slammed the door behind him.

The thud of the door echoed in the silence.

Asher's gaze settled on me.

His words wouldn't leave my thoughts, nor the look on his face as he ordered me to leave. My lungs squeezed and made it difficult to breathe.

Jax had accused me of stealing and Asher had kicked me out.

Sure from an outside perspective, it was his brother versus me, but I had given him everything, willingly. I'd expected a little more defense on my behalf.

Asher dropped to his knees and his waist hovered by the top of the tall bed.

"What happened, Catalina?" He gingerly touched the top of the cast on my leg and I stiffened.

"Don't touch me," I wheezed, inching back a little more. It sent a shockwave of agony through my limbs. I squeezed the pillow I still held to my chest.

"Don't be stubborn."

I gritted my teeth. Stubborn? How was this stubbornness? It was only self-preservation!

"No," I shouted in his face.

Asher's blue eyes widened and he studied my features.

"Why are you angry?"

I blinked, no way he was serious. It was enough to calm the verging hysterics. His expression didn't waver.

"You lied and . . ." I trailed off, taking a beat to get it

together again. "You didn't believe me." Despite my attempt to keep it in, my voice cracked with emotion at the end.

"Oh." His eyebrow raised. "Nothing came of it. I should have handled the situation differently."

"That's not the point—"

"I do not understand."

Of course he didn't understand, he wasn't human.

"Are you ready to explain your bargain with Calliope? It will help me convince the others to spare your life."

I couldn't believe what I was hearing.

"Are you expecting my thanks?"

Both of his eyebrows raised this time.

"You do not understand, traitors are not tolerated, but I will speak on your behalf." He drove the metaphorical stake deeper into my chest.

I didn't have the energy to defend myself. He still thought I had tried stealing the urn with their precious Imogen's ashes in it. He wasn't asking me if I did, he had no doubt I had.

I would stick to my written boyfriends from here on out. Only the characters I wrote never failed me. I'd also take pleasure in creating one named Asher and killing him in the most painful way possible.

"Catalina. You are mine. I will protect you."

"I will never be yours," I spat.

His sharp incisors elongated. In a movement so quick it made my head spin, his hands cupped beneath my thighs and he pulled me to the end of the mattress. The pillow slipped out of my grasp, falling off the side of the bed. My thighs spread and a pinch twinged the leg with the cast.

"Calm yourself, Pet," he murmured, with the corner of his

lips curled up seductively. His eyelids lowered, framing his eyes with those long dark blonde lashes.

Pet.

His palm dragged down my side in a gentle rub. His waistband pressed between my legs, widening my thighs.

Was he getting frisky with me?

He grazed his nose against my cheek and down to my neck, inhaling deeply as he hovered over my pounding pulse.

Instinct bade me to clench my legs together. I wanted pressure at the swelling throb. His fangs flashed in my memory, the feel of them sinking into my throat.

I shivered.

I'd let my body get me in this situation in the first place. I turned away from his mouth and hugged my chest as if I could contain my lust within my body.

I would not give in to my desires.

I slammed my good knee into his dick.

Christ! A throb radiated down my knee and to my ankle. Did his stiff cock break my other leg?

He erupted in a string of curses in Swedish.

He rolled to the side, flopping onto the bed. Good to know that the move was just as effective on vampires.

"Don't touch me." I wouldn't be fooled. Fancifulness would lead me nowhere.

Guttural grunts escaped from his mouth and his shoulders twitched.

Waiting to die was my last resort.

catalina

"MY TURN." A hiss reached my ears, then a harsh grip at my neck.

I found myself on my back staring up at the ceiling beams. The grip around my throat squeezed, cutting off oxygen. With my good hand, I clawed at the fingers digging into my throat.

Jax's upside-down features blurred. I couldn't breathe. My eyes felt like they'd pop out of the sockets.

Not too long ago, I'd been stretched out between the twins like this, but they'd been fucking me instead.

"Jaxon," Asher snarled, gripping his wrists, but Jax didn't release me.

Dots blurred my vision. What would he do with my dead body? Peter wouldn't know what happened to me—I would just disappear.

I could feel each beat of my heart.

The skin at the side of my throat burned and darkness crept over my sight. His fingers loosened.

I sucked in a gasping, burning breath. His release of my throat spread numbness along the column of my neck. On the heels of the dullness came painful pricks like pins were being stabbed into my throat.

The front of Asher's body pressed over my body. He'd stretched over me to grab his twin who stood along the length of the bed. He straddled my waist, eyes focused on what would be his mirror image if it weren't for the shorter hair. Their hands hovered over my head and a droplet of my blood dripped onto my cheek. The slow glide of my blood tickled as it traveled toward my ear.

They were too still as they stared at the blood on Jax's fingertips. Fangs exploded from their gums. Jax's eyes flashed red and his head lowered.

Screaming, I hiked my shoulders to protect my neck. It went against the initial instinct to bare my throat.

"You will not bite her," Asher hissed. "Not until you can control your anger. You gave up your claim to me. She is mine."

Jax had a 'claim' to me . . . when did they have this conversation?

"She is a traitor," Jax spat. "We dispose of them. *Hon måste dö.*"

"*Nej.*"

Jax wanted to dispose of me. My pulse bounced erratically. I peeked up at him. His features settled in an angry cast. A muscle ticked on his jaw.

"I will not kill her, but she needs to talk."

I never should have let my curiosity force me to peek at the fucking urn. That's what got me here. I never planned to give it to Calliope, and it was my luck that the temperamental vampire was the one that caught me snooping.

If I'd gone straight to them when I'd arrived, none of this would have happened.

Asher released his grip on Jax and sat back. He braced on his knees so his weight wasn't fully settled on me, but I could feel the press of his thighs.

I flicked my wide eyes to Asher's curled mouth. The earlier threat disappeared from his expression. His white, loose silk shirt fell open, exposing the curve of his muscled torso. As always, he reminded me of a pirate.

Like he should grace the cover of one of those smutty historical books.

Nope, couldn't go down the road of admiring his beauty. That would lead to lust, and I wouldn't give in to him.

Still, the smooth glide of his pierced cock sliding in my pussy couldn't easily be forgotten.

Asher's thighs tensed and his eyebrows wiggled as he stared at me knowingly. He could smell my sudden desire. My cheeks heated and I scowled.

Squeezing my thighs together sent a spike of pain down my broken leg and I gasped.

Asher pursed his lips.

"We can't have you whimpering with every graze." Asher straightened and stared down at me.

"She doesn't deserve the blessings of our blood."

For once, I agreed with Jax. I didn't want anything from any of them.

Asher dropped his gaze to his brother. "I understand your aversion but you were outvoted. She stays."

Jax hissed at his brother, his face set in a scowl and so much anger in his eyes it could have lit me on fire. He glared down at me and I could see in his eyes that he wanted nothing more than to kill me, right here and now. Asher cleared his throat and Jax hissed again.

"Fine, but I'll do it." He brought an arm forward and ripped his teeth into his wrist, holding it out to me. Light reflected off the bright red liquid. Before it reached my lips, I turned my head. It smeared across my cheek.

"Pet, be a good girl."

I clenched my teeth tight to bite back my retort.

"I'll hold her, Jax."

Asher gripped my hair, and his large palm clasped my jaw. I couldn't fight to pull away if I tried. My neck pinched as he forced my head sideways, so that Jax's wrist could reach me.

"Open up."

I glared up at Asher. He settled more of his weight on me. His fingers dug into my cheek. The pressure turned agonizing, but I fought against the force. I managed to hold on until it felt like my jaw would break.

I finally opened my mouth with a cry.

Asher's fingers flexed in my hair.

"No—" My shout was cut off by Jax's skin pressing to my lips.

My lips became wet from blood and the sweet taste exploded on my tongue. I held back my urge to suck down his sweet, familiar taste. Laying there, I glared at them both over his arm.

"Suck," Asher ordered.

I hummed my 'no' against Jax's arm.

Asher sighed, his lips turning down. He plugged my nose.

Not this again. I didn't move my eyes from Asher's. He believed I was sent here to betray them. My heart thumped painfully. Although he hadn't physically hurt me and went as far as to protect me, he didn't believe me innocent. I'd become a true 'Pet' in his eyes.

And that knowledge viced around my chest with thorny vines, opening a new wound.

I could no longer hold my breath—I gasped, and Jax's sweet blood spread on my tongue. A second later, I helplessly swallowed once as I gulped on oxygen.

Asher's lips parted and his eyes became half-lidded. He liked watching me like this, I could tell.

His stiff cock pressed into my belly.

Jax lifted his wrist and as soon as my mouth was free, I spit the pooled blood I managed to collect. Red sprayed across their faces in little droplets and some of it dropped on my face.

"Kill me or leave me alone," I said, panting.

A muscle jumped in Asher's jaw and he swiped his thumb across his cheek. He looked at the smear of blood. The perpetually upturned corner of his lips twitched.

I waited with bated breath. Would he finally end my torment? Adrenaline worked its way through my system. My fight or flight had fully activated.

At this point, they couldn't do any more damage. More than anything, I thanked my distrustful instinct that hadn't allowed me to disclose the fact that I had a brother—my only weakness.

Asher suddenly burst into laughter, his sharp fangs peeking from behind his lips.

I sucked in a breath.

Jax didn't seem to find the humor in the situation like Asher. He hissed and rubbed the back of his hand across his face, sneering angrily.

"Ungrateful whore."

My heart stuttered and tears flooded my eyes. I'd been trying to hold them back this entire time, but his hateful words unraveled me.

I was a whore. I'd given in to their bite when I knew better.

Asher stiffened while I lay limp under him.

"Out," Asher hissed, his weight lifting off me. They volleyed insults back and forth in their language.

Swiping at the tears that trickled free, I gulped in breaths, but nothing abated the pressure that settled on my chest.

The door slammed, but I didn't move.

"Catalina." Asher's voice held a gentleness that destroyed the progress I had made with my tears. The bed dipped and his arms slipped under my body. He lifted me with ease, settling me higher on the bed.

I leaned against the headboard, squeezing my eyes shut, counting back from ten. Asher hovered near my face, so close that his nose grazed mine. I jerked back so fast, the back of my head hit wood.

Wincing, I swallowed hard.

He cupped the back of my head gently and pulled me towards him.

"If you drank more, you wouldn't need these." His knuckles rapped against my arm cast.

I winced. It still hurt, but I couldn't deny the insufferable agony had abated slightly.

"What happened to you?"

"You think I betrayed you, so why are you trying to take care of me?"

Asher went quiet and he moved to the edge of the bed. The mattress was clearly good quality because it didn't dip under his massive body. He arranged my legs straight and the movement didn't hurt as much as before.

"I don't know what to believe, Catalina," he murmured. "You admitted that Calliope sent you to us."

I pursed my lips.

"You didn't hear me out." My voice cracked and I paused to clear my throat. "She asked me to bring it to her, but I wouldn't have."

"I want to believe you," he murmured with his gaze unfocused. "Everything would be simple if I could compel you. Then there would be no doubt."

He may as well kill me now if he thought this way.

"I get you have trust issues, but your vote of confidence is really appreciated," I said sarcastically.

"I've seen too much to believe without questioning."

I clamped my lips shut. Even after I explained, he didn't believe me. Sure, it didn't look good that I'd been snooping around, but hadn't I garnered a little consideration?

His fingers wrapped around my good wrist and then something soft tickled my skin. My eyes rounded on the fuzzy cuffs leading to the other side that he held.

"Don't worry, Pet, they're brand new, just for you." He lifted his arm, taking mine with his, pulling as he hooked it around the sturdy headboard bar.

I jerked against it, but the wood wasn't fazed.

My heart pounded in my chest and I jerked again. The edges dug into my wrist.

"Don't," he murmured. "You'll hurt yourself."

But I couldn't stop. I wanted to get out of the tight grip.

The vampire that captured me held me in place, shackling me with his grip and wouldn't let me go. He'd kept me there as his emaciated body lay over mine, cutting off my breathing. While bugs skittered over my skin.

"Shh. Shh." Asher pressed his cheek to mine. His nose grazed my ear and he licked the sides of my neck.

A shiver coasted down my spine. His warm tongue lapped against my throat. I hadn't felt the scratches Jax left until Asher brought attention to them.

"I can relax you," he whispered against my throat.

His arms caged me, and he hovered over my restrained body. I shuddered while my pussy responded to his words and tongue.

My body begged me to give in and open my legs. To have him fuck me and bite me all over.

His head lifted from my throat, mouth smeared with my blood. His head lowered to capture my mouth with his.

I bit his lip and slammed my leg, the one in the cast, up, hitting him right between the legs—again.

Asher dropped to his side like a rock, cupping his dick.

"Don't touch me."

He stood with his shoulders hunched forward, shock widening his eyes and pain furrowing his features.

"Catalina," he chastised, his tone strained.

"Let me go," I ordered.

"I'll return at sunset," he said, backing away with a hitch in his usual glide.

"Asher," I shouted. "Let me go."

My voice bounced off the walls, echoing.

I screamed again, ignoring the agony ripping through my abused throat.

SIX

asher

I'D NEVER BEEN REJECTED for anything, much less a fucking. I braced one hand on the door as Catalina screamed from inside my chambers. Her fury was a sight to behold . . . spitting brown eyes, her face pinched with an adorable scowl . . . I'd been making note of all of that when she'd slammed her knee into my cock. And this time my arousal didn't work in my favor.

I gingerly limped away from her door.

If I'd been human, her kick would have rendered me cock-less. I shivered in horror. I may as well stake myself if that happened.

The remnant throb was beginning to wear off, but I never wanted to be dick-kneed again. I'd rather be staked through my arm.

The waxed wooden stair led to the third-floor landing and split into two directions like the other floors. I turned toward the left-wing living room and unlike the second floor, this one did not have multiple rooms lining it.

I'd lost count of how many 'homes' I'd had—they were interchangeable. Suitable for only one thing.

A bit like women.

Until Catalina. And I was beginning to grow fond of this estate.

The small entrance opened to the ample room we hosted company in. My uneven steps echoed on the wooden floors. Right as I crossed the threshold, glass shattered into pieces. Familiar fragments skid across the floor and toward my loafer. Fuck.

Not the cobalt vase.

"That was a limited edition piece from Versailles," I gritted out between my teeth.

"I know." Jax sneered and without removing his gaze from mine, he stepped on a large piece that settled next to his foot. The crunch reached through my sluggish heart, shattering it.

"You monster." I staggered forward, clasping my forehead. "I need to take a seat." A few more steps had me around the curved sofa in the middle of the rug, with a clear view of Jax where he stood next to the marble column that had hosted my vase.

Jax snorted. Gleeful bastard. I whipped my head toward him.

"Do you know who I had to fuck to get that art?" I'd kill him. I'd kill him this second. I clasped my chest. "I'm going to hyperventilate." Not really a thing for vampires since we hardly even breathed, but it encapsulated how I thought I'd be reacting.

Jaxon lifted an eyebrow.

"Dramatic fuck. Don't act like you didn't enjoy fucking the Rouge Coven leader."

"He reeked," I hissed. For vampires, he was disgustingly unhygienic. Imogen knew of his proclivities and taunted me into a bet to take his prized art. She must have known about his fascination with shoving candle sticks up asses. I'd tired the male out so I could steal it, but the event was not an experience I reveled in remembering.

A piece of China settled near my heel. That lovely piece of art that had made the disgusting endeavor worth it was gone.

"And what exactly did this solve?" I hissed.

"It pissed you off."

I narrowed my eyes at the smirk. There were two of us, but if one of us poofed from existence, then good riddance. I'd be doing the earth a favor ridding it of such a bitter fucker.

I lunged at Jaxon and drove him into the ground. Any harder and his body would have dented the flooring.

Hissing into his face, I wrapped my hands around his throat.

Grinning into his scowling face, I sank my fingers in harder. He slammed his fist into my side. My rib cracked.

Grunting, I squeezed harder, breaking skin with my nails.

"You kill him, then we lose all those he sired," Ren drawled from somewhere behind me.

"I do not care," I hissed and dug my claws into his throat. Blood gushed from the punctures. Jaxon's shape morphed into a cat, slipping from my grip, then just as quickly became a large mountain lion to slice his claws into my thigh, almost hitting my prized cock.

"Watch it!" I shook his blood off my hands. "You'll tear my shirt."

"Is this petty squabbling what you two have been up to in my absence? Such a weak minded—"

"Shut it," I hissed. "You talk about weakness when you burned her house down?"

Ren threw his head back and laughed.

"So we're back to this, eh? Since when do you care about humans?" I walked over to my twin, still in his feline form and wiped my bloodied hands on his fur.

Jax slinked away with a snarl and morphed back. "The fuck?" he snapped, glaring at his sides where my hands had left prints. I returned my attention to Ren.

"Just one human. Mine."

Ren raised his hands. "You've made your ownership clear, but since she's a Pet, you should keep her in the basement."

Any humans we'd kept stayed locked up down there, so they could not escape while we slumbered. Although the bedrooms on the second floor designated for each of us were properly sealed off from the sunlight, a vampire that could burn to a crisp couldn't be too careful.

"Bastien is down there now," I said, simply denying his comment instead of shouting. I also didn't mention that her wrapped in my bedding pleased me.

"What I would give to be your Sire."

I narrowed my eyes at Ren. He'd abuse his influence over me. The sensation had been compared to when vampires used compulsion on humans, except a vampire was aware of the Sire's influence.

Which I knew well since Imogen was my maker. She used to take perverse pleasure in forcing her will on me.

"You," I jerked my chin at my brother, "turn into her cat."

"You're worried about her right now," Jax scoffed and shook his head. "She tried to take Imogen's ring and you want her to have her fucking cat?"

"Turn into a fucking cat," I repeated.

"No."

"Jaxon." I narrowed my eyes.

Catalina needed comfort and she would not accept it from me.

She no longer called my name with her sweet tone. It held an underlying vein of disgust. Nor would she tell me how she got hurt.

"Get it together, Asher," Jax said. "She betrayed us. Stop protecting her so vehemently."

I didn't acknowledge the statement. She betrayed me, and I didn't fucking care.

How had a human wrought me this uncertainty?

It'd been centuries since I was human, and that was the last time I encountered weak emotions like this. I didn't think I would care this much—ever.

"And?"

"Fuck you, brother," Jax snapped in our language and left the room.

Like clockwork, the metal shutters descended, cutting off the windows. Weight settled on my eyelids as it did when dawn approached. Even rubbing my face took effort.

I made no comment to Ren as I passed him to find a bed to fall into. As much as I wanted to curl up with Catalina, I couldn't sleep with her, not while I didn't know her intentions.

Our decision making had never been so compromised. Our unique Coven functioned because we let Imogen make ultimate decisions, or Imogen imposed her will. I could only think of one instance where I'd ever argued, and that was on how to handle Bastien's blood madness.

A slip of a human caused this much conflict.

If it was up to Ren and Jax, Catalina wouldn't have survived the night.

Our laws demanded her death. From the beginning, she should have been handled because she could not be compelled. I couldn't even comfort her with the promise of turning her into a vampire, so she had no choice, she would have to live as my Pet.

And she had better come to terms with it, because she would not die for centuries to come if I had my way.

SEVEN

SCREAMING HADN'T DONE ANYTHING. No

one could hear me outside of their gated mausoleum. Not just because the place was huge, but also because no one lived down this street.

They wouldn't even hear me in their coma-like daylight sleep.

And now I had a sore throat. I jiggled the cuff, tugging at it uselessly.

I wasn't sure how long I'd slept after the effort sobbing had taken. Even if I didn't know the exact time, it had to be close to sunset. If I could go back and not move into the house next door to vampires, I would do anything in my power to do it.

I thumped the back of my head on the head board again.

Everything I owned was gone.

I lifted my knees. My leg no longer hurt with every twitch. Some vampire blood had made its way into my system and healed it enough for me to apply pressure without wanting to tear my hair out from the pain. Pressing my heels into the mattress, I stretched my spine. This position killed my lower back and my cuffed arm pinched with each twitch. My body screamed for release. This was torture, plain and simple.

No-good vampires. I gritted my teeth, glaring up at the ceiling. My eyes burned and it felt like sand coated them.

Asher had to let me go. I'd tried pissing him off enough to kill me, but nothing.

And he continued calling me his Pet. Did he really think I would stay without a fight? If not now, as soon as I had the sliver of a chance, I would bolt. I could never trust him to care for me again. Reality had walloped me good, leaving behind ragged scars.

A low hiss exploded through the room. The metal shutters began to rise.

Vampires equated unreliability and their seductive qualities were a trap. Vampires were made to invite, seduce, then destroy.

These weren't the fictional, caring ones I'd written; they were death, madness, and danger. I re-learned that the hard way.

My original captor, the Pale One, should have been enough to teach me a lesson.

The doorknob wiggled and I clamped my eyes shut as footsteps encroached. I kept agonizingly still. The soft tap of footsteps neared the bed.

"I know you are awake."

A lilting accent caressed my ears: Tobias.

My stomach rumbled with the worst timing.

Tobias chuckled and I couldn't help but tense up. No point in acting asleep, now.

Straightening from my slump, I glared at my lap when all I wanted to do was cry and take off running.

A whoosh of air pushed my hair back. His presence hovered

close enough that I saw the edge of his shoe, but I didn't look up.

I was a bit proud of myself, actually—I hadn't been startled by their speed this time.

"Asher has not fed you?" Tobias' words whipped through the room. I kept my head down, not turning to look at the tray Asher had left at the bedside. I'd eaten exactly zero off it.

Giving my clamped arm a wiggle, it sent spikes to my elbow, and I pressed my lips together to hide my whimper.

Tobias gripped my caught wrist in a gentle hold, and he shielded it as he reached over me with his other hand. The cotton of his sweater brushed my cheek. It took everything in me not to turn my face up and rub my cheek into his hard, muscled torso. My mind wandered to when he'd held me against him, and I'd felt his hard cock pressing into my side.

Thinning my lips into a stiff line, I grappled to bring myself back to reality.

His presence radiated calm and urged me to lean toward him, but I wouldn't fall for the trick again.

The fur around my wrist banded close to my bone. I couldn't help but tense, expecting the worst, even if I didn't know what that would entail. The chain clanged, then ruptured and instantly, I pulled my arm to my chest. The fur around the cuff lessened the dig of metal, but the angle still stung. I rolled my wrist, stretching it in all sorts of ways to release the pull on my tendons.

Tobias straightened, and as he retreated, his hand grazed my head, rustling the strands around my face. My pony tail had fallen into a disarray with hair all over the place. I lifted my trembling hand to smooth it back, but could only do so much with an arm in a sling.

"I will help." He leaned forward with his large hands extended.

"No," I croaked and jerked my head back. I didn't want him touching me. Yanking my loose hairband out of my hair, I finagled it onto my wrist. The mass of hair waterfalled around my shoulders.

His eyes lingered on the mess of locks.

Swinging my cast off the bed and using the momentum, I scooted to the end of the bouncy bed.

Tobias pressed a palm to my shoulder, stilling me on the edge.

He hovered with a few inches between us. I craned my neck to look him in the eyes. Boyishness hinted within his angular features. The tall, leaner vampire looked the youngest and closest to my age even though he was the oldest.

"For someone claiming innocence, you're not doing a good job convincing them you haven't done anything."

My heart slowed and as if it were electrocuted, it bounced to life, pounding faster. I dragged my eyes to his, my eyebrows furrowing close together.

"I keep saying I didn't do anything—you believe I didn't do anything?" I gripped the bottom of his sweater, curling my fingers into the soft cotton.

"No, Love," he murmured. "Your character does not indicate deception. And if you did, you must have had a reason." Sometimes . . . the way he spoke about human behavior and feelings seemed stilted, like he was reciting from something he'd heard.

A knot ballooned in my throat, making it difficult to swallow.

"Then let me go," I choked out.

His cold, gray eyes didn't move from mine.

"That's not how our Coven works."

Sounded like a no without him saying no. The smidge of hope that blossomed, fizzled away. I loosened my fingers on his shirt and dropped my hands in my lap.

"Just say, no." I gritted my teeth.

"I will bring it up again, but our decision must be unanimous and Jaxon and Ren will not be swayed." He crouched and lowered his head since even bent and with me sitting, he was still taller.

He couldn't help.

His fingers gripped mine and I yanked them free. He let me do it, I had no doubt that if he'd fought it, my fingers would have snapped.

Tobias sighed and rose.

"I need to go," I said, hastily tipping my nose toward the bathroom across the room.

I hobbled toward the bathroom, half dragging the leg cast behind me. A small part of me expected him to stop my progress, but he didn't. I shut the door and enclosed myself in the dark. I scrambled to flip the light switch. My pulse calmed with the glare of the light. I slumped against the door.

God, my hair was a mess.

Limping to the sink, I washed my face with one hand, scrubbing at the mascara that flaked beneath my eyes. I hadn't been able to do my skin care routine, and it was messing with my head. The vampires were messing with my self care. Combing my fingers through my wild hair, I managed to untangle the mess until my hair fell around my shoulders and to the middle of my back in a mass of waves. Water dripped and trickled off my fingertips.

Smudges of exhaustion marred beneath my eyes. I hated how tired and beat down I looked.

I scowled at my reflection. Stop, I narrowed my eyes at myself and rubbed my face one last time, then turned to exit.

Tobias replaced my spot on the bed with his ankle over his knee. He roved his gaze over my face and focused on my hair.

"Would you like to stretch your legs?"

Immediate denial came to my tongue but I bit it back.

I flicked my eyes to the bed and then the door. Getting an idea of the exits wasn't a bad idea. If I had the opportunity to escape, I would. After all, I could wait until sunrise to make my attempts.

I'd behave so they didn't lock me up tonight. Then I'd find a way out of here.

I hesitantly nodded.

Tobias moved carefully and with grace. He reminded me of the lull of a calm ocean. And as deceptive as one, too. Underlying lack of control battered along the surface. I could feel it.

He held the door open for me.

A key remained in the doorknob on the outside, and there were no bolts anywhere else. They only kept me in with a locked door. Perfect.

He waved a hand down the hall, the opposite from a wide window at the end. Stars glittered in the sky. That was the only opened window on this floor.

Other than Asher, Bastien, and Tobias's bedroom, I figured the other two had theirs on this level too considering how long it spanned. Fortunately, I could see to the end of the hallway even though it was needlessly long.

I gripped the banister at the top of the second floor. The

large front door was yards away from the base of the wide flight of stairs. If I ran . . . I peeked over my shoulder. Tobias would catch me before I touched the doorknob. Clenching my hand, I took a deep breath and released the banister.

"Where to?" I slowed to match Tobias's relaxed gait. Smiling, he tilted his chin down toward the first floor. Another staircase continued up to the third floor. I hadn't been up there before, but based on the structure from the outside, that was the final level.

The manor stretched tall and wide, and it seemed much more ostentatious since it rested on an incline.

My cast thumped loudly on the wooden staircase, and I stopped at the foyer.

Plaster and stone littered the entrance of the living room. A broken couch lay burst into pieces across the ground, like a tornado had ransacked the home.

I turned back around. Was that a male sized hole in the wall? I caught myself before I asked what happened. None of my business.

"There was a slight disagreement," Tobias murmured. His palm pressed against my spine to guide me toward the kitchen. I shuffled forward, and he prodded again, so I picked up speed until he no longer touched me.

Asher leaned on the kitchen island, elbows propped on top as he stared off with obvious contemplation. He caught sight of me and a smile spread on his lips.

Jax stood near the stove with his hip leaning against the granite as he downed a blood-filled bag. His eyes settled in a half-lidded position. He saw me and pulled it away from his mouth, blood staining his lips and dripping off his chin. Red splattered on the front of his shirt, absorbing into the cotton fibers.

"What is she doing out?" Jax stormed forward and I stumbled until my back slapped against Tobias. His anger bared down at me, the blood painting his lips, and his flashing fangs caused an uptick in my pulse. Flinching, I hugged my chest with my good arm.

"Even Pets get to walk around."

I whipped my head toward Asher's drawled words. Asshole!

He strolled close with the slightest smile and tapped the bottom of my chin. I yanked my head away from his touch and backed away from Tobias.

"The construction crew is arriving to fix the mess you all made at the entrance." He looked at Jax derisively. "We had to pay a pretty penny to get them to come in the middle of the night." A hollow knock echoed down the hall from the front door. "And there they are."

Asher's silk shirt flowed with his quick steps, his loafers brushing against the floors. People were here. I could try to sneak them a look, or give them a sign to get me help—

Jax clutched the back of my hair and jerked me a few steps forward until my front was flush against his chest. I exhaled in a hissed breath, wincing from his tight grip.

"Try anything and I'll kill them in front of you."

I pressed my lips together. That was pure evil since he could compel them to forget instead of straight murder. But I kept my seething thoughts under wraps.

"Do you understand?"

A boulder settled in my stomach. He treated me so harshly. I turned my head away from him, refusing to speak.

"Enough." Tobias wrapped his fingers around my arm,

pulling me tight against him, the stern hold Jax had in my hair tugging at my scalp.

I stiffened, but didn't move away because at least Tobias wouldn't feed from me. I also enjoyed the ripple of irritation in Jax's features.

He leaned down and I shrunk into Tobias, but I could only get so far.

"You think he can stop me if I want to kill you?" His sweet breath brushed against my cheek.

Panic viced around my chest and my limbs locked when I should be running the other direction. I kept my lips shut and focused on his mouth. His angled jawline rippled with irritation and bowlike lips tensed into a thin line. If he could incinerate me with his glacial blue eyes, he would have.

"Get out of her face," Tobias said casually as if he were commenting on the weather. Jax's eyes narrowed, and he straightened. I followed his retreat with wide eyes. He didn't turn left and down the hall upon exiting the kitchen, instead, going straight through a metal door facing the kitchen. I'd seen it, but never saw one of them open it.

He gripped the handle latching the door shut and pulled it up. It rubbed with a hiss and upon opening, the metal handle thudded upright.

A flood light powered on, and he disappeared downstairs, leaving it open. Any semblance of energy leaked out of me, and I leaned against the solid form against my back.

Everything about vampires drained me.

Fingers pressed into my waist with a large palm spanning my side. Tobias squeezed. I sucked in a breath, freezing up. Something grazed the top of my head.

Was he sniffing me?

His cock swelled against my back.

Fuck no.

I jumped forward . . . at least tried to. Tobias didn't release me, so I bounced back against him.

His arm banded around my stomach, flushing me tight to him. He exhaled shakily.

Every facet of his torso curved into me.

He pressed his cheek against my temple. Smooth, silky skin rubbed on mine.

I squeezed my eyes shut—I would not react. Why did he have to smell so good? Why did I have a weird obsession with getting bitten? I wasn't a blood-whore, I could control myself. I could tell myself that's all I wanted, but my pussy knew otherwise. His cock in me would satisfy all sorts of cravings . . .

Shut it.

"No," I spat out. I didn't know how I mustered the will, but I did it.

Tobias stiffened. His chest shuddered.

The low tones of conversation echoed from down the hall. Then the loud sounds of some sort of machine revved to life.

"It appears you will have to eat later." He grabbed my arm, still gentle, but tension remained lining his form. I stumbled after him, struggling to keep up.

A man with work goggles sliced into the damaged wall dividing the foyer and the living room. I stumbled past, trying to look at the man, but Tobias hauled me upstairs. Once reaching the landing, he turned a sharp right to Asher's room— the third door.

His palm urged me forward at the small of my back. I quickly stepped forward. If I did as ordered, he might not chain me up, giving me an opportunity to run.

Just as I hoped, he waited for me to cross the threshold and grabbed the edge of the door as he backed out.

"Tobias." He hesitated with one foot out the door. "Can you take this off?" I thumped my heavy foot cast on the floor.

Tobias's expression was unreadable. A moment passed and then another. His stiff expression didn't twitch. He seemed to sink into his mind. I cleared my throat. Finally, he looked at me.

"I'll have Jax remove it." Why Jax?

"No!" I shouted, before he shut the door.

Tobias frowned.

"Jax has experience with injuries." I didn't give any shits how much experience he had. I wanted that vampire to stay away from me. All of them should, but I needed this off.

"You . . . please."

I needed to be unhindered if I wanted to try to escape, and Tobias was the only one I could semi-handle.

As selfish and self-centered as vampires were, Tobias seemed to try not to be. Even if he failed.

He sighed. In a few steps he knelt at my feet and slipped his fingers into the edges of the cast. He tore it easily. With the same precision, he removed the one on my arm. It happened so fast I didn't have the chance to be shocked.

The plaster thumped on the ground and without saying anything more, he left.

The knob jiggled with the turn of the lock from the other side. I hurried to check. He'd locked it.

I gritted my teeth and hugged myself. The night had just begun, and I had no doubt another vampire would visit.

EIGHT

tobias

I EXITED the front door within moments. As much distance as I could put between myself and the delectable human, the better. I paced into the narrow pathway of the garden until I reached the patch of cement surrounded by rose bushes framing a stone bench to the edge. I slowed and laced my fingers behind my back. The stiff undulation in my chest forced me to inhale. My chest expanded, and I exhaled with an audible sigh.

Vampires did not need to breathe often. Only extraneous exertion . . . or emotions caused the vexing urge.

I'd almost given into her scent and destroyed my efforts to keep my distance. I had touched her, and she had not reacted as she used to.

She was no longer pliable and sweet against me. She stiffened with distrust.

I abhorred it.

Madness. Everything she caused within me was pure madness. Wanting a human.

Urges to not only worship her body, but to fuck her hard, ravaged against my insides. Like some sinful beast.

Even still, I wanted to gather her to me and sink myself deep inside her.

I reached into my slack's pocket and plucked out a tin canister.

I'd taken to popping these orange candies in an effort to distract myself. Food offered no substance, but these bitter orange sweets managed to distract me from the memory of her luscious long hair. Hair I wanted to yank as I—

I groaned. These thoughts would never leave me unless she was at a distance, but even at that point, I did not believe I could leave her.

We were self-centered, egotistical vampires. We could have done so much good to the world. Yet, we could not be bothered. Even I struggled with the concept of caring. Because I did not feel it.

There was some truth to Jaxon's claims on humans. Their selfishness, their cravings for materialistic possessions. Unrest that continued to plague current society. Astounding how things can change so much, yet remain the same.

All of those desires were emphasized within creatures of the night, yet emotions came with such difficulty. But once a vampire's loyalty is given, it cannot be dissuaded. Staying away from Catalina was imperative for that reason.

Asher had already reached that point. He never gave himself to Imogen, so all that fixation he'd been incapable of accessing narrowed in on the human girl.

He'd thought and called her 'Älskade' too much, leading me to discover the truth. He viewed her as his beloved. A vampire mate in essence. But that was not possible. Humans could not be a vampire's mate.

And she could not become one of us. Asher's surety in himself never craving another was what caused his downfall.

Ren was morbidly fascinated with the human's taste as much as the rest of us. I didn't think he would falter. He didn't have the capacity to care about others more than himself.

Bastien and Imogen argued the most, leading to Jaxon and him exchanging blows.

I would keep my distance to avoid becoming just as besotted as Asher.

Jaxon would never claim to believe Catalina was his beloved because everything in him belonged to the memory of Imogen, his female. The only male in this Coven that had given everything of himself.

That did not mean the others did not have loyalty, but the surface-level loyalty stemmed from self-interest.

My sister was no saint. Young, impulsive, and often cruel. She never thought her actions through, leaving me to pick up after her much too often. My ability to contain her was how I ended like this, an eternal vampire.

Many centuries ago, she'd arrived at the parish I served, her face coated in blood.

I'd prayed over what I believed was the demonic entity, all while she laughed.

I will offer you a gift. Her words of that night invaded my thoughts. *There is no God, dear brother, but I will make you invincible.*

In the face of my rejection, she sank her teeth into me and began the process of turning me into a vampire.

When I woke up, I no longer cared. I had the veiled memories of fear in the distant past, but they slipped away from my grasp when I tried to grab onto them. That is how it was with all emotions. Morality did not come easily to us, which was why I had taken to reading novels exploring the complexities of the human psyche. Reading human minds allowed me to understand the origin and the description of the emotions. This was how I recognized the danger Catalina posed. Yet, I could not bring myself to rid the Coven of her.

When I met her—no—when she saved me and sweetly offered her blood, an internal shift, a deadly craving, had bloomed. One that may be my downfall. One that would be undying.

I tired of keeping my distance. The tenuous strands of control frayed. How much longer could I contain myself?

NINE

catalina

I FOCUSED on my hands resting on my knees. I'd donned the same clothing after rinsing my body of the dirt and blood crusted on me. Sleep beckoned me, but I didn't want to see Bastien, either. No longer could I just disappear because he awaited me there. Hunger twisted my stomach. How long had it been since I'd eaten?

The doorknob wiggled, and though I stiffened, I kept my gaze fixed on my clenched fists.

"Follow me," Jax said in his usual delightful tone. I didn't look up at him. From now on, they didn't exist to me. I curled my legs up and settled my chin on my knees, closing my eyes tight. As if my cocoon could protect me. "Girl."

I didn't react to his barked word. A wave of air fluttered my hair against my cheek. He took a fistful, yanking my head off my knees so I looked at him. "I will drag you out by your hair if you keep ignoring me."

I dropped my eyes to the droplets of blood on his shirt. His grip tightened in my hair, making it hurt. I let my body go limp and it turned agonizing. I couldn't hide my wince.

"Stubborn idiot." Jax hissed and swept me over his shoulder. I lay limp, not giving him any reaction. His shoulder dug into my ribs and every step he took was excruciating.

My nose rubbed against his back with each aggressive step. He always walked with a perpetually angry, jerking gait. Tears sprang to my eyes from the pinch in my side. It only got worse as he went down the stairs. The rug flashed in my blurry peripheral. Breathe. Breathe. I chanted to myself. Blood rushed to my upside-down head and the crevice between my shoulder and neck pinched.

There were no longer the loud noises of construction, but I couldn't look up to confirm the human men were gone. A ringing started up in my ear—agonizing and dizzying. Jax took my hips in his big hands and easily lifted me off him, thumping me down on a stool.

My head swam and I clutched the edge of the granite counter, vomit crawling up my esophagus. I glared at Jax's retreating back.

Asher's cheerful whistles filled the kitchen, happy as a fiddle. Like I hadn't slammed my knee into his cock a few hours ago. He stirred a spoon into a pot over the stove. I helplessly watched him flit from corner to corner, moving so fast it frankly made me dizzier than I was. Asher reached up to the cabinet and a sliver of his lower back peeked. His silky skin—I forced my gaze down, set my elbows on the counter and fixed my hands in front of me.

"Having someone to feed is quite nice." He thumped a ceramic white bowl in front of me.

I didn't react to Asher's statement or to the food.

"You have to eat."

I remained silent. He could talk all he wanted, I wouldn't

eat. What if they put something in it? I didn't think it would be poison, because they didn't have qualms with straight up murdering me, but I wouldn't put torture past them. Asher appeared next to my stool, moving so fast my hair swayed.

He gripped my chin. I flinched, scrunching my face.

"Cat, *Älskade*, please eat." Exasperation coated his words. I yanked my chin out of his hand in answer.

He gasped as if I'd just stomped on his puppy. He took hold of my jaw again, the cold palm enveloping the bone. He pressed a warm bread roll against my clamped mouth. Glaring into his frustrated gaze, I didn't give in.

"Fine, if you want it the hard way." He worked his thumb into my cheek, forcing my teeth open. Turning my head, I chomped on his finger.

He freed himself and shook his hand.

"*Du bet mig.*" He scoffed.

I didn't know what he said, but whatever. I turned my head. My body wasn't at full capacity and my shin still ached. I shouldn't have asked Tobias to remove the casts, I still needed them since I hadn't gotten enough of their blood to fully heal me, but they would be an overall hindrance if I had a chance to escape.

Asher sighed and gripped the bottom of the stool I sat on and pulled it out. I wobbled unsteadily, gripping the bottom of it. The legs screeched against the tile until there was enough room for him to step in front of me. He brushed hair behind my ear. I stiffened, yanking away from his touch.

He sighed again.

"You haven't eaten since you arrived, Catalina. Humans need food."

My stomach was about to eat itself with my hunger, but I

didn't care. I wouldn't eat even if the salty butter he'd pressed against my lips made my mouth water. It took everything in me not to lick it off.

Since he invaded my space, all I could do was turn my head to the side. I wouldn't be able to strong arm him away from me, but I could nail his dick with my knee again.

Another sigh. He was breaking a record.

"Do not shut me out, Pet," his voice lowered, verging on pleading, this time, twisting his torso to get in my face.

No reaction from me.

A look of contemplation settled on his expression and the bun thudded on the counter. His statement didn't move me. I kept stiff and unyielding. "If you eat, I'll reward you," he murmured, thumb caressing the side of my neck.

I inhaled sharply as his touch flared my lust to life. I clutched the sides of the rectangular bar seat. He dragged his fingers into the collar of my shirt and grazed the hollow of my throat. As much as I wanted to give in, I shouldn't—no, I wouldn't.

I squeezed my eyes shut to block the sight of the playful curve to his lips. He'd hurt me so much.

"Why are you bargaining with a human?" Ren's deep voice intoned.

"Why are you everywhere?" Asher muttered, and his sigh brushed against my cheek.

"Your Progeny is on a call with Jaxon. She's been trying to contact you."

Asher frowned and with a final spine-tingling graze against my skin, he straightened.

"Looks like the cat is out of the bag." His grin held a secretive edge.

Progeny, like a child? Asher was a father?! Vampires could have children?

"Do not injure her," he drawled and gave Ren another warning look. "Call for me if you need me." He gave me a final shoulder squeeze.

Over my dead body. I didn't say it, as much as I wanted to shout it at him.

Now that I was alone with Ren, I tensed up. He was as unpredictable as they came.

Ren gripped the back of my neck and forced my cheek flat on the counter. My gasp became muffled, and I scratched against the granite, unable to breathe. It happened so fast, I didn't have time to brace. One second he was across the room and the next his hand clamped around my mouth. My chest seized, a burn working through my lungs.

I sank my teeth into his palm and Ren chuckled.

"I do not give a fuck if you live or die."

I whimpered and wiggled so hard my knees slammed into the bottom side of the island. Agony wove around my bone that'd been broken just a few hours ago. He dragged me higher so my stomach pressed into the edge and my feet dangled.

Ren covered my back with the front of his body. I bucked to get him off, but it was pointless. I was a human and he was a vampire, ten times stronger than me. Even if he wasn't a vamp, he would have overpowered me as a human man.

He pressed his stiff cock into my ass.

"Keep writhing just like that."

I froze and my pulse stuttered.

Ren rubbed his cock harder against me. The edge of the counter dug into my belly, wrenching a gasp free. My arm and shin burned like hell.

Gritting my teeth, I clenched my thighs tight together. I would not call for Asher. His smug face was the last thing I wanted to see. I didn't want to feel like I owed it to him if he came running in.

He'd take it as me giving in to him.

Ren's fangs grazed against my throat. A shiver coasted down my spine. Need breathed to life and I ached.

Oh God no. I couldn't hold back my whimper. The hair raised on my arms.

He chuckled in my ear.

"The little human enjoys being bitten," he said huskily. "You react like a needy little blood-whore."

Every facet of my body begged for the bite. I couldn't weaken—but it felt so damn good—no! I cinched my eyes shut.

There was the pain of his fangs as they punctured my throat and the mental battle ceased. Lust flared and my clit throbbed. Ren's grip tightened on my chin and his head burrowed in between my neck, pushing his lips harder against my throat.

His cock ground against me and I rolled my hips toward him, rubbing my ass against his hard dick. With each suck at my neck, it drew me tight as a bowstring. He drank another mouthful of my blood and lights flickered behind my closed eyes.

"Mm, I can't forget how good you taste," he whispered against my throat.

A tingle blazed to life and caused my knees to weaken. He sucked again and launched me into an orgasm. Sparks burst behind my scrunched eyelids. I kept grinding against his jeans, riding out the wave of release against the denim. It allowed me just enough pressure, but I wanted him inside me, fucking me, devouring me.

No. No. No. I stiffened.

"Enjoy the memory, blood-whore, it's the most you will get from me."

Humiliation slapped me in the face.

"Let me go," I croaked, breaking my self-imposed silence. There wasn't a doubt of how wet and ready I was for him. He only bit me and I came.

I was fucking twisted. Every muscle went limp and his grip loosened. I fell to my ass and curled my legs into my chest, huddling under the island.

A sob wrenched free.

He stared down at me, cool and collected as he swiped his tongue across his lip.

I swore I wouldn't cry in front of them and here I was.

Swiping the back of my hand across my damp face, I hiccupped in a painful breath.

My chest tightened painfully with my inhales. Like a hand wrapped around my lungs and continued to squeeze.

The grip on my lungs engulfed my throat, sending my heart racing. How embarrassing, instead of going out in an escape attempt, my fear would do me in.

"Human, get up." Ren tapped his toe against my ankle but my body was starting to go numb. I clutched his jeans, clinging to him. My surroundings blurred.

I wheezed, my grip weakening.

I'd lost a lot of blood in the car accident and the little droplets Jax forced down my throat only served to make it manageable to get around without a cast. To not be taken down due to my crippling fear, I needed more of their blood.

Over my dead body.

Movement from the kitchen entrance dragged my focus to the approaching blur.

"Pet," Asher murmured, gripping the back of my head.

I let Ren's jeans go and tipped to the side. If Asher wasn't holding onto me, I would have banged my head on the hard floor.

His arms snaked around my waist, and I collapsed against his hard chest.

I could get through the attack. I could do it. Getting my heart to chill out was the only way and as much as I wanted to deny it, his arms warmed me. A wave of calm settled over my mind and cinched my eyes closed. His palm rubbed down my back in soothing rubs.

It was like he was a life-sized inhaler calming my squeezing lungs. It sickened me how well being held and petted calmed me.

"Ren doesn't fuck humans, breathe." Asher's voice rumbled in my ear, but . . . it held a thicker accent. This wasn't Asher. "He will not hurt you."

I locked up, keeping my eyes shut. This will all disappear like a bad dream. I'll wake up in my seedy LA apartment, the last place I had been before moving to Washington.

When I opened my eyes, it would all be gone . . . my lungs stopped constricting in my chest. I opened my eyes to clash with Jax's blank gaze. It wasn't a dream. Tears welled again, but I beat them back. His attention dropped to my throat where it tickled and felt wet.

"Why will you two not leave the girl alone?" Tobias said and crouched. His nose twitched and fangs exploded from his gums.

I gasped, cringing into Jax, but immediately stiffened. Jax was the furthest vampire I'd seek comfort from.

Tobias frowned.

"She's bleeding. Close her wounds."

Jax's jaw fluttered and he loosened his hold at once, yanking my fingers from where they curled around his shirt.

"I'm not healing her."

Tobias's jaw ticked and he looked at Jax like he thought he was scum.

"Very well, hand her over." Tobias slid his arm around my back to prop me up. "I need to close your wounds."

I had no energy to fight Jax transferring me over to Tobias. I was limp and aching. My legs slid against the tile, scooting as Tobias cradled his arm behind my back to drag me close. He had no right to be so gentle. Who was he trying to fool, me or himself?

Electric pinpricks traveled through my limbs. I shoved at his chest. My move caused the wetness at my neck to trickle toward my cleavage.

"Shh," he murmured and brushed my hair back from my face.

I blinked tears away, too weak to make an appropriate effort to get away from him.

"I won't hurt you," he murmured and his head lowered, gaze fixed on the rise of my breasts. His tongue slid up the column of my throat. The warm lash of his tongue was a smooth caress that brought my goose bumps to life.

I shuddered, closing my eyes tightly.

His tongue paused mid-lick and his fingers tightened around my waist. I waited between the precipice of not knowing what he would do and wanting to beg him to keep touching me.

When he finally moved again, it was to sigh, his warm breath puffing me with sweet orange as he retreated.

"What happened?" Asher scowled. "I left you alone for only minutes."

Tobias smoothly stood and extended his hand to help me up. I ignored it and struggled to stand on my own. He must have had enough of my fawn-like movements because he cupped my elbow and hoisted me to my feet.

I wavered. It couldn't be good losing as much blood as I had. In addition to that was the hunger twisting my stomach. My head swam and I swayed. Tobias's grip tightened.

Asher tsked and plucked at the blood drenched collar of my shirt.

"We need another outfit."

I didn't like him talking about us like we were a unit.

I glared at him and yanked my arm from Tobias's grip.

"He burned all of my things," I spat, letting my temper get the best of me. Ren's eyebrow raised and he lifted his hand. A bright flame sputtered to life across all of his fingertips. The five small flames were faintly blue at the base and brightened toward the tip.

"Would you like me to set *you* aflame?"

"Go ahead," I said, gritting my molars, with more bravado than I felt. I tensed so much it hurt, but it was the only way I stayed in place instead of pointlessly running like a bat out of hell.

"Enough," Asher muttered. He clapped his hands. "I have some gowns in the upstairs storage."

The flames hovering over Ren's fingertips sputtered and extinguished. Only then did I process Asher's statement.

"I'm not wearing one of those hideous gowns belonging to that vampire woman."

The entire room went utterly still. I swear the oxygen sucked out of the room with my words.

True fear skittered down my spine. If anything would drive them to rip my head off it was talking about their precious Imogen. Instinctively, I crowded closer to Asher.

He grinned and swept me close to him.

"My Pet is quite funny," he cooed, and he strolled out of the kitchen with his arm around my shoulders. The foyer was devoid of workers, but the space was swept clean and the broken, jagged edges of the walls were smoothed with plaster. "That will be finalized and painted tomorrow."

Whatever. I didn't think I'd be alive long enough for it to matter. There was only one place this could possibly head to, and that was my death. Once Asher grew bored of me as everyone that knew him insinuated he would, I had no doubt he'd toss me to the side. If he didn't off me, then it would be Ren or Jax.

The cold truth settled into my heart.

Either way, there was no use dwelling on the inevitable. Ren attacking me like that couldn't have made it more transparent and with that came the realization that I didn't care to hold my tongue. In fact, if I could get all of this over with sooner, then all the better. I'd try to escape, but if all else failed, inciting their wrath to kill me quickly would be my way to go. I was too much of a coward to off myself, anyway.

"Why can't I wear something from the stuff you ordered?"

"None will suit."

He shuffled me up the two flights of stairs until he reached the rounded alcove that broke into two directions. He headed left and dramatically shoved through the two swinging doors. This side was as large as the one that mirrored it.

"We moved back in here a few months ago. We try to rotate through our homes every ten years or so as to not raise suspicion by staying in one place."

In the corner of the room were four large leather chests fastened with metal bands. A large rectangular object under a white sheet leaned against the wall behind it.

Setting me on my feet, he flipped the latch of the closest chest and rifled through bright colored tulle, releasing a burst of musk with his movements. Skirts spilled out from the edge and he pulled the ends of a dress. All I could focus on was the gaudy purple that would wash out my tan skin.

Imogen didn't have good taste, there, that was the truth. And evidently a truth these vampires were unwilling to hear. Other than Asher. He'd been the only one willing to speak about her to me.

They were so secretive about their precious Imogen.

It wasn't kind, or nice of me to think this way of a dead person, but I couldn't lie to myself when her shadow hung over me at every moment in their presence. All this drama was caused by her in the first place. They were angry that I took her ashes. The fact that my mouth became as dry as sawdust at the thought was something I'd happily ignore.

He hooked the dress over his shoulder and the clingy, silky skirt molded to his chest. In a few steps he was in front of me.

"Hey," I gasped as he disrobed me as easily as if I were a doll. He jerked my shirt over my head. I sputtered. Then I was standing in my bra and panties. He paused, admiring the swell of my breasts. "Hey." I crossed my arms over my chest, scowling.

Asher smirked and jerked the dress over my head. I remained stiff and unrelenting. He gently pulled my hair through the collar.

"Hurry it up if you don't want Jaxon seeing your gorgeous body."

Gritting my teeth, I slid my arms through the long scratchy sleeves. As soon as my arms were through, Jax slammed through the doors. They swung behind him. Asher didn't even look, he just

continued straightening the skirt. Turning me so my back was to him, he pulled the string of the corset until it banded around my stomach.

"She shouldn't come," Jax said through gritted teeth.

Did he ever say anything while not angry?

My lips tightened, but I tried to keep my expression neutral.

"Leave her here."

Asher paused for so long that I peeked over my shoulder, in time to see him throw his head back, laughing. "She is mine to do with as I want." He tightened the corset another rung. "Unless you would like to share my Pet, but you gave up your claim when you voted for her death. That means anything to do with her will be handled by me and Tobias."

Jax scoffed and walked toward a large open window at the furthest end of the room. Then returned to where Asher and I stood in a few clipped steps. A pacing vampire.

I focused on Asher and pressed my hand to the ribbed corset compressing my stomach. The dress pushed up my cleavage and the tight fit didn't make them any less prominent. Asher popped another chest open, unveiling a bunch of shoes.

I pursed my lips at the glittering heels. The stilettos would kill me since my leg wasn't fully healed. That wasn't taking into consideration that they weren't really my style. I peeked up at him under my eyelashes. He stared at me without a twitch. Whatever, I'd grin and bear it for the chance of getting outside of this prison. I didn't have any false hopes that I'd manage to escape, but at least I would get fresh air.

"She would make you pay for allowing a human to touch her things."

"If she were alive, Jax," Asher drawled. "But she is not, so I have nothing to worry about."

Eesh, that must have stung. I rolled my lips between my teeth to stop my smirk.

Asher crouched and lifted my good leg, leaving me on my aching one. I gripped his shoulder to balance. I could stand on it, but a dull pain speared through my shin.

His shoulder bunched. The muscles were quite nice—

I clenched my teeth and shoved on the other heel and let him go. Fucking vampire was too tempting to be around. My mind and body battled. They drew me in like a month to a flame. I'd get incinerated soon enough.

As they argued, I hobbled over to the window to peek at my obliterated rental.

The charred, half-turned-to-ash building, sprawled below. I had a clear view of my driveway from here.

I pressed my palm to the cold window pane, and an outline of condensation formed around my hand.

My room no longer existed. It was a gaping hole now, just like the one in my chest.

Believing in vampires got me that. I couldn't make the mistake again.

Not that my decisions mattered since I'd be dead soon.

TEN

jax

IF SHE WERE ALIVE, Jax. The truth of Asher's words stung and I stepped on the gas, speeding down the winding road as fast as the sports car could handle it.

I grew tired of denying myself. Catalina needed to go. Death by my hand or death by Ren's hand. Those were the two options. And the only way she would no longer haunt me. If she was alive out there . . . I would hunt her down. To fuck her, to feed on her—to keep her.

I'd be like pathetic Asher, following the whims of a human.

I shook my head. Fuck that.

As good as her pussy was and as sweet as she tasted, I would deny myself. She was nothing. And as a human nothing, she should not be touching Imogen's things. The thought came with less hostility than I liked, and I found that happening much too often.

The clothes did not suit her. I didn't want them touching her . . . but, it was because I didn't want the reminder of what I'd lost.

Catalina and Imogen were absolute opposites.

Imogen would rip the human apart if she were around. The human would run in fear, cowering.

The thought unsettled me.

I ran my palm over my jaw. Meaningless thoughts to have. They would never meet, fortunately for the human.

She was too weak, as displayed by the state of her body when she arrived. Broken down, wrapped in casts, and bruised. The image returned me to the dirty streets of the Kingdom of Sweden in the late 1700s where I'd survived as a thief. Imogen found me beaten, on the brink of death when she changed me. I squeezed the steering wheel a brief moment before releasing it.

She'd changed Asher for me, as well.

I owed her everything.

Then why did *she* affect me? Seeing the broken human caused a violently visceral reaction in me. I could not contain the things happening in my chest. I'd gone deep into the woods, morphed, and slaughtered every animal I came into contact with, relishing in their squeals of pain.

I scratched the back of my neck so hard I gouged into my skin.

I craved a traitor.

catalina

ASHER REACHED OVER and around my hip to unclip the seat belt of the fancy car I could only dream about owning. I'd have to sell my soul to afford a vehicle of this caliber. I bit back a scoff. Some could argue I'd already sold my soul for money.

His arm brushed my boobs as he retracted his arm.

I gritted my teeth. I could do it myself, but he seemed determined to treat me like the Pet he kept calling me.

Asher's face hovered near my nose. I could see every blond eyelash. His sweet scent enveloped me and as much as I tried to steel myself, my muscles relaxed. His blue eyes peered into mine and the barest flash of red leaked into the irises. I exhaled slowly through my nose, legs clenching together.

He retreated with his bow-like lips curved in a knowing smile. I verged on panting. I rubbed my temples with my fingertips and exhaled slowly. With my shoulders stiff, I shoved open my door, smacking Asher's leg in the process.

"I was going to open that for you," he said in an overly

pleasant voice. "There was no need to dent her." He crouched to look at the metal.

As I swung my legs out, the silk skirt rustled around my legs. I begrudgingly admitted that although Imogen didn't have the best taste in colors, the dress flowed beautifully.

Jax appeared near my face, making me reel back a step until the bottom side lip of the car dug into my calf. His hands rested on the vehicle, corralling my head as he leaned into my face.

"Do try to run, human. You're mine to kill if you attempt to escape."

I gritted my teeth. If he was trying to taunt me, it wouldn't work, I'd already decided to accept fate.

Jerking my chin up, I straightened. My movement forced him back a step, otherwise I would have ended up against him. And the precious vampire couldn't be touching a dirty, traitorous human.

"Stop talking about it and do it already," I said through gritted teeth. I wanted to sound angry and defiant, but ended up sounding exhausted.

Jax scoffed, and with him being so close, I had a straight shot of his already pointy canines extending into long, intimidating fangs.

"Enough, you two," Asher drawled and captured my hand, pressing it into his curved arm. I scrunched the cotton of his loose long sleeved shirt. The top buttons gaped open to display his collar bone.

Meanwhile Ren's wide shoulders were already smoothly heading through the parking garage.

Asher's grip on my arm forced me after him. My heel's click echoed on the cement until we exited the dimly lit garage and onto an inclined pathway.

I gripped the vampire tight as I kept up with his long stride. I was a little more than half their height, so I had to do some serious hoofing.

A woman in a black dress with the hem cutting off near her ass shuffling from foot to foot came into view. A few steps further and another girl stood a bit in front of her. Rounding the corner of the building, an entire line came into view.

Women and men dressed in skimpy night club outfits waited in the chilly night. We didn't stop at the end of the line but kept forward until reaching the front.

An awning red light shined a reflection on the ground, the cursive letters blinking.

Crimson Nights

"Is this a club?" A bouncer met Ren's eyes and slightly widened. He pressed a finger into his ear and the wire in his shirt wavered.

I couldn't hear what he said, but he unclipped the felt rope opposite from the one he was allowing people through. No one waited on that side.

"Sire," he inclined his head at Ren who only grunted.

Sire?

I blinked. What? Like a maker?

I didn't take my eyes off the man as we passed him—his eyes held an intense aura to them. He looked like any normal guy one could come across in a grocery store, but his skin seemed too smooth—like he had no pores. I ignored the intrigued expressions of the female next to the male. She tilted her head down in an almost deferring motion as she moved to the side to let us pass.

Why were they staring at them like that? Even Asher hadn't gotten looks like these when we went to Saphire Lounge. A few steps further and we crossed through a fluttering velvet curtain. And on the other side there was another . . . and then another. Red lighting lined the top side of the walls, offering just enough to see my way, which continued to be curtains. They blocked what lay ahead until we crossed a few more. A dull throb of seductive music pulsed, becoming louder with each step. Then we were on the other side.

Black sconces lined the tops of the wall and reflected a low red glow toward the ceiling. Bodies writhed on the dance floor, so close that they practically fucked.

"Where's Tobias?" Jax asked. He stood so close that I felt suffocated, smushed between them . . . and a little too aware. With the hand not clutching onto Asher for dear life, I gripped my skirt.

"He went through the back," Asher said, squeezing my hip.

I frowned. Why couldn't we have gone through the back?

This place was different than the one we'd been to . . . a lot more seductive.

"Sire," a girl flounced over, her hair bouncing with each little hop of her step. She pressed her palms to Asher's chest, practically feeling him up.

"Talia, my little Progeny," Asher patted her blonde head . . . affectionately? My fingers folded into my palm. I wouldn't fool myself into thinking he hadn't felt me tense up.

"Meet my Pet." He tipped his chin toward me.

She turned her shocked eyes toward me, her smile twitched and she breathed in once. I didn't think her eyes could widen any more, but they did. Her face suddenly invaded my space, too close to my neck for comfort. I flinched.

Both guys had a grip on her in an instant. Asher gripped her ear while Jax's hand enveloped her throat.

"She smells so good," she breathed, fangs poking out with her words. "Could I have a taste, Sire?"

"I said, *my* Pet, Talia," a threat echoed clear in his tone. "Do not touch her or I will end you." I'd never heard such a threat uttered in his silky tone. A chill traveled up my spine.

Talia's expression turned to shock.

"Yes, Sire," she mumbled, lowering her head.

Asher released her ear and an affable smile spread on his lips like there had been no threat seconds ago.

I eyed Talia. She could end all of this uncertainty...

"Is Amira's human here?" His voice lowered, but I was close enough to hear his question.

Talia nodded and a frown spread on her lips. She pressed a finger into her ear.

"Do not let that human in again. Make sure you scrub the location of this place from his mind." She dropped her hand and turned back to Asher. A devoted expression settled on her expression.

I shouldn't be jealous. I really shouldn't be, so I focused on breathing to save my sanity.

"In the pink room."

Asher's fingers flexed on my hip and he pulled me away. I staggered, using his side to balance myself. He almost made me fall on my face. Inconsiderate vampire. I struggled to keep up with his long stride. Did he forget my legs were not even half the length of his? And this slippery ground wasn't a good match for heels. It had only been a few minutes of walking in them and my shins burned, especially the not fully healed one. He wove me through throngs of thrashing bodies. Random hands caressed Asher, tugging and pulling at the hem of his shirt. He kept moving like he couldn't feel the touches and murmured invitations.

I smacked away a hand that landed on my boob. Jax caught the wandering hand and squeezed. His fingers bent in ways that shouldn't have been possible.

The human sucked in a breath to scream.

"Shut it."

The male clamped his lips tight.

Jax shoved him away and a vampire dressed in black, similar to the bouncer out front, appeared to take him away.

I couldn't focus on the utter lack of humanity in Jax. Such viciousness edged every word and action. His true self.

My toe slammed into a metal stair as I scrambled up the steps, trying not to set down the back of my heel since there wasn't a doubt in my mind the thin heel would go through the holes. This caused a whole other burn in my leg.

I glimpsed a small bird's eye-view of the dance floor before I was pulled through a door and into a hall with black walls. The path led us into a circular room, a bright red circular couch adorning the middle of the room, while the lighting remained the same as the dance floor, lending a seductive ambiance.

Asher pulled me in front of him, one arm across my chest, and forced me against his front. Each brush of his body against my back flickered memories of our bodies tangled with each other. I wet my lips, as he guided me through one of the doors.

I understood why they called this the pink room.

Everything was medicine pink. Even the big bed in the middle of the room.

"Mr. Crimson!" A woman jumped off the edge of the mattress. She shuddered and her eyes closed for a beat—long enough to be odd.

"Sire," she intoned, her voice decidedly huskier and accented. "I've not found information about that human. Calliope keeps everything between her and Freya."

"Is this what you've been up to, Asher?" Jax hissed.

Wait a moment. That was about me. Asher was looking into if I was a plant.

I stiffened, trying to jerk forward and out of the cage of his arms.

"You mean trying to find factual information instead of throwing out accusations?" Asher grinned. "I can't take full credit. Tobias inspired the idea to question my Progeny currently undercover with Calliope. She compelled this human to meet me here."

The girl suddenly shuddered and dropped to the bed again. She panted and pinched her temple.

Jax's gaze blazed on my face. I scowled at him. A flicker of uncertainty washed across his features, but it was gone too fast for it to bring me any hope.

Whatever.

"Amira told me to give you what you like." The human pushed into an upright position on the bed.

Leaning back, she spread her legs, announcing to everyone that she didn't wear underwear under the glittering dress. She let everything hang out.

"Ah," I choked, startled.

She sliced her wrist and blood rose to the surface, she held her wrist over her pussy. Red splashed on her folds and dripped down.

That didn't seem, like, sanitary.

Who was I kidding, these were vamps, they didn't care.

I cleared my throat and focused on the painting of a flamingo over her head.

My hands slipped off Asher's arm, and I shuffled on the heels. His palm flattened on the small of my back to steady me.

"Lovely proposition, flower, but not interested."

Jax approached the girl.

Despite myself, my lungs seized. There was no reason I should be disappointed. They were never to be trusted—

"Leave and forget you spoke to us." He stared into her eyes, and spoke with his voice lowered.

She clamped her thighs together with a slap and mechanically stood. With stiff movements, she left the room. The slam of the door perfunctory.

I peeked at Asher from the corner of my eye.

"What?" I grumbled. He wouldn't stop looking at me, and it put me on edge.

"I told you, I only want you."

Fluttering exploded in my belly. *Ohhhh.*

I regained my senses and I sucked in a breath.

"I don't care." I let him go and backed up. I didn't like the look in his eyes.

He flashed his fangs.

"Your vamp child wasn't able to confirm my innocence. So what now, you kill me?" My heart thundered in my chest.

"Silly girl, you are mine."

Panic squeezed my lungs tight. Red from the sconces reflected off his teeth.

They still wouldn't let me go.

"You know what? I did it," I spat, the desperation unbearable. I wanted it to end. "I was sent by Calliope to get info on you guys. Like how you have your people over in her Coven."

Jax snarled.

My heart jumped painfully. The twins stared at me, expressionless. They should have lunged at me. Torn my throat out, something.

Defeat took out my legs and I dropped to the ground, clutching my chest. God, it hurt to breathe.

"Cat." Asher scooped me off the ground and curled me in his lap. The bed dipped under our weight. His palm rubbed down my back. "Your asthma is acting up again."

Jax moved into my peripheral and I cringed against Asher, holding him tighter.

"Don't touch me." I shot toward Jax.

I squeezed my eyes shut and my head rested on Asher's chest. A door slammed.

"There, my bitch of a twin is gone," he cooed.

I choked on a laugh and it made it harder to get my lungs to work properly.

"You're panting, Catalina." His nose grazed my cheek. "Let me feed you my blood and my cock, Pet."

My stomach tightened at his low tone. I closed my eyes tight. Being enveloped in his arms soothed my panic and I hated it. He'd conditioned me for this. Every caress to calm me had ended up here. I squeezed my eyes shut. If I didn't see his lying face, then I could accept the comfort.

He inhaled so deeply that his chest expanded. Was he sniffing me? Vampires didn't need to breathe much at all.

"You smell divine." His cock swelled under my ass. My eyes widened and heat flushed over my cheeks. "I've fucked you like mad, and you still pinken whenever you hear naughty words."

His chuckle spiked to my clit. I wiggled my hips on instinct to soothe the ache.

I stiffened.

"Drink from me," he murmured in my ear. I turned my head away and he sighed. Frustration. I could work with that. Maybe I could piss him off enough to drain me. "Catalina."

My body trembled at his purred order. I swallowed hard. I would give in to him. Tension leaked from my limbs. He must have taken it as an acquiesce because he lifted his wrist to his lips and sank his fangs in. Upon removing them, blood painted his mouth. A droplet of blood trickled down and upon touching his sleeve, bloomed.

Vampire blood was a deeper red than human blood. I'd only had the slightest bit each time I'd drank it. Asher told me about the side effects, and other than that it healed a shattered ankle, and turned me on, it also caused a bond. Which was why vampires never shared their blood. If humanity found out about aging slower, healing, and the aphrodisiac qualities of their blood, it would create chaos.

I turned my head away, teeth clenched. I'd had Jax's and Ren's blood. I couldn't add another even if what they gave me had already run its course—

Asher forced his wrist to my lips and his blood slipped onto my tongue. Electricity traveled over my nerve endings. And the sweet taste exploded on my tongue. Each time I attempted to think of a descriptor, it faded from my grasp. I fought to turn my chin away but his other hand gripped my jaw, keeping me in place. I gasped and swallowed another mouthful.

And then another.

A shiver crested up my spine and I took hold of his wrist

with both my hands. So, so good. His cock throbbed under my ass and I arched my spine, grinding my hips downward.

I couldn't control the lust riding me. My grip tightened on his wrist. I swallowed the ambrosia again, humming against his silky forearm.

Asher hissed, his hips jolting up, thrusting his dick into my ass.

I opened my legs and tipped forward, keeping hold of his arm in front of my chest. The stiff cock rubbed exactly where he would enter me. Oh, yes. I groaned against his wrist and tugged another mouthful of blood into my mouth.

The liquid coated my throat and warmed my belly. Pressure in my ribcage tapered off and I breathed without my airways constricted. Blood leaked from the corner of my mouth and tickled as it trailed down my chin.

Asher clicked his tongue.

"Greedy, Pet," he murmured huskily and gripped the back of my neck, bracing me as he pulled his arm away from my mouth. A whimper crawled up from my throat and he guided me back until I rested against his chest. I rested my temple against his jaw.

Everything seemed brighter and shiny. My body drooped, warm and needy. The hand on my shoulder slid to the front of my neck and his long fingers pressed up the underside of my jaw. He lifted my chin so I could see his eyes blazing with lust. Half-lidded and hungry.

His lips curled with satisfaction. Then he dipped, delving his tongue into my mouth. The skillful kiss remained soft and searching as he swept his tongue against mine. He pulled back slowly, keeping an inch between our mouths.

His blue eyes were so bright and pretty. His fingertip

rubbed across my lip, the soft touch rubbing gently, then followed the line down the column of my throat to my cleavage.

I shuddered.

"My reactive, Pet." He tutted. "Watch me."

He reached inside the corset and popped my breasts free. Cupping his hand under one swell, his large hand wrapped around the mass. His thumb rolled across my nipple.

I moaned and my head fell on his shoulder.

"I said, watch me."

I sank my teeth into my lower lip and forced my eyes open. He squeezed my breast once more then inched down. The low scrape of his fingernails dragging across the fabric encased whalebone corset echoed loudly in my ears. With a quick rustling of my skirt, he pulled them to my waist.

"Lift your heel to the edge of the bed."

I immediately did as he ordered and my shoe dug into the mattress, the pointy stiletto pressing hard into the pink comforter.

Asher bunched the skirt over my waist. His long finger delved into the waistband of my panties and he curled his finger into the material.

"You're so soft," he murmured against my ear. In a quick motion, he ripped off my panties. "Watch," he repeated.

He inched over my shaved pussy, creeping closer to my clit. I held my breath, on the precipice of shouting at him to touch me. Finally, his pointer finger pressed against the bundle of nerves. A rush of lust flooded my core.

"Your pussy weeps for me," he murmured, finger grazing over my wet entrance.

"Asher."

His body shuddered, causing his fingers to curl against my

core. Slipping his fingers into my need, he swirled those long, male digits. My channel clutched at his thick fingers. He added another one.

Oh God, I wanted his pierced cock inside me, too. I squeezed my lips together to cage the words inside.

"Give me more of your delicious need."

His husky order caused another wave of liquid to throb free. Moisture glinted on his hand. He withdrew his fingers, exposing more of his wet hand, then he shoved the two thick fingers back into my entrance.

The sound of his fingers fucking me blazed my lust to an excruciating level. His palm pressed against my clit as he kept the motion steady. My eyelids lowered into slivers, I couldn't close them because I couldn't look away from his hands.

His nose grazed against the side of my throat and I sucked in a harsh breath. Goose bumps exploded across my flesh and I stiffened in his arms. My orgasm slapped me across all my senses, and I wriggled to the rhythm of his fingers, trying to get more pressure. Pants exploded from my lips. So, so good. Oh . . . my God.

Asher didn't stop moving and the wet gush of my need drenched his hand. His movements slowed, riding out the aftershocks of my orgasm.

He raised his fingers to his mouth and skillfully licked my moisture clean off.

His cock throbbed under my ass. He returned his licked clean fingers to my pussy, shoving them deep.

I cried out and clutched his arm banded in front of me, trying to pull his hand from the overly sensitive spot, but it was like trying to move a statue.

Biting into his other wrist, he lifted it to me again. I

clutched his wrist to my mouth without hesitation. He shuddered, his moan vibrating against my ear.

"I want you filled with my blood." He nipped my ear. "To smell of me, and only me."

Yes, please. I gripped him tight to my mouth as I took from him . . . and he let me. Warmth spread down my throat and expanded in my belly. The buzz in my ears raised by a few notches.

Talia whipped the door open.

"Ren is—" Her smile slowly faded away and she balked. Her attention didn't leave his wrist at my mouth.

"Out," Asher hissed and his grip across my chest tightened.

I gripped his wrist tighter and drank another mouthful of sweet nectar.

Talia's shoulder jerked and she disappeared from the threshold, leaving Jax standing behind her. Moving so slow, he reached over without removing his attention from me and shut the door. His nose flared and he focused on my wet sex.

I wiggled on Asher's lap. Raw and needy for more. Moans melded with my whimpers.

In the next instance, Jax kneeled before me and burrowed his head between my thighs.

His nose rubbed against my clit, wrenching a gasp from my throat and my hips gyrated forward. Asher opened my sensitive pussy for his brother's tongue.

The sight was too much for me to handle. Jax hooked my leg over his shoulder and sank his teeth into the crevice where my thigh bent. I shot into another orgasm.

My hearing went out, replaced by static. I could have been floating for all I knew.

A sharp sting radiated outward from the spot where Asher had been nuzzling at my throat.

Nonsense spilled from my lips but I didn't care at the moment. I could have been giving my soul away and it wouldn't have made a difference.

Finally, the swell calmed enough for me to hear my ragged breathing. Jax licked my pussy clean of the blood that had spread into the aching folds. Each touch jolted me against Asher. His grip hadn't loosened.

He hummed against my throat and since my ass was bare against his slack-covered cock, I could feel the dampness beneath him.

"Was that me or you," I croaked and then hiccupped.

"Both of us, Pet. I can't control myself where you're concerned."

Satisfaction licked up my spine. Making a vampire come in his pants seemed like a skill I really should be proud of. Jax's shoulders moved once in a jerking motion. What could Jax be feeling so intensely that he had to take a breath?

The floating sensation hadn't abated. I wiggled my fingers in front of my face and the sight of them seemed to be enhanced, like I could see them under a magnifying glass.

I licked my lip to lap up whatever blood still painted my mouth. I'd never had so much vampire blood before. The short-haired twin's shoulders moved again. He wanted my death, but knelt between my legs?

"Get off of me." I jerked to the side to remove his grip from my leg. Blood leaked from the wounds he hadn't licked shut.

He gripped my thigh and hissed. It wasn't a damn chicken wing.

"He's going to heal you."

I didn't care if he was about to sacrifice himself at my feet. I rather he killed me.

Using my other foot, I kicked out and slammed the bottom of my shoe into his shoulder. The heel punctured his shoulder and he sneered.

"No, thank you," I slurred.

Jax suddenly leaned in my face, a violent glint in his eyes. I tipped my chin up, waiting for him to tear my head off, but no dice.

Asher poked a finger into his chest, stopping him.

"No attacking other vampire's Pets." Asher tugged me tighter against his chest while I jerked my skirt down to cover my legs. A trickle from the blood and my still wet pussy mingled between my legs.

Jax narrowed his eyes and straightened. His thumb swiped across his lip.

"When you no longer have his protection, be ready." His threat hung between us.

"Looking forward to it," I said without inflection in my tone. I squinted, was he multiplying into two of him? I rubbed my eyes.

Jax raked his hand through his hair and the short front strands stood up.

"I'll find Tobias."

The door slammed behind him.

I went limp against the hard chest behind me. The floating sensation became stark as the adrenaline fizzled away. Rolling my head to the side, I met Asher's satisfied gaze.

"Let me leave." My voice sounded far away. Asher's features were unfairly pretty. And it wasn't just because he was a vampire because I'd seen some ugly ass vampires—Asher was born with his gorgeous features. All the Crimson Coven vampires were. Maybe they had some sort of beauty standard requirement listed before they could join their group. "Or kill me."

His head tilted and confusion marred his perfect features.

"You will never leave me, Cat."

I would never leave.

A snorting laugh slipped free from my mouth.

I'd escaped the other vampire that tried to keep me captive in that cave. Years later, I found myself in the very situation I ran from.

Hopelessness settled over my shoulders. According to their laws, humans could not know about vampires. The truth was compelled from them . . . and I could not be compelled.

A tear trickled from the corner of my eye.

Asher frowned and leaned down to lick it clean.

catalina

I LAY on the mattress of the pink bedroom, with the mesh canopy—in the same bright pink—hanging over the bed. As conscious-less as they behaved, I used to believe there was a semblance of humanity in the vampires, but I'd fooled myself. Asher sprawled next to me, causing the canopy to sway. He set an elbow on the bed and perched his chin on his fist. God, I felt too hot and needy. Why was he so attractive?

I'd sunk into his dark embrace and ran with it. Asher's grin widened, giving me a peek of his long incisor teeth. The very ones that elongated in preparation to bite me.

This was my life now. My chest swelled with emotion, and I wanted to burrow my head into the ground and never come out. An invisible band wrapped around my neck and tightened with each second. I clutched at my throat like I could make the suffocation go away. This was different than the pressure from asthma.

A choked laugh escaped me.

"Is something wrong?"

Everything. The room swirled at my peripheral.

"Not at all." I waved Asher away and stifled the burst of laughter bubbling behind my lips. No way was this my life now. Vampires, blood, sex, getting tongue pillaged . . .

I licked my lips. Some more of that tongue pillaging sounded so great. My gaze dropped to his wrist, the wound I'd fed from already closed up. My mouth watered. I wanted his cock inside me while I tasted him again. His face swam in my vision.

"Stop moving around." I squinted and reached for the front of his shirt to keep him still.

Droplets of blood had bloomed across the front of his shirt. That was my blood. The corner of my lips twitched. I shouldn't be feeling all proud of it. Right?

But why? I liked him. I peeked at him under my eyelashes.

Asher was keeping me, and here I was, happy about belonging to him. I shouldn't feel like this . . . right?

"What are you staring at?" Asher poked the middle of my forehead.

"You're pretty," I announced.

Asher's eyebrows raised and the corner of his lips quirked.

My brain was definitely not okay right now—worry floated out of my hands like an elusive cloud.

I just wanted more of him.

The bedsheets rustled from him scooting closer. A tingle spread across my skin.

"Stop moving, Ash." I patted his cheek with my fingertips.

Asher's eyebrows furrowed.

My attention dropped to the hollow in the middle of his throat. I wanted to lick and bite it.

"Why am I so hot?" I whined.

Grabbing my skirt, I scooted it up my thigh, baring my skin inch by inch. His gaze lasered in on the movement. I clenched and unclenched my thighs. I was drenched with need. Finally, air hit my pussy and I grinned at the red flash of Asher's irises.

The door swung open. Tobias entered with his head down as if he was thinking deeply about something. He slammed the door behind him.

"What is taking you so long . . ." He trailed off, his steps slowing as he focused on my soft flesh. My clit throbbed at his attention. I spread my thighs for him to get a better view at my aching folds.

I pushed up on my elbows.

"You're bleeding," he choked out. He was talking about Jaxon's bite wound that hadn't been healed.

"I know," I said huskily.

His gaze unfocused and his knuckles popped. He took another step closer and froze, shaking his head.

"I think . . . I think she has a blood-high," Asher breathed.

"But that is simply not possible." His English accent deepened and took on a rougher edge. "Only vampires get blood-highs."

I couldn't care less about whatever they were going on about. I was still too hot! Tobias ran his tongue over his lower lip. I wanted it on my pussy.

"Tobias." He returned his gray gaze to me. "Heal me." I widened my thighs and stretched out my leg.

"Please," I breathed.

Fangs sliced into his lip and his eyes turned red. He blurred with how fast he moved.

My head fell back as his mouth settled over the wound. A

tongue swipe had my lips parting, then he drank from the wound. His eyes focused on mine—the red hadn't left, he snarled, fingers digging into my ass.

Tobias bit me again. Right next to the original wound.

His eyebrows furrowed and he didn't look away from my gaze, keeping me captive with the blazing lust splashed across his face.

"More," I moaned.

I ground my ass on the bed, aching for him to touch my clit.

The bed shifted as he gyrated his cock into the mattress. I clenched the sheets under my ass. His brown hair fell forward and into his forehead.

He groaned, the vibration of the sound reaching my clit. His warm mouth crept close to my clit until he finally tongued the slit of my pussy.

I jolted my hips up.

"Yes, Love." He groaned and rubbed his nose against my clit.

"Tobias," I moaned.

"Such a good girl." He lifted his head to look me in my eyes. Red and gray flickered in his irises. "Come for me, Love." His sharp incisors flashed with his words.

Blood and my need dripped off his chin, then his gaze turned fully red again and he sucked on my clit.

Crying out, I gripped Tobias's shoulder, curling forward as a massive wave crashed into my pussy. I jerked against his mouth, riding out the roll of the orgasm as it dragged me into oblivion.

Asher gripped my chin and turned me toward him. His head dipped and he claimed my mouth. I flicked my tongue against his long fangs, swirling my tongue around them. He moaned and pulled back with a gasp. His gaze blazed with lust —I'd stretched out the collar of his shirt.

The aftershocks of the orgasm throbbed through my channel, needily clenching for something it ached for.

Tobias stiffened and withdrew his tongue from my throbbing clit. He slammed his hands into the bedsheets, and bunched the fabric so hard a loud rip echoed through the room.

With his hair in a disarray, he seemed even more youthful. He breathed in once, and his jawline bunched. I wanted to bury my nose into the smooth, creamy dip of his throat.

"I . . . I apologize," he croaked and backed away, his gaze wide with horror. He wouldn't stop blinking. Why was he so upset? Another retreating step.

I pushed to sit up.

"Priest," Asher called, but Tobias was gone.

I frowned after him, but the room was spinning even more. What had I done wrong? Rubbing my face, I pressed my pointer fingers into my temples.

"I'm dizzy," I muttered and then collapsed.

Asher's arms curved around my body and he flattened me against his hard chest. He had such a long torso—the long, Viking vampire. Unfairly tall and muscled. And there were two of them!? Unfair.

Asher had rolled his sleeves up to his elbows. The arm on the bed slid under my ear. Veins bulged in his forearm. Blood ran in those veins. Delicious blood. A sweet taste that offered that expanded warmth in my belly. I just wanted more.

I nuzzled closer. His skin was warm against my cheek as it always was after he'd fed. I grazed my nose against the soft skin on the inner side of his elbow.

It tasted so good . . .

I sank my teeth into his bicep. The sweet tang spread on my tongue. Asher hissed near my ear. I managed to swallow twice before the grip on the back of my neck forced me to let go.

Vampire blood made me feel strong and capable. Something I'd sorely lacked for such a long time.

The door slammed open and Ren stared at us from the threshold in only jeans. I shoved upright, Asher alongside me.

Ren's gaze focused in on me.

"Hand her to me."

Asher's fingers dug into the back of my neck where he hadn't released me after I'd bitten him. I grimaced. That bite didn't look good and I was surprised the hold he had on me remained relatively tame. Blood pooled at the surface of the indents of my teeth on his skin.

The rushed footsteps coming behind Ren snapped me out of my drooling. A slim woman with dripping bite marks in her neck rushed into the room. Her chest heaved over the collar of the strappy, black crop top.

"I can send another donor to please you, Mr. Crimson." She careened to a stop, her eyes widening on Asher and me. "Asher." She breathed, and the tone made it clear they'd spoken before.

"She's one of our human donors," he murmured in my ear.

I scowled, before I could smooth my expression.

Asher smirked.

"You still have it in you to be jealous."

And why did he sound pleased by that?

"I don't care what you lot do." I tried to keep my tone even, but my voice rose slightly at the end, ruining the attempt.

"We have your usual human with another vamp right now, but I'll get her for you, Ren."

"No other will do." He focused in on me and I clutched onto Asher—lesser of evils and all that. "I've developed a preference, it seems."

"No," Asher intoned threateningly.

"We share everything. Our Coven is powerful because we do not divide." Ren grew eerily still. A threat rang in his voice and his nostrils flared. His low words made his anger clear even though he didn't raise his voice.

"You gave up the right."

Ren suddenly stood at the end of the bed. I had to crane my neck to look up at him. The top of his head brushed the pink canopy.

The corner of Ren's lips went up, but it didn't seem like a smile. More like a threat. He pinched my chin and forced my face up toward him.

"She belongs to Crimson Coven. Is that wrong?"

Asher's arms stiffened around me.

A laugh escaped and I clamped my lips tight. They were fighting over a blood bag. A human sized, female blood bag that had no control over her life ever since she got involved with vampires.

Ren leaned down, blood still painting his mouth.

"You have . . ." I pointed at my lip.

"Lick it."

The order . . . the smug look. I gritted my teeth.

I smacked him across the face.

The human girl gasped, then I gasped. What had I done? My hand hovered in the air and I gawked at it. What the hell was wrong with me? An evil, death craving entity must have possessed me.

"Asher," I said, cringing into his chest. But he was no help since his body shook with laughter.

I peeked over at the vampire. I hit him like he couldn't tear me apart with his hands. Ren still hadn't straightened.

I'd wanted to do that since I found out what an asshole he was, but I never would have done it. What the hell was wrong with me?

Especially towards him. He was the last Crimson Coven vampire I should have attacked considering that not too long ago he'd bent me over the counter and drank my blood just because he wanted to.

Asher couldn't be with me 24-7. How would the massive vampire make me pay? It wouldn't be the easy death I wanted.

"She's high off blood."

Ren gripped my hair and forced my face out of Asher's chest. His knuckles pressed into my head as he squeezed my hair to the point of pain. I cinched my eyes shut, blocking the view of his sinister expression.

"Careful, Ren," Asher warned.

"Open your eyes." Ren's demand vibrated over my skin.

I cinched them tighter.

"Now."

The low-toned threat sent a shiver down my spine and I popped open my eyes. A grin fixed across his lips. Not at all what I expected and honestly it was much more frightening.

My heartbeat stuttered.

The narrow bridge of his nose arched high and the planes of his cheeks dipped with deep dimples.

"I confirmed after trying to feed off the other human."

He directed the words at me, but I didn't know what to make of it. I licked my lips.

"Enough, Ren."

Even though he looked at me, he hadn't been speaking to me based on Asher seeming to know what Ren was going on about.

"Don't act like you don't taste the difference in her blood." He raised both eyebrows. "Isn't that why you've held onto the human so intently?"

catalina

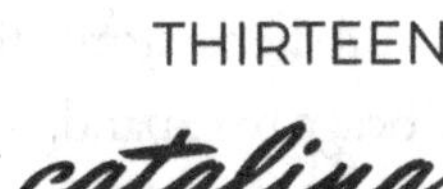

THE AIR SUCKED out of my lungs like a vacuum had been attached to my organs.

I understood the words, but I couldn't make sense of them.

"Her blood hums for *me*," Asher hissed. "She's meant to be mine."

Ren straightened. The tattoos slithering up his throat moved when he stretched his neck side to side. I hadn't had the opportunity yet to study the intricate ink spanning his golden skin.

The left side of his neck hosted stretching branches with pink cherry blossoms. The mass of flowers became lush at his chest and waves interwoven with koi fish painted his skin and melded into each other seamlessly. A lotus bloom curved over the side of his stomach and wrapped around to his back.

Each inch hosted a blend of beautiful artistry.

"Then if that's the requirement, she belongs to me as well."

Asher and Ren stared each other down. Tension mounted in the room.

My position clutched to Asher's chest became increasingly uncomfortable. I squirmed, but he didn't react.

"Humming blood?" I croaked. It sounded super loud to my ears, but neither of them looked at me.

"Yours?" Asher scoffed. "I was willing to share until . . ."

Asher's arms flexed tighter, making it difficult for my ribcage to expand.

His tirade turned into a buzzing sound as my vision wavered. I couldn't get words to push out from my throat as he slowly suffocated me.

A wheezing cough expelled from my mouth, but Asher didn't seem to notice my struggle.

"No other will do, Asher . . ." Ren said and his voice faded into the distance as Asher constricted his grip around me even more.

My ribcage tightened around my lungs. God, this was how I would die?

Being human fucking sucked sometimes.

REN

THE WAY he looked at me, knowingly . . . smug, but I didn't give a fuck. Catalina became limp in Asher's arms and the Swedish fuck didn't seem to notice. I lunged forward, hands outstretched to rip my human from Asher's clutches.

She could not be dead. Pressure on my chest compounded. Such a foreign sensation. I cradled her against my chest and her head rolled until her cheek pressed into my shoulder.

Her chest moved rhythmically, and the flutter at her neck showed she was alive. But her limp body and unresponsive features—I did not like this.

I focused until the slightest thud of her heartbeat reached my ears.

She was okay.

I brushed the long hair away from her face. Her lips pouted even while at rest. The dark, long eyelashes rested against the crest of her cheekbones. She was quite a beauty.

"Catalina," Asher shouted, panic filling his tone as he snatched her out of my arms. *Now* Asher noticed that he'd been constricting her to death. His twin barreled in a few moments later. As if he'd been waiting nearby. He usually kept himself at a distance, but it'd worsened since the human's been around. Jax's gaze focused on Catalina, alarm flickering over his expression.

"What's wrong with her?" The pitch of his voice differed from anything I'd heard from him since I met him. The day Imogen pitched the idea of creating a Coven so large that none would dare move against us, I'd been intrigued. A Coven that could work together? I'd never heard of it.

She said to leave everything to her.

Less work for me.

Then she'd come home with the moody criminal and his twin, a whore for hire.

She was incapable of softer emotions, but the criminal was besotted, following her every command with a smile. The discord between the twins wasn't lost on me, but he never said anything or endangered the Coven. I'd still been prepared to rid us of Asher if the time came. Until now, it had not happened, and he'd proven himself a useful Sire and resource.

"What happened?" His sharp gaze focused on the girl draped in Asher's arms. I straightened.

Jax shouldered into my space. I observed him. The eyes flicking side to side, his hands hovering out to touch her and then retreating. The looks he sent his brother.

He was jealous.

I had seen that emotion in action but have never seen it from him. Much less because of a human. The corner of my lips twitched. I settled on the edge of the bed beside Asher, the bed dipping and creaking from my weight. Asher's side glare didn't escape me. I reached out to comb my fingers through her long hair, the silky strands slipping between my fingers. Her hair was so soft . . .

I shook myself out of the fixation before it swallowed me whole. My original plan was to set Jax off into a fit.

I looked up at him. His mouth pursed with displeasure. A glare fixed over his features. I contained my smirk.

"Such a lovely little human," I murmured, still peeking at Jax from the corner of my eye as I combed her hair. Having never done such a thing, it felt strange, but it was oddly fascinating.

"Ren, what the fuck are you doing." Such incredulity from Jax.

"Your jealousy is showing."

"What are you talking about?" he sputtered. "I'm not jealous over some human."

He'd never seemed so . . . emotion riddled. The corner of my mouth twitched.

Vampires easily displayed all of the negative emotions, but this? No, our reaction to her was not normal.

"Let's kill her and be done with it. If Asher and Tobias are so set on being *kind*," Jax spat the word out like it was a ludicrous concept. "Then we can end her right now, she would just be gone. No pain."

Her death? No. It would not happen. The taste of her blood settled in my memory. A rampant need to sink my teeth into her now urged them to extend.

"You are here because your brother is convinced that you truly want this human. Do not think of murdering her. She must be savored." Like fine wine. His jaw twitched. Such bitterness lived in this youngling; he let himself be run by it. "Do not make moves without thought, Jaxon, you will not survive long."

I would not allow him to damage our Coven or our new belonging. Even if I had to infect him with blood-madness. I'd had to do it once per Imogen's convincing that it was in the best interest of the Coven. If I hadn't, then Bastien would have left us, and we needed him to maintain our numbers.

I needed to follow my own reminder. A human would not come above me or power. As delightful as her blood tasted, she would not bring my Coven down.

FOURTEEN

catalina

"I FORGET HOW FRAGILE HUMANS ARE." Asher's sweet breath ruffled my hair and caused it to tickle my ear.

With consciousness came a dull soreness at my torso. Groaning, I pressed my palm into my side. There was less room to stretch out, and peeking at the seat fabric behind Asher, it informed me it was because we were in the car.

Asher clicked his tongue like a disapproving parent. I didn't have the energy to glare at him like I wanted.

"Don't move too much, Pet. Here's some more of my blood." Soft skin pressed against my lips. I shook my head, smearing the blood across my cheek.

My mouth watered, but I pressed my lips together to not let any slip through. My head felt fuzzy, like I'd woken from a long nap instead of essentially being boa constricted into unconsciousness.

Asher cradled me in his arms, enveloping me completely. My cheek pressed into his pec and I drooped against him.

My ankle pinched from the position of my foot with my heel wedged between Asher and Jax's thigh. I wiggled my leg and it sent shockwaves to my knee. I sank my teeth into my lip to hold back my whimper.

Jax, angry looking like always, gripped my calf and jerked my foot out from between them. My heel settled on his jean clad thigh. Tingles spread through my foot.

"You could be gentle," I whimpered.

Jax looked at me like I was talking crazy. Must be such a foreign concept to him.

My attention lifted to the driver's seat where an unrecognizable person sat there with an old fashioned driver's suit on him. He didn't even turn. As for the passenger, all I could see was her long hair. The bright red hair gave it away as the girl from the club. Asher's Progeny.

"Pull up here," Asher ordered.

The car slowed in front of their gate. The ornamental wrought iron fence rounded at the top. Roses intertwined with the black bars and both sides had a wall of red bricks stretching to surround the place with the black of the gate adorned around the top. Like spears embedded into the top.

Asher moved and the door popped open with a click. If he didn't brace me I would have fallen.

"Hop off." I gingerly slid off his lap and wobbled on my numb, still tingling feet. "Up to the manor, Pet." Asher patted my ass.

I shot him a glare and he only smiled unrepentantly.

The flippant vampire was asking for a stake to the heart.

He slammed the door shut, cutting off Jax's words and leaving me alone outside the car.

The cold breeze ruffled my loose waist length hair around my arms, and I hugged myself. Such silence. I should have been used to it considering I'd spent much of my time alone. The car detached from the sidewalk, moving forward at a crawling pace.

The long street was quiet except for the caw of a bird perched on the sill of the window. It almost blended in with the dark backdrop of the home.

Asher thought I was a mole, but he didn't hold it against me. He'd offered me a semblance of a leash. I wouldn't be fooled into taking all of it, though. They became obsessive and compulsive with what they considered theirs. That was where Asher was. He didn't have to explain to me or take my feelings into account, but he did. Since they couldn't be tempted into killing me. I'd remain at their side until I could escape, which meant settling into their home.

I unlatched the gate and swung it wide open, setting off a swarm of bats. The fluttering sound of their wings no longer sent my heart pounding. Once I reached halfway up the cement stairs, I could see the wide doors yards up. And the large metal upside down bat knocker.

Their home rested on the slightest incline, and rose bushes bloomed on both sides of the steps. The beautiful blooms coated the breeze with their scent. Growing them in this colder environment took skill.

Crows cawed from their perch on the iron welded into the brick. My foot slipped to the side of the shoe and bent my ankle again. With a huff, I crouched and jerked the little latch off out of the strap, shoving the skirt out of my way. I wiggled the heel off and hooked my finger in the strap and went to the other one.

A crow flapped its wings to my left. I followed the

movement and to the . . . hair? It'd settled on the head of a dead woman. I gasped, falling backwards onto my ass.

Her heel rested on the edge of the stair, her body on its back within the tangle of rose bushes as if she'd fallen backwards. Her eyes were open, unseeing, and the raw open gash across her neck explained the 'how' of the dead girl. A pool of blood bloomed beneath her neck, painting the thorny vines.

A scream ripped out of my throat. I scrambled back, scraping my palms and ankles against cement. Crows and bats exploded from wherever they hid on the property, filling the night with their fluttering wings and blocking out the pale moonlight. My heart thundered in my ears. A hand yanked me back and I screamed, fighting to get away.

"It's me!" Asher shouted.

In a blink, my face was buried in his chest, and I clung to him like a monkey.

"She's still warm. This happened recently," Jax said.

"No one knows where we live. How did this happen? *Jag måste ringa*, Jax." They continued volleying words back and forth in their language. I breathed in deep and let out a steadying breath. The girl looked like me. I breathed in and out again. Nausea swirled in my stomach, but I needed the confirmation.

I lifted my head from its burrow against Asher's chest. His arms that were banding around my back squeezed around me, but I still had room to turn my head to the side. She did look like me, eerily like me. Hispanic, with long black hair plastered to her bloody skin. Even her body type. Her shirt had been ripped and it hung off her shoulders in tattered strips. Across her belly were the ragged openings of skin peeled back. I could see the layers from where someone or something carved into her. "Whore" was written out in curving letters.

I gagged and pressed my hand to my mouth to stop the vomit from escaping. Had *he* found me? The Pale One?

Asher gripped under my elbows and hoisted me up to my unsteady feet, keeping me balanced. He caught my hands and pressed them to another chest. I gripped onto whoever he directed me toward. All I could see through my blurry sight was a wide chest, which meant it could be anyone.

Fear rode me hard, and I didn't care who I held onto. I sniffled and dashed the back of my hand across my eyes. My cheek pressed against the hard chest, and I clasped my arms around his waist. It tapered too much for it to be Ren, and yet was too wide for it to be Tobias. Which left Jax. I blinked, clearing my vision to watch Asher swipe through his cell.

"Is Tobias with you?" Asher said. "He disappeared? Find him, we have an issue." Asher paused to listen to the voice on the other end of his call.

Jax pressed his large palm into my lower back, then slid it around my waist. He pulled back so I was no longer plastered to his front. He prodded me up the rest of the stairs with me hobbling on one heel. The other one likely fell into the rose bushes.

Although he didn't stop me from gripping onto him, he didn't help me keep my balance, so I clung onto him as he half dragged me.

He made a sound—a cross between a scoff and a sigh of exasperation—and lifted me into his arms. I swayed in his cradle until we reached Asher's bedroom with dizzying speed.

He dumped me on the bed.

"Wait," I gasped, bunching the bottom end of his shirt. My skirt tangled around my legs as I tried to get up.

He was going to leave me. I didn't want to be alone for a second. My hands trembled.

"Don't go."

His sharp jawline bunched, but he gave me his back, easily sliding out of my grip. Panic bloomed into a ball in my stomach.

"I did it!" I shouted right as his large hand wrapped around the door knob. I repeated the admittance of guilt. The other three wouldn't kill me, but this one . . . this one ached for my death. I untangled myself from the skirt and stood at the end of the bed oscillating my weight from foot to foot. He hadn't left and that was what mattered.

He was suddenly in my face, hand wrapped around my throat. I choked on my next words.

"I know." He leaned down so close his nose grazed mine. If it weren't for his thumb digging into my trachea, it may have caused butterflies having him so close to me.

Even though he closed in to choke me, he wasn't leaving and that was what I wanted.

I blinked up at him, silent.

The edges of his hair mussed at the top and his blue eyes, more of a blue lapis in color, and deeper than Asher's, flashed with red before fading away.

I couldn't erase the memory of the dead girl and how closely she resembled me. It couldn't be a coincidence. Factor in 'whore' and then it was a given; someone targeted me. Someone other than the vampires currently holding me hostage.

I bunched my skirt in my fingers.

All I needed was to be held. Jax would never hold me, though.

My second-best option was having him end this crippling fear nipping at my heels. But here we were, alone this time, after I told him I was guilty, and he still wouldn't kill me. All he needed to do was squeeze a little harder. He was eerily still as if made of stone. He loomed over me intimidatingly, not moving a centimeter. As much as I struggled to breathe, I was still able to drag in a lungful.

Why wouldn't they just kill me?

"You will not last here, pathetic human. Asher will grow bored of you." He sneered and released me, straightening to his full height. He may as well have punched into my chest and taken my throbbing heart in hand.

He turned on his heel. Leaving again. He always turned his back to me. I understood I wouldn't mean anything to him. His contempt didn't surprise me, but I couldn't help that it hurt.

My heart jumped into overdrive, the swelling balloon in my stomach preparing to pop.

"Not as pathetic as being hung up on some dead girl."

Every muscle in his back tensed up.

I held my breath.

I'd crossed the line, but I couldn't care. His quick move toward me caused my hair to flutter around my face then he dug his fingers into my throat.

I grabbed his wrists, holding onto them as I was pulled to my tip toes. I blinked up at him. If I was finally going to be snuffed out, I'd look him in the eyes the entire time.

Stupid tears welled to blur him. I blinked and they rolled down my numb face. His bowlike lips stiffened into a thin line. His hand around my neck flexed, then I went flying and landed on my back with a hard bounce, the mattress squealing with protest upon my landing. He sprang on top of me, sneering into my face.

Weight settled over me and I struggled to expand my chest. Jax took hold of my wrists, slamming them beside my head. I clenched my hands so hard that my fingernails dug into my palm. The furious vampire was so damn large. His wide torso hovered above me, and his chin was pointed down as he sneered at me.

Jax's weight settled between my legs, so heavy that he forced them to splay apart. Pressure on my clit spiked lust through my veins. I gasped, my eyelids fluttering. Oh God, their violence was an aphrodisiac. Everything about them turned me on. It was a truth I couldn't hide from after accepting my twisted desires.

He rose higher onto his hands, pinning me more securely as he rose over me. His movement rubbed against my core. A whine crawled up my throat, but I kept it contained. The desire flushing my face and body was embarrassing enough in the face of his demeaning expression. His nostrils flared and a muscle jumped in his jaw.

"You like that? Needy little human?" His teeth flashed, his perpetual fangs extending. "You're sopping wet, aren't you." It was more of a statement. "I can smell you." His eyelids lowered, blocking half of his deep blues. Ecstasy played over his expression.

His hips moved and the hard bulge at the apex of his thigh flared pleasure through my clit with each of his grinding thrusts. The pants needed to go. I whimpered, still trying to move against him, though it was pointless.

The gyrations curled through my limbs with delicious temptation. I moaned, trying to move, but he kept control of me.

I panted, arching my hips to push my aching clit against

him. His sinfully strong body that could fuck me hard. Having his skin against mine—I craved it. I wanted to sink my fingers into his short hair, but he didn't let me loose despite my attempts.

Submitting to his dominion, I lay limp under him.

"More," I begged.

His eyes turned red in the blink of an eye. Jax struck his teeth into the swell of my breast with such violence that I screamed. Tears flooded my eyes, but they quickly turned into ones of pleasure. A long suck of my breast had me writhing for more, trying to arch my spine to get him to continue sucking. With him inched over my chest, his torso settled between my legs, my thighs wide.

He hummed, the vibration tingling to my nipple. His weight slightly shifted and he held my ribcage.

I panted and my breasts pushed against the curve of the whalebone adorning the top. One jostle would expose me completely. A shiver trembled up the large vampire's body as a rush of feminine power heightened my lust. I made him feel that way, not Imogen. His tongue flicked across the bite, the warm lave inciting another gush of moisture. I lifted my hips, grazing my needy core against his hard abdomen. When he lifted, he no longer had the red irises.

"Never speak of Imogen."

The threat sliced through me and nasty emotions surfaced. My face heated up and I curled my fingers into a fist, desperately trying to yank free from his shackle-like hands that had yet to release me. Unbelievable fucking vampire.

Despite my irritation, his hips slamming against my core flared lust to the forefront. I wanted him to want me like that. To only desire me.

The way he was with me before he thought I betrayed them. At this point, I may as well have done it. It was the cruelest of realities.

"Why?" I said between pants, grinding my wet core against him. The mix of frustration and jealousy melding together to create a perfect storm of I-should-have-kept-that-thought-in-my-head. "She's dead." My panties were a damp mess. If only I could get the clothes out from between us to feel his smooth shaft.

He bared his distended fangs then gripped my hips, turning me in a smooth motion. I landed face down on the mattress. My skirt pooled at my waist and in seconds my panties were gone.

I braced my forearms under me. There was a rustling sound behind me and then Jaxon grabbed my thighs, securing them around his hips, simultaneously lifting and spreading my legs to the point that it hurt. He held me suspended and poised.

"What—"

He slammed his cock into my channel and his thighs slapped against mine. I jolted forward, losing balance as my cheek flattened on the mattress. My core clasped onto him like she could keep him inside her forever. He never fucked me while looking me in the face.

The bed muffled my groan. He easily kept my hips high, and with a slow glide, he slid out until only the thick tip remained inside me. The walls of my pussy fluttered around the mushroom of his head. The shallow tease of his tip reinforced the overwhelming thickness of his cock.

He pounded forward and another slap rang through the room.

Breath left my lungs with a cry.

"Fuck. *Jag kan inte motstå dig.*" Whatever he said seemed to spur him on harder. The rhythmic thrusts turned disjointed and volatile. With every thrust, my cheek rubbed across the fabric of the red silk sheets.

I clawed my fingers into the bed, moving my hips to try to meet his rutting, but he kept me still, turning me into a whimpering mess.

"More!" I panted. "Jax!" No sense of self-preservation remained. He snarled and the sound caused my pussy to constrict around him as if in answer. The orgasm crashed into me with suffocating strength. My ears rang with my scream. He continued pounding into me with hard, claiming thrusts, dragging out my release.

I twitched to get away, to get a smidge of relief from the onslaught of his thrusts, but it was a fool's attempt. His hands flexed around my waist, and he continued owning me.

My arms completely gave out and I slumped against the mattress, taking his attack. The wet smack of his glide in and out of me invaded the bedroom. I whimpered, my sensitive folds constricting around him. Jax angled my hips higher, and the tip of his cock shoved hard against something deep inside me—I could feel him in my throat. A gasp escaped and he continued pounding. Another swell built with a flurry. What was he doing to me? I was so close. So close.

His guttural groan sent me over the edge a second time. His cock throbbed in my core, and my pussy clasped onto him with repeated wrings. Gripping tighter and tighter. He thrust once more and then kept his hips flush against my ass, hands painfully clutching my hips. He gasped and my channel squeezed him. Another throb of his cock caused moisture to leak from around him and trickle onto my thigh.

Half his body settled over me, smushing me against the

mattress. He curved over my back, his weight settling over me. As heavy as he was, the compression felt good.

His nose grazed against my ear. That felt so good. He'd tired me out.

He stiffened, stopping mid-nuzzle, cock still deep inside me.

"You can't compare to Imogen." It was like a bucket of ice-cold water was dumped over my head. The fogginess clinging to my thoughts ever since drinking from Asher faded.

Nothing Jax said could have hurt me more. He could have tossed me around and it would have stung less. His weight disappeared off me. I rolled to sit up. My chest still heaved with exertion. God, him choking me had hurt less. I hugged myself, my chin dipping to my chest. With ease, he ruptured the blissful cloud I'd floated on. This place could never be my true home. And I could never belong with them. I curled my legs to my chest, pushing my skirt down.

Jax stood at the end of the bed and efficiently buttoned his jeans, his jaw working as he stared at me with dead eyes. I watched the smooth glide of his fingers work through his short hair.

"Don't expect anything from me."

"Wouldn't dream of it." I almost choked on the words.

His eyes narrowed at me but I meant it. I honestly didn't think he was capable of it.

With a final look, he turned. It spiked my pulse into action. Panic crawled up my throat. If that vampire that held me captive had found me, it meant the end of me. The remembered feel of insects crawling all over me forced nausea to the surface.

"Don't leave!" I choked out and I hurried off the bed. My feet got tangled in the dress and I fell to my knees. Pain vibrated through my legs.

Jax stared at me on the ground. One beat, then two beats passed. He slammed the door.

My eyes stung. I wanted him. It was too late to save myself. That chance was gone and I'd embrace the darkness while I stayed put until the time came to escape or die, whichever came first.

tobias

"TO WHAT DO I owe this pleasure?" Calliope's tone was biting. She perched on the edge of the plush red seat cushion, leaning forward so her elbows rested on the edge of the table. She swirled a cocktail glass, swishing the red liquid side to side. The loud booming from the speakers assaulted my ears. Saphire Lounge was in full swing. I never understood how others enjoyed the raucousness of places like this. I smoothly glided into the seat next to her.

Damn mind reader—her thought cut off. I didn't react. Thoughts from vampires came and went.

"Would you like a drink?" She waved a hand at the wine bottle. "I had it siphoned from a severely intoxicated human."

"No, thank you." I leaned forward, lacing my hands on the surface.

She snorted, shook her head and tipped her glass back. *Never understood this one—*

"I will get to the point before you continue to disparage me," I said.

She stiffened.

"I must remind you, if you act against me, I will—"

I put up my hand.

"Yes, yes, you will cause all sorts of havoc against us. The threats are unnecessary." I sighed. "Today we had an uninvited visitor. Do you know anything about this?"

Her dark eyebrows furrowed. *Someone attacked them?*

"Why should I tell you anything when you killed one of my people?" Vampires and their notorious grudges.

I sucked in one breath to contain my aggravation.

"Cease with the melodramatics. I did you a favor." My tone held the slightest bite. "Now, tell me, did you attack my Coven?"

She stiffened and met my eyes.

"No," she snapped. "I didn't send anyone to attack your precious Coven. I swear it on my dead Sire." *I'm not that stupid.*

I CROSSED the threshold into our home.

Jax's thoughts shouted at me from where he paced in the living room. He made the simple act of walking seem angry. Usually, I was able to stifle the ability so whatever thoughts filtered through became background noise, but since I focused on it with Calliope, my ability was especially sensitive.

*She seemed so desolate. I took it too far—*I entered the living room to find him pacing to and fro. So distracted that he did not see me. What was wrong with him? Like a storm on a rampage. He never relaxed enough for me to get much more than a few thoughts here and there, but words blared at me. Although Jax did not, or could not put into words what he felt, his thoughts indicated his guilt.

"What have you done, Jaxon?"

He jerked to a stop, and slowly turned to look at me. His eyebrows remained furrowed. Instead of waiting, I would find out myself. I made quick work of the stairs and was in Asher's bedroom in seconds.

She lay on the floor, curled on her side, eyes closed. Her cheek pillowed against her hands, stained with tear tracks.

"You left her in this state?"

"I . . ."

Had she fallen? I'd caused this. I . . . hurt her? His thoughts continued. A stream of thoughts I'd heard in plenty of human inner dialogue. Guilt.

"What have you said to her now?" I hissed. My patience wore thin. I scooped her up into my arms.

"Where are you taking her?"

"I'm going to get her cleaned up," I retorted stiffly.

I want my *scent all over her . . .* his thought cut off. I scoffed. He had no right. I offered him a glare, but he was too deep in his head to register my disapproval.

I said her name on purpose. To drive a wedge between us. I couldn't keep denying the tempta—the thought faded into static.

catalina

COBWEBS COATED my brain and I slowly crawled free of them. With a gasp, I shot straight up. A mattress dipped under my ass. The bed sank under my weight. I curled my fingers into the brown comforter. Tobias's room.

The events of last night rushed to the forefront of my memory. One after the other slammed into me.

Giving into Asher, Tobias . . . Jax.

A priest ate me out and I was all for it. If there was a hell, I was heading straight there. I tempted a fucking priest out of their vow of celibacy. Guilt nibbled on my conscience, realistically, though, I understood I wouldn't have been able to force him. Oh, no, but it didn't stop there. I incited Jax into fucking me even though I knew he hated me. All because I didn't want to be alone. I rubbed my temples. My lust toward them was nothing new, but last night I'd turned over a new shameless leaf.

I pressed my palms into my eyes. So much happened last night. My brain reeled as events flashed behind my closed eyelids.

Asher claimed he wouldn't let me go.

Glee surfaced, expanding in my chest, about to pop. *No, calm down*, his words meant nothing. I could never truly belong.

Asher was why they hadn't offed me. Him and maybe Tobias, but that could have flown out the window with what happened last night. The dead body on the steps flashed to the forefront. My stomach twisted.

I was so tired of being scared.

Staying with them . . . as much as they could never truly care for me, was my only option other than death. I could make a stake out of something, except I knew myself. I didn't have killing them in me—not even a little bit. I was a survivor . . . more of a runner, and above all: not violent.

I stretched out on the bed, soreness kissing my muscles. The cotton sweater tickled my thighs. I plucked the front of the top that Asher must have dressed me in. Wait, I wasn't bound to the bed. The sconces framing the door emitted a soft glow and I scanned Tobias's room. The metal shutters were down.

"Asher? Tobias?" I shouted. Silence. No answer. It had to be morning.

They never left me unbound or alone until now. I eyed the doorknob. Had they . . .? Maybe my opportunity had come sooner than I anticipated. I jumped to my feet, rubbing my palms against the large sweater. I dropped my gaze to the doorknob. No way they left it unlocked. I gripped it . . . and it turned. A smile twitched the corner of my lips, and I caught myself before it turned into a full blown one. No celebrating until I was long gone.

A lovely, sweet scent reached my nose and I lifted the front of the sweater to sniff it. My eyes shuttered as I inhaled deeply.

With my move, my hair fell forward, so I brushed the wavy masses back. It had puffed up much more than usual, like it did after I showered and fell asleep without blow drying it. I sniffed a lock. That didn't smell like my shampoo, there was an earthy musk mingling with a sweet scent. Tobias. All the Crimson Coven vampires had the same distinct vanilla smell. Not overwhelming or cloying—a scent I could breathe in forever. I sighed and marched forward.

Each step was accompanied with a twinge of soreness. Whoever bathed me last night had done me a favor; it was something I could begrudgingly admit. I bet I'd feel ten times worse if I had woken sticky, naked, and in pain.

I padded across the carpet, down the hall toward the staircase. A few steps more and I would be within the faint light filtering up the stairs. The only beam spearing through the hallway since the shutters covered the window at the opposite end of the hall. I descended the steps. No one stopped me. There was no sound or a vampire springing out to yank me to their side. A smile bloomed to life.

I tiptoed as I crept forward, trying to be as quiet as possible. They were deep in their vampire slumber, but I could never assume what precautions they'd taken to ensure I stayed put. I was counting on them assuming I would be out for the entire day considering last night's events.

The exit, freedom, taunted me from a few steps away, but I kept my pace steady and quiet. If I stepped out unscathed . . . where would I go?

I didn't have anything. My things had all gone up in flames, from my laptop to my clothes, to most likely my cat. That included my debit cards. My heart pinched at the thought of all I'd lost. Wondering if Binx had escaped or if he was truly gone. I slowed. Sunlight spilled in from the half-circle window at the top of the wide door.

But even if I had nothing on me right now, I might not have a chance like this again. I'd just have to find a ride to the bank . . . except they'd request identification. If I went to the police, they wouldn't be able to protect me against vampires that could compel them, and even less against their deadly strength.

Then there was the dead girl. Whoever had killed that girl, and all signs pointed to the Pale One, could kill me. What if Crimson Coven was the only reason I'd survived this long?

Who was I kidding, they were also the reason I was *in* this mess.

The doorknob twitched, like someone was trying to open it. What the . . .? A thin knife looking object jiggled between the hinge and the frame. That didn't look legal. I backed up, at first hesitantly, and then I bolted into the living room and crouched behind the thick red curtain. The shutters were drawn down in here, too, so it left me within a veil of darkness.

I was just in time for the click of the lock giving to reach my ears. I kept my breaths shallow, but in my flurry to hide, I disturbed the layer of dust coating the velvet fabric. I clasped my palm over my nose, trying not to sneeze.

Whoever snuck in shut the door quietly—sneakily.

I nudged the curtain to peek out. A tall, slim form paused in the middle of the foyer, a swinging machete in hand. The weapon was half the size of my body.

My lungs seized. Was he here for me? I clenched the soft curtain in my fingers. Breathe. I forced an exhale out. Were there more people outside? Ready to catch me if I fled? I licked my lips. I'd have to take the chance.

The footsteps became louder and then the man came

within my view. His gaze scanned the dark living room I hid inside. I dipped to hide my mass of hair. Gashes marred the man's face and . . . I squinted. Were those bite marks on the side of his neck? He continued looking around and anger flitted over his expression, then he started down the hall.

Slipping out from the curtain, I oh so slowly tiptoed across the living room, stopping shy of stepping into the foyer.

What would the person wielding a machete do to the vampires? I clenched my teeth.

Not my problem. I tiptoed out and leaned to make sure it was a clear path to the door.

From the light, hollow steps echoing down the hall, he was in the kitchen. He seemed to be sweeping the area.

Would he use the machete on the vulnerable sleeping vampires upstairs? Or was he just after me?

I sighed and squeezed my hand into a fist and peeked at the steps. He could kill them, and the Crimson Coven would be no more . . . revulsion roiled in my chest. I didn't want them to be gone. At least not all of them. Could I live with their death on my conscience? I only had a moment to think about my next act. My body moved before my mind caught up and I dashed across the open foyer and up the steps. I skidded to the left side of the hall. The first door was my target. Since I had woken up in Tobias's room, then maybe he'd gone to bed there as he had before. I opened the door as quietly as possible, sliding inside the room and gently shutting it behind me. Closing the door left me in the dark. My heart jumped frantically. *I can do this*, I chanted repeatedly, almost like a prayer.

With my hands in front of me, I navigated from muscle memory since I couldn't see anything. My knee bumped into the mattress and I ran my hands over a cotton sheet until my fingertips nudged a foot. Please, please be Tobias. Using it as a guide, I dragged my palms up the muscled body.

This didn't feel like Tobias. He was too bulky. I trailed my hands up the large body. All of them were ungodly tall. Tobias was compact and the leanest of the three, and this one had too much muscle.

I touched a hip and the divots on the stomach dipped dramatically, marking his abs. Ren was the only one who had this many distinctly chiseled abs. Hands were interlaced on his belly and I ran my fingertips over the knuckles. Definitely Ren. He had scars on his knuckles like he spent most of his time as a human beating on people or punching poles. Could be either one, honestly.

"Ren," I whispered and nudged my palm against his shoulder. He didn't budge.

Could I even rouse him? My hand smacked into a corner of a nightstand and I flipped the lamp on, knowing it might bring attention to this room. But I had no choice, I needed to see. "Wake up," I whispered. "Ren."

I clenched my fist, poising to strike his face. I pursed my lips, winding back. I sighed and opened my hand. My aversion to violence was annoying. He'd hunted me down. He'd laughed at me. He'd stood by with that irritating smirk—I smacked him across the face. His eyes sprang open so suddenly. I hissed a breath out, clenching my stinging hand.

He lashed out, grabbing my arm so hard I landed on the bed. My bounce on the mattress cut off as he flattened me under him. Ren grabbed my throat with one hand, the ease in which he moved, frightening.

He didn't blink as he loomed over me. I lay unmoving, struggling to breathe. He inhaled sharply, lowering the tip of his nose to brush it against my cheek. The suffocating grip loosened. I dragged in oxygen.

"If you're trying to kill me, you'll have to do better," he said, voice husky.

I fervently shook my head.

"Someone broke into the house." My whisper broke mid-sentence.

He turned to granite and after a beat rolled to the side. As soon as he was upright, he wilted to the left, staggering slightly. Each blink of his eyelashes seemed to weigh him down.

He braced himself on the wall. He shook his head and slid to his ass.

"The weight of the sun." He paused and his shoulders moved. Vampires didn't breathe unless they seriously exerted themselves. "It's at the highest point."

Time of day could make it harder for vampires to move around? That was news to me. If this was him at his most vulnerable, then we were all screwed with me as the defense.

Ren's head fell forward.

"Shit. Shit." I combed my fingers through my hair. I didn't have time to freak out when that was all I wanted to do. I yanked the quilt off the bed.

"Just stay here, I'll stop him," I said, wetting my lips. *I'd try.* I tossed the blanket over his head. It would hopefully give him a chance of survival if the man killed me. He looked like a mass against the wall. I didn't know if the person was here to steal or what, but the fact that he brought a machete made it pretty clear that this was a full-on murder attempt for someone.

Two large samurai swords hung above the bed. It was closer to the ground, the style distinct to Tatami beds.

With my heart pounding, I hopped on top and reached for

the handle of one of the dangerous looking slim swords. The cool metal settled in my palm and I pulled it off the hooks it rested on. The blade immediately thudded on the bed. I grabbed it with both hands and struggled to lift it.

God, this was not the time to rue my unathletic body. I swayed to the door, moving ungracefully because of the weight. Resting the tip on the floor, it immediately gouged into the wood. I winced at the destroyed flooring.

Opening the door, I slid out, dragging the weapon behind me while holding it with two hands. How did people fight with these every day? Imagine the arm muscles . . . and that explained Ren's muscle mass.

I inched past the stairs and crossed to the right-side hallway. Jax's bedroom door was open.

The broad shouldered man stood at the end of the bed, staring down at Jax. Oh God. He was a big guy. Bigger than I'd thought. Broad and tall and wide. A Mack truck of a human. But he stared down at Jax without movement. The floorboard creaked. In a sudden jerky motion, he turned on his heels. There went my element of surprise.

His features tautened and his blank expression became suddenly animated as he narrowed his eyes on me.

He lifted the machete and bum rushed me. My lungs seized and I scrambled to lift the sword as I backed away.

I managed to get it pointed at him as he came at me.

Maybe I had this! . . . the hopeful thought evaporated as he smacked the machete against the samurai sword. The vibration stung my hand and I dropped it with a pained grunt.

The back of his hand flew at me, and I rolled from the force of his backhand. My hip hit the ground, and I used my heels to drag myself backwards. The sunlight spilling in from downstairs fell across his face as he stormed up to me, giving me a better look at him.

Those eyes only held rage.

I used my palms to scoot back.

He bunched the front of my shirt and lifted me only to slam me against the wall. He was human and I still couldn't hold my own against him. My head ricocheted off the wall with a frightening thud and my sight swam.

He crouched and grabbed my neck and pinned me to the wall. He slowly lifted me until my feet kicked in the air and my eyeballs felt like they would pop.

I dug my nails into his forearms, but the long sleeves didn't allow me to draw blood.

He stared at me, watching me struggle. Taking pleasure in my frantic movements.

My face throbbed. Something dripped into my eye. Blood from my aching eyebrow.

I couldn't breathe out of my nose because it hurt and the scent of copper tinged every inhale.

With his free hand, he lifted his phone and snapped a picture of me. Efficient and quick, like photographing a landscape.

He slipped the phone back into his pocket and his free hand joined the one at my throat.

catalina

PRESSURE EXPANDED IN MY TEMPLES. My head would pop soon. I dug my nails in harder, but he didn't loosen.

I thought I'd die at the hands of vampires . . .

The man suddenly jolted. A thin line of red slowly spread across his throat in a diagonal, then his head slid right off leaving me staring at bloody severed bone. My stomach lurched, but since his hands still remained around my throat, it dissuaded vomit from rising.

In a sudden breath, he collapsed and I fell in an ungraceful bundle beside his decapitated head. I pressed my trembling hand to my mouth to muffle my scream.

Ren staggered and dropped the sword with a thud that vibrated the ground. His palm pressed into the wall over my head.

His shoulder faced the sunlight spilling in through the front door window. Steam floated off his shoulder accompanied by a low sizzle.

His eyelids shuttered his brown eyes and he dropped to his

back. Light fell across the front of his chest and within moments, the steam started at every point the sun touched him.

If he stayed like that, he'd end up boiling alive.

I forced my attention away from the dead body and crawled to block the light from hitting Ren. Blood puddled under my legs, the slippery sensation coating my skin and making it harder to scramble over to him. As soon as I blocked the sun from his body, the smoking tapered off. He'd crossed the sun to save me. He could have waited for the human to come at him.

I would need to move fast to get him covered. Jax's room was closest. Sliding my hands under his shoulders, I used my legs to drag him.

Little by little, I nudged him toward the bedroom. I panted from exertion, but adrenaline must be working through my system because I managed to not stop until he was safe behind Jax's door.

The threshold was as far as I could drag him if I didn't want my lungs to explode. He draped across the entrance ungracefully, muscled limbs all over the place.

The scent of burnt flesh singed my nose from the wounds that didn't sizzle any longer. Still, they remained open and nasty. If he'd burned any longer, the tattoos would have been a jumbled, unrecognizable mess.

I pressed my wrist to his parted mouth, but he didn't react. Blood dripped off my chin and splattered on his chest. I gingerly touched my forehead. A gash split my eyebrow. Using what was smeared on my fingers, I rubbed it on my wrist before placing it against his mouth.

His nostrils flared and fangs distended. Yet, he remained peacefully slumbering. Shoving my wrist to his teeth, I awkwardly punctured myself with one fang. I winced from the sting.

Blood leaked from the puncture and into his mouth.

Ren grabbed my arm.

I grunted, forced down from his pull. He suckled sleepily, hugging my arm. He only swallowed a handful of times before his tongue lapped against my wound.

I tried to pull free, but he didn't release me, keeping his lips against my wrist. The sunlight wounds at his shoulder reunited inch by inch. Amazing how it didn't ruin the mosaic of tattoos. My neck pinched at this position of bracing up while he hugged my arm.

It would leave me even more sore than I already was. I moved my elbow so it poked out enough for me to lower.

I lolled with my ear against his abs.

My head pounded and as my body relaxed and adrenaline leaked away, each wound became startlingly easier to feel.

The human male had done a number on me.

Being held like this, even if he didn't know it was me, comforted me. Tears pricked my eyes and they drooped with each blink, but I couldn't fall asleep.

I missed Peter.

As soon as I had the chance, I was sending an anonymous email to my lawyer informing her of my demise. From there she would know what to do to pass along my estate to Peter. He could continue having a life without worry. That would be enough.

Ren groaned and the vibration traveled to my ear.

As much as they hurt me, they'd also protected me. If the Pale One found me, they were my only chance at surviving. I'd been waffling about all my options, but this event cemented it.

I'd die before going back to that cave that creature kept me in. Where I'd become acquainted with the smell of wet rock and the sensation of being held at the edge of death.

I huddled against Ren, waiting for the vampires to wake . . . as soon as my brain wandered, my surroundings faded.

Familiar with the fuzzy backgrounds of Bastien's dream realm, I turned to find him looming over me.

He wore no shirt and his broad shoulders tapered to a muscled torso. His abdomen hosted the slightest indent of abs. He was the largest of the five, which was a feat all in itself. Bear-like in stature. He was also the most unhinged.

But him being crazed wasn't a choice. Bastien was blood-mad. The only vampire illness in existence, according to Asher.

That must have been what was wrong with the vampire that took me, except that one was sickly and thin. Practically a skeleton.

Bastien approached with quick strides and in one fell swoop, he lifted me into his arms, cradling me close.

"Oof," I grunted. As much as it hurt, I embraced the feeling of being held. Bastien was the only one that hadn't been so mercurial with me, if anything, he always made me feel wanted. Sure, he was slightly psychotic, but I was used to it. At least he didn't keep me guessing.

I buried my nose into his chest, inhaling his sweet scent.

I wouldn't question my sexual preferences anymore. If anyone looked at them, they'd salivate as much as me.

My readers could attest that the vampire kink was alive and well. Only difference was that the ones I created were much sweeter—unlike these monsters.

Bastien hoisted me higher on his chest until my thighs spread on his torso and he could dip his fangs into my throat.

He sucked. The pleasure was veiled behind a curtain, nothing close to what it truly felt like. His exhale verged on frustration.

As good as fucking in this dream world felt, when I woke it felt like I had a really good wet dream. In better terms, it lived in my imagination. It must feel the same for him when he bit me.

Bastien never spoke to me. Honestly, I didn't think he could. He moved his head back and looked me in the face, glowing red eyes not holding much behind the depths.

He tilted his head, nostrils flared.

The surroundings incrementally darkened and melded together as it blurred into something else.

I grabbed a handful of his long pale hair before my disorientation took me to the floor. Not that I would have hit in the real world, but it felt like I was falling.

A bed with soft cream pillows sprawled across it came into sight. My stomach dropped—my bedroom no longer existed. Now it consisted of piles of ash.

My nose burned and a tear slipped free.

Bastien's head jerked and he narrowed his eyes. With his speed, he had us on the bed with me on his lap.

He licked the tear traveling down my cheek.

What was it with them eating my tears?

I sighed and rubbed the back of my hand against my face to dash the wetness away. Bastien settled me on my back and slid down, delved under the hem of the sweater and buried his face between my thighs.

Gasping, I trembled under his touch, bunching the fabric under my ass. The cotton felt eerily close to how mine had felt, but it wasn't exact.

Bastien's tongue flicked out and he ran his long warm

tongue through the folds to find my clit. I jackknifed upright and pulled his long hair. He hummed against my pussy. I pressed my heels into the bed and shoved up against his mouth, rubbing myself so hard his teeth grazed against my sensitive sex. The rasp of his teeth felt delicious.

An orgasm swelled to a painful peak. Bastien didn't stop suckling my clit. His jaw worked as he ate me out.

My head fell back and I choked on a gasp. Bastien steadily feasted. I wanted this in real time.

I shivered from the after effects. I came with him watching me. He crawled up the bed and I sifted my hand in his hair—he enjoyed when I played with his silky locks. I sank my fingers close to his scalp, and he hummed. A gush of need made my clit throb.

A LARGE PALM rubbed against my head. Groaning, I leaned into the touch, enjoying the tingles that were traveling down my spine.

I popped my eyes open, and Ren stared down at me with his eyebrows raised. He propped himself on his elbows, staring at me over the expanse of his muscled, tattooed torso where I currently rested my head. We were still on the hard ground, but half of me was all over Ren's body.

I'd been rubbing my cheek dangerously low on his stomach, damn near his dick. Fortunately the low-riding black sweats covered the tented front.

"Continue please," his deep voice had taken on a husky intonation I hadn't heard before. Up until now, everything he said had been angry, abrasive, or rude.

"You're like a little cat."

"Like a kitten," Jax said with his deep accented voice. He stood leaning near the door with his back against the wall, arms crossed.

Ren raised an eyebrow at Jax who cleared his throat and crossed his arms.

I popped up so fast.

Four pairs of vampire eyes stared down at me.

Asher crouched and curled the blanket that had pooled at my waist around my shoulders.

"Good job, Pet," he crooned, clasping my cheek in his large palm.

I scowled, but he only smiled.

"What . . .?" The answer reared to the forefront of my memory. "Oh."

"Are you struggling?" Asher asked, his eyebrows furrowing. "Considering humans have difficulty with death."

"I'm fine," I said stiffly. I rubbed my eyes to get rid of the sand sensation rubbing against the insides.

"Our Pet is stronger than what you give her credit for."

Our? I snapped my head to Ren so quickly it hurt my neck. His gaze hadn't moved on from me.

His keen focus freaked me out.

"Back to the important bits," Jax interjected. I didn't miss the backhanded comment. "Calliope had to have sent him. She's the only one that could have known. You."

I swiveled to look at him. "When she sent you here as a spy, did she ask you to give her the lay of the manor?"

"For the millionth time, she didn't send me." I was getting tired of repeating myself. He'd believed me when I admitted to the transgression, but refused to doubt, just a little, that I worked for Calliope? Ridiculous, trust-issue riddled vampire.

"As mentioned," Tobias interjected from his stiff stance behind Asher's crouched body, interrupting whatever diatribe Jax was about to embark on. "No one knows of this manor unless we're being watched."

"The question to answer is why now and why was a dead human dumped on our doorstep. It's targeted to—"

"Me," I croaked. "He found me."

My stomach might as well live outside my body with how often it fell. The hollowness caused nausea to rise. It could be the only explanation. He'd found me. I'd begun to suspect, but the picture the man took of me, and the—

"Breathe, Catalina," Asher murmured and smoothed his palm down the back of my neck. "You're safe. No one will touch you."

The words swirled in my brain, but my body had a difficult time believing it. A tremble coasted over my hands.

Asher sat back on his haunches and swept me onto his lap and clicked his tongue as he rubbed my shoulder.

"Come, sweet Pet, tell me who is after you? I will not allow it to happen."

A large, heavy palm wrapped around the back of my neck and forced my head up. I met Ren's eyes who'd sat up.

"No one will touch you."

The clear threat in his brown eyes served as another layer of fear.

I swallowed past the knot in my throat. If I wanted their protection, I needed to spit it out, but dredging the words to the surface compounded on my shoulders.

"A long time ago, a vampire held me captive." I thought

they'd been still, but I had never felt the quiet fall upon a room like this. Even Jax took a step forward and froze as if he'd shatter in a moment. "He fed from me until I was near death. And kept me like that, chained in a damp, dark cave, for weeks."

Asher caught my trembling hand and it offered me the strength needed to keep talking. His body had tensed up against mine. I'd told him the surface of being hurt by one of his kind, never going into detail.

"There was something off about the intruder." I shrank a bit.

"Go on, Pet." Asher caressed the side of my neck with the back of his finger.

"Like he was compelled. He stood over Jax. He had a chance to slam the machete in him, but he didn't, but as soon as he saw me, he came at me full force." I shook my head. "And when he looked at me, there was this eerie blank glaze to his eyes." I squeezed my eyes tight and slumped against Asher. "The person behind it has to be the one that kept me all that time ago." I swallowed. "A-and the man took a picture of me. Was there any information on his phone?"

"No, *Älskade*, I scoured the device and there was nothing but the picture he took of you," Asher said, his arms tightening around me.

Jax suddenly straightened, his attention fully on his brother.

"We need to find this vampire," Tobias snapped. He hadn't looked me in the eyes, and he still didn't when I looked over at him.

He was making it startlingly obvious he was avoiding me. Warmth washed over my cheeks and I cleared my throat, forcing my gaze away from his mouth. His delicious, tempting, sinful mouth. A shiver traveled down my spine.

Ren suddenly leaned close and inhaled deep. He hummed, making a point in letting me know he smelled my arousal. I cinched my legs tight. The heightened sense thing was a menace. It didn't help the heat on my face.

The deep intonation of the doorbell echoed through the halls.

"You guys have a doorbell?" I usually used the bat knocker. Jax strode out.

"Bastien's meal has arrived," Asher murmured into my hair.

Meal? Like he was about to feed on someone?

"What do you mean?" My voice came out high pitched. The muscle in my chest paused and restarted. "Wait!" I thrashed in Asher's arms, trying to get free.

Jax definitely heard me, and he definitely ignored me.

catalina

I HURRIED AFTER JAX, trying to keep up, but when I turned the corner, he was gone. My aching throat didn't make my effort any easier.

My bare feet padded across the clean carpet. There wasn't a single indication of the massacre from earlier. Good, the severed head would haunt me enough as it was.

I descended to the first floor.

Jax had already opened the door for a woman. I slowed to a stop halfway down the stairs.

She smiled sweetly up at him. Like he'd hung the moon, stars, and universe. I bit back my scoff but couldn't stop from narrowing my eyes.

There was no use in trying to charm the ornery vampire. Their lips moved, but the words were too low for me to hear.

"Don't worry Pet, she's from a high-end escort service run by a reputable vampire Coven. She understands the risk and is paid handsomely for it," Asher said into my ear.

I startled, catching myself on the banister before losing my footing.

Jax guided her down the hall and past where I stood gawking. The girl had to be around my age. Her blonde hair flowed behind her as she swayed past in her short, barely-there dress.

"Bastien can't bite her." The words burst from my mouth. I could hardly hear them because of my heart pounding in my ears.

"Jealous again? Over the blood-mad vampire?" Asher blinked at me as if he couldn't fathom the idea. His eyes took on a faraway look.

I had no idea what could be passing through his mind.

"He won't fuck her—"

"There's nothing to worry about, Cat," Ren drawled, seemingly appearing out of thin air. "Bastien will drain her." A slight smirk curled his lips and he pinched my chin. "If that's distasteful to you, then you're in for a rude awakening."

"Like that's any better," I muttered.

"Of course it is." Ren's response didn't hold any sort of indication that he joked. He paused at the base of the staircase.

Sometimes I seriously forgot how deadly vampires were. Their human forms were shells to the inhumanity within.

"Whatever," I mumbled, continuing my descent.

"You should stay up here."

"No." I reached Ren's side.

He curled his hand around the back of my neck and pulled me, walking me alongside him. His thumb rubbed against my scalp, wringing a shiver to life. At this point, I wished I *was* just a blood-whore. At least that would help me explain away this . . . this attraction. A straight explanation for my utter obsession with their touch.

Asher's words from yesterday echoed in my ears about

getting high off blood. I'd had vampire blood before, but yesterday I drank it to a different level. The sensation their blood gave me frightened me . . . but also made me feel frenzied. Even now, as I thought about their blood, my mouth watered.

Speaking of the slightly unhinged vampire, why was he so touchy all of a sudden?

I had to crane my head to look at his side profile. Cherry blossoms on branches stretched up the side of his neck. I followed one branch until the tip ended just shy of his jaw line. His broad, strong jaw was smooth and his pore less skin, enviable.

A perk to being a vampire aside for the extended life span. Only if I was prepared to no longer feel emotion on a deeper level would I go through with something like—

"Watch the ledge," Ren snapped as we crossed the opened threshold of the metal door opposite to the kitchen. It was much too dark . . . I couldn't see anything. Nerves clenched in my stomach. Darkness . . . uncomfortable, suffocating . . . but with Ren's touch and Asher's presence, I didn't have the urge to bolt.

I side eyed Ren. Incredibly deranged vampire. His moods changed faster than I could keep track of.

My bare foot slipped on the edge of the metal of the second step. I gasped, my leg flying out from under me.

Then I was straightened by the hold on my neck. A muscle in my shoulder pinched from my weight being lifted from one spot.

Ow.

I full on glared at him, but not one peep from him.

Huffing, I said nothing considering he'd saved me from

getting my head split open. Especially since I had to rely on his guidance downward.

"Why was Bastien moved down here?"

"After his little escapade, we needed to secure him better," Asher said from behind me.

"You guys are acting like he's an animal," I mumbled.

"He is."

I glared back at Asher, hoping he could see my face.

Ren tightened his hold on my neck, forcing me forward again. "Watch where you're going."

"It's not like I can even see."

He grunted.

"His life is a blur of craving. Nothing matters in his endlessly devoid existence—"

"Here he goes. Asher, wax poetic some other time."

A scoff escaped me before I could hold it.

"You're laughing at me, Pet?" The end of Asher's words titled at the end from surprise. I pursed my lips tight and shook my head. One of my strands of hair stuck under Ren's grip and pinched at my scalp forcing me to stop.

We reached the landing, and a faint light beamed across the first step, allowing me to see where they brought me. A spacious room with a russet, traditional carpet rolled out in the middle of two half circle couches facing each other. Across from us was a door that was wide open and the origin of the lighting.

A raised female voice echoed.

"You didn't say I'd be feeding a blood-mad vampire." Her voice trembled.

I wrenched free and dipped to escape Ren's grip. I hurried into the room and discovered exactly why she'd shouted.

Bastien stood at the corner, tensed and ready to strike. The bear-like stature, standing snake-still. His unfocused gaze seemed to see through her.

His look screamed that he wouldn't have mercy. Ren's words echoed through my thoughts. She'd die at his hands.

"Why'd you bring her?" Jax asked, eyeing me with irritation.

I chose to ignore his bitchiness.

Bastien's head slowly turned to face me and his nostrils flared. In a millisecond, he burst forward, hands outstretched to grab me.

He stopped a few feet from me, the chains shackled to his wrists forcing him to a stop. Bastien hissed and jerked at his hands causing metal to clang with his harsh moments.

"Reinforced steel, you're not getting out of those," Asher called to him. Of course, Bastien didn't react.

"Do what you were paid to do." Jax shoved the shaking girl.

She stumbled forward, into Bastien's reach. I lunged forward to intercept the stumbling woman. Bastien's eyes screamed death. He swept me behind him and slammed his palm into her chest. She flew backwards and hit the wall with a sickening thud.

I gasped and lunged to hang onto his arm before he went at her. The girl groaned, curling her legs under her as she clasped her temples.

"Fuck," she hissed, eyes cinched tight.

Bastien didn't like that. He moved toward her, head lowered like a bull.

"Stop," I shouted and smacked Bastien's arm.

He slowly turned his head toward me.

The girl finally opened her eyes and swiped the back of her hands against the blood dripping from her nose.

She staggered to her feet with eyes as wide as a kewpie doll. She scooted against the wall as she moved away.

"I can't do this," she said, her voice wobbling. Jax sighed and pinched the bridge of his nose.

What an asshole.

"I'll feed anyone but that thing."

I clenched my teeth and swung my glare toward her. He threw her against the wall so she was well within her right to be hateful, but he didn't mean to hurt her. "So which of you need some blood?"

The corner of my eyelid twitched, but I forced my attention to Ren. Whatever they did, or whoever they bit, was none of my business.

"Leave, vampire food. No one wants your blood," Ren drawled from near the door frame. He leaned against the sill, blocking most of the exit with his body.

The sliver was all she needed to squeeze past him and out of the room. Her hurried footsteps echoed.

When I turned back to Bastien, his face hovered an inch away from my face. His red, eerie eyes peered into my face. Unlike how he blankly looked at the girl, he actually seemed to see at me.

I clicked my tongue.

"Why don't you ever put clothes on him?" A robe split at the top, exposing his smooth tan chest. His skin tone's hue was nicely bronzed and his white, long hair fell in messy waves down his shoulders, about mid-bicep.

He settled his chin on my shoulder and sniffed my hair. This bedroom wasn't as cozy as the one upstairs. The cement made the room colder and the bed resting on the floor lacked any sort of bedsheets.

Clutching his arm like I could protect him against the twins and Ren, I whirled. "And why is his bed on the floor?" I didn't allow Asher a word edgewise. "Not only that but couldn't you have put blankets or even a sheet on the bed?"

"It's a new mattress . . ."

"And what is this?" I shook the chain at Bastien's wrists. They clanged against the bolted metal plate over his bed. "Is there really a need for this?"

"Is . . . the human scolding . . . us?" Ren blinked.

"Did you not explain Bastien's mental state, Asher?" Tobias's voice came from behind Ren since he blocked the entrance. "Love, he doesn't care what he sleeps on. He doesn't care about anything. It's difficult enough getting him to feed instead of simply murdering."

They could go on and on about how he was a mindless vampire who wouldn't care about comforts, but then why did he create bedding and clothing in his dream world?

I couldn't be convinced that not a single bit of memory remained in Bastien, even if it was muscle memory.

"I'll feed him." I met Tobias's focused gaze. "But I have a request." The words spilled forward. They could deny me or ignore me, but I would ask regardless.

I bounced my gaze to Ren, then Jax, and lastly to Asher who looked delighted.

"And what is that?" Asher sounded too excited.

"Get him a proper set of clothes, unchain him . . . and . . . buy me a new computer." I tossed in at the end.

Ren closed his eyes and tilted his head back. The corner of his lips turned down and caused his dimples to dip.

Was he about to laugh at me?

"A human caring about a feral vampire." He opened his eyes. "Quite refreshing."

Oh no, he seemed even more intrigued by me. Hunger glinted in those brown eyes. "We will do that." Ren nodded.

Jax sighed and turned. "How did the meeting with Calliope go?" Tobias shouldered past Ren, walking into the room.

"She did not do it. She swore on your shared Sire, Ren."

The relaxation faded from Ren.

"She is not lying, then." Ren turned to me.

"Aren't you guys, like, enemies?" I asked. They seemed much too nonchalant about her.

"Some days."

I was even more confused.

"What he means is they like to play little games in the face of bored immortality," Asher offered.

Kidnapping each other, sending murderers to each other's house—they had an interesting way of pranking one another.

"That's your entertainment?" I scoffed. "So what, do you even believe it's the vampire hunting me?"

Bastien banded his arms around my waist and his fangs grazed against my neck, eliciting a shiver from my soul.

"We needed to eliminate every possibility, Catalina."

I hummed.

"What about vampire hunters," I said jokingly, but their expressions didn't change.

"We finished eradicating the vampire hunter bloodline a decade ago," Ren said, deadpan.

Well there went my joke, whittling away like a deflating balloon.

I cleared my throat.

Just as I thought then—it was the male vampire after me. My stomach dropped and I pressed closer to Bastien. In his arms, I felt safer than I'd felt in a while. I should have come to him sooner.

"So will you release him or what?"

Asher's head fell back with his laugh.

Ren straightened and he seemed suddenly serious. His attention focused on me, but he didn't say anything. He just studied me.

"Not cautious anymore, Cat? Did you grow up or have you succumbed to madness?"

I shrugged and picked at my chipped nail polish. Option two.

"You could kill me. Whatever vampire is out there can kill me." I waved my hands in the air. "At least Asher and Tobias will make sure I go gently if one of you off me."

Nerves bubbled in my stomach from his perusal, so I returned my attention to Asher. He yanked Bastien's cuffed hands out and gingerly turned Bastien's wrist to reach a latch on the underside. The circle had a line in the middle that needed to be turned to line up with the outer section.

Asher shook his hands as if the touch of the metal bothered him. I reached to unhook the other cuff from Bastien's wrist much faster than Asher would have.

"You understand you will be in charge of him?" Ren interjected, eyebrows slightly furrowed.

I scowled at him in answer.

"Imagine, we wouldn't have this entertainment if Imogen got her way with Bastien and had us kill him." Asher chortled again.

Kill him? I mouth, horrified.

"She knows the value in keeping him. She was testing us." Ren snorted.

Tobias raised a haughty eyebrow. The truth was being stretched if his expression meant anything.

"The ease in which you two speak of Imogen—" Jax stopped mid-sentence and looked at me. "All because of the influence of a meaningless human pussy."

His words sliced through my heart.

My lungs felt like they deflated.

Even though I wouldn't be fooled into thinking Jax ever cared for me, he'd been close to looking at me with affection.

I turned my attention to the vampire that actually made me feel safe. Clasping Bastien's hand, I tugged him past Ren. Bastien easily shouldered past him and forced Ren out of his way.

"Where are we going?" Asher asked as he caught my other hand. Sighing, I stopped fighting him, twinning our fingers together.

"Don't know, but I didn't want to hang around that prison cell." At the base of the stairs, I had to let go of their hands so I could make my way up with quick steps. "Can I add some slippers to the things I want?"

"I'll order them." Asher's voice echoed in the tunnel-like hallway leading to the main part of the house.

"You like ordering stuff online don't you?" I asked, knowing the answer.

"I even have a membership for speedy delivery—"

"He was chronically online before you came around, Love," Tobias's deadpan voice floated up to me.

"I don't know if you can call his porn addiction—"

"Now reel the judgment back in." Asher interrupted Ren.

Asher's offended tone caused a smile to spread. I quickly stifled it, hurrying to the kitchen island and hoisting myself up on the granite. Bastien wouldn't need to lean down too much with me up here. Pressing my palms into the cold surface, I leaned back. The long sweater hem caressed my thighs. The cold counter touched a sliver of my skin. I hissed a breath out between my teeth.

"Bastien?" I called and tilted my head to the side to bare my throat for him.

His red eyes traveled over my body, and he inhaled to smell me, releasing a hum with each exhale. I bunched the collar of his robe and tried to force him to me. All I managed to do was loosen the sash and expose his long, tapered body.

Wide, strong, and thick, were only some words used to describe him. He was also ethereal with his white hair, bronzed skin tone and red eyes. His cock hung between his legs, still large even though blood didn't fill it.

I caught Bastien's arm and pressed his palm to my neck. My pulse jumped and he groaned, sniffing audibly. His fangs popped free and my body responded.

With a hard swallow, I sank my teeth into my lower lip to keep my libido in control or at least contain a semblance of it. Then Bastien was all up in my face and burying his teeth in the side of my throat. I gasped, twitching against his onslaught of sharp pricks at my throat, then the dash of pain was swept away with him sucking. He tugged at me so hard he tore the fabric of the sweater and the scraps pooled under me.

A moan left my mouth and my eyelids shuttered. I wiggled, until I practically ground down on the granite. My hands fluttered at his biceps, fingertips brushing against the silk robe.

His cock nudged my calf.

Bastien pressed his palm into the middle of my spine forcing me to arch my back and press my breasts toward him. My nipples rubbed against his chest with each of my harsh breaths. Lust blazed across my skin.

I couldn't close my legs to stop the moisture from trickling onto my thighs because his mass stood between my knees. God, my clit felt sensitive to the max and all I wanted was a bit of pressure.

Bastien slurped another mouthful, licked the wound, then straightened.

My gaze dropped to his straining cock.

I wanted to please him.

I pulled his arm until he followed my tugging onto the granite counter. He hoisted himself on with ease. Shoving his shoulder, he followed my demand, settling back with his elbows on the hard surface.

Curling both my legs under me, I hovered over his member. It pointed up, veiny, thick, and uncircumcised. Clasping my hand around the girth, he jolted up with an audible gasp. Bastien's wide, red gaze settled on me. I couldn't help the corner of my lips twitching.

His reactions were always endearing and uncontrolled. He felt without restraint and I loved it. I lowered and the curtain of my hair brushed across his thighs. He must have liked how it felt because his thigh muscles twitched.

I wrapped my mouth around the mushroom tip. Immediate precum spread on my tongue as I lapped it. I lifted my head and watched it surface in fascination. There was a red tint to it.

Peeking up at him, I smiled and then took as much of him as I could fit in my mouth. I had to open so wide my jaw cracked. Flicking my tongue up the side of his shaft, I licked the silky side. His thighs tensed and both of his hands bunched the back of my hair, forcing me down to take more of him. His tip prodded against my throat.

I struggled to swallow with his tip shoving at my tonsils, but he seemed to like it very much because his hips gyrated upward. Bastien would choke me on his cock if he didn't let me breathe. My vision grew spotty.

Forcing a breath through my nose, it allowed the dizziness to fade. I couldn't panic. I swirled my tongue again and Bastien gasped.

It didn't take long. With another drag of my hand up his dick, Bastien exploded into my mouth. Cum spurted into my mouth, tartness mingling with a sweet taste different from how their blood tasted.

His hands slowly slid off my head to the granite, and I lazily licked him clean.

A harsh groan ripped through Bastien's heavy breathing. I sat up, stretching the kink in my neck.

Ren and Asher watched, lust blazing in their gazes. In a few quick strides, Ren gripped my hips and slid me to the edge of the counter, Bastien sliding off to stand beside me.

"What are you doing?" I asked breathlessly as Ren spread my thighs apart as far as they could go.

"You're feeding all of us, Cat," Ren breathed against my wet pussy.

catalina

ASHER GRIPPED one of my thighs while Ren kept hold of my other.

Ren watched me from half-lidded eyes, his fangs poking out from between his lips.

"Decadent scent."

While I rested in the middle of the rectangular island, Ren stood to one side, his large body overwhelming my senses, but not enough to erase the feel of Asher's fingers digging into my inner thigh, keeping me wide open from where he stood near my legs.

Ren reached across my body and pressed the tip of his fingers near my pussy entrance, but still not touching me where I wanted. He lowered and those dimples made a showing. I attempted to close my legs to shield from the sensitivity. There was no use. They held me open with their advanced strength.

"Such a damp Pet," Asher tsked, his gaze fastened on the apex of my thighs.

I could see my wet, needy flesh and the bundle of my

throbbing clit. Ren's fingers pressed into the dip where my leg met my entrance.

Licking my lips gave me another second to think of what to say. Ren's torso angled toward me.

"You can feed from me, but I don't think—"

Ren's fangs sank into my throat. I gasped, my body going limp.

Asher's palms flattened on the counter, and he leaned forward, hovering over my nipple.

"That's right, Pet, don't think," Asher murmured against my skin. His sweet breath caressed my areola. The hair on my body stood on end and then he sank his teeth in.

Crying out, I jerked against the stiff hold. I couldn't see it, but I could feel liquid trickling down my collarbone and making its way down between my boobs.

God, my own blood traveling down my body shouldn't feel as erotic as it did.

I shuddered and another wave of need throbbed through my core. I needed to be touched. Writhing to get Ren's fingers to move over my weeping core proved unsuccessful. Asher's grip fastened on my hip, stilling my movements.

I felt like I would go crazy.

Sliding my hand to my pussy, I pressed on the needy sex and rolled the hard nub.

"Oh," I whined, but before I could lose myself, Ren caught my hand and forced it to his unfairly hard stomach. I felt up his muscles through his shirt. He lifted his head, leaving my wounds open and dripping. His chest pumped up and down a few times.

Asher straightened, his smile painted red. Inch by inch, he lifted himself until he stood straight, standing at the end of the counter, scanning the entirety of my bare body with a satisfied glint to his blue eyes.

"Such a pretty sight," Asher murmured. I dropped my gaze to see what had him so riveted. Lines of blood marked the inner swells of my breasts, leading down over the soft curve of my belly and down my pussy. Asher's long, pale fingers smeared the blood on my mound and dragged it over my clit. I gasped.

I thrust up to get more of his touch, but he moved away with a sly grin. He dipped and licked the trail of blood, stopping shy of the spot aching with need. He moved to the left, kissing down to my knee. Asher's hair tickled my thigh.

I cried out in frustration, bunching Ren's shirt harder. Ren groaned deep, gutturally. He took my wrist and slowly unclasped my hand. Stern and demanding. A step later and he was beside Asher, staring between my legs.

I sucked in a breath, in time for Ren to shallowly slide his finger inside me. He swirled once and lifted glistening fingers. My need mixed with the blood Asher had smeared. He sucked them clean in a swift move, humming as he did it.

So quickly, he lowered until his tongue lashed across my clit. I sucked in a breath, my lungs refusing to work.

One dark haired and the other light haired. Night and day but so individual and beautiful.

"Stop playing with me." I whimpered.

Asher's smug expression didn't assuage the maddening need.

They were having too much fun with my desperation.

Their attention dropped to my clit. Since they hadn't closed the wounds, blood continued trailing down to my torso.

I wrapped my fingers around the edge of the counter. "Ren!"

He finally gave in and licked up the new trail of blood traveling to my pussy.

This time he didn't stop. He dipped his tongue into my folds. Gasping, I gyrated forward, but he retreated with a deep, dimpled grin. Asher gripped my hip, shouldering his way to take Ren's place. He dipped his tongue, swirling it in my channel. I whimpered but could not move to the rhythm of his fast tongue. Ren wrenched my thigh wider, and sank his teeth in. I screamed from the overwhelming swell of pleasure. Their heads hovered so close to each other . . . I wanted them both licking me at the same time.

Warmth bloomed in my stomach and my breasts bobbed with my harsh breaths. I pushed myself up to my elbows.

Asher lifted his head slightly.

"Ren. She wants more from us." His eyes held a hint of surprise. "Tell me what you want, Pet." His murmur curled heat through my body.

Ren hummed and lapped his bite marks, eliciting a shiver over my flesh.

"I . . ." I breathed hard. "I want you both to lick me." My voice trembled.

Asher's smile turned wicked. Ren's grip on my right thigh flexed while Asher took my left and they spread me more than I had been. I yelped, struggling to breathe.

My heart drummed in my ears. Anticipation coiled through my gut. Asher dipped and licked the slit of my entrance. He left enough space for Ren to bow over my leg. Another tongue delved inside me. I moaned, gyrating pointlessly since their hold kept me still. Both their faces buried close to my aching core.

I gasped, reflexively trying to press my knees together.

"She likes that," Asher purred. "Do you like to see us tongue you together, precious Pet?"

I couldn't form a thought, much less a word.

Ren lifted his face and raised an eyebrow at me. My need painted his damp mouth.

"I need a response," Asher purred. I pushed to my palms, propping myself up.

I held my breath and nodded hard.

Asher dipped back next to Ren and I had a full view of Asher's tongue fit into my pussy with Ren's. Ren didn't stop the slow glide of his tongue into my folds. Their tongues touched as they wrung more moisture from me.

My breathing elevated and my lips parted. So erotic.

The warmth in my stomach finally exploded and I screamed. A swell crashed into me and I grabbed onto both of their hair and yanked at them with harsh tugs. Mimicking the violence of my orgasm.

I couldn't stop grinding against their faces if I wanted to. My head tipped back and I gyrated, thighs pressing into their ears.

As if synchronized, they each grabbed their respective thigh and forced my legs wide.

"More," I whimpered.

They delivered.

A pair of fangs pierced my clit while two fingers were stuffed into my pussy. My hearing gave way to buzzing.

Unmatched pleasure vibrated down my lower spine and exploded through every nerve ending. Each little touch, from the flick of the fingers inside me, to the tickle of Asher's hair grazing my inner thigh magnified the orgasm.

"Yes. Yes," I exclaimed.

When my mind floated down from the massive high, my shoulders rested against the cool counter surface. I panted, still not able to hear. A shadow fell across my closed eyelids, turning my red eyelids dark. Opening my eyes, I found Bastien staring down at me.

The fingers in my pussy turned in a circle, causing me to jolt from the sensitivity.

Ren's heated brown gaze focused on me as he popped wet fingers in his mouth.

I struggled to swallow.

"Such a good little meal," Ren murmured.

"One we should feed," Asher added from where he leaned against my leg, his elbow propped on the granite by my hip. His wide shoulders didn't allow me to close my legs. His blond hair waterfalled between my thighs and tickled.

My gasp turned into a moan as his tongue lashed across my clit. Asher chuckled.

"What would you like to eat, Pet?"

My head lolled to the side and I blinked up at Bastien. He stared into my features like he'd been studying them. Having those red eyes looking at me should have skeeved me out, but the focus comforted me.

Asher's hair tickling my legs retreated.

"Catalina?"

I angled my head to watch him as he rolled his sleeves up, baring his forearms. His blonde arm hair glinted on his arms, the dusting faint. Unlike me with my too obvious Hispanic arm hair.

"I don't care," I said awkwardly.

"Soup sound good?"

They have soup? Where did they get soup from? I nodded,

drowsily blinking. With a big yawn, I stretched out my arms, shaking a bit from how good my body felt. Bastien still watched me, his large body hovering near.

Ren held his hand toward me, and I slipped mine into his. He pulled me upright.

I tried to let him go, but he didn't until I scowled up at him. His grin told me he thought I was funny.

Huffing, I inched off the counter, the torn sweater under my ass aiding my slide off, and I dropped to the floor. My feet tingled and my knees buckled. Ren gripped my elbow, helping me balance. Another yawn crawled free and I rubbed my eyes.

The scratch of a spoon against the side of a pot echoed through the kitchen. I should clean the island if I was going to eat.

"Do you guys have cleaning supplies?" I wrapped my arms around my bare breasts and tried to stuff down my embarrassed flush. I should really get some clothes on after I cleaned the counter.

Asher paused his stirring and turned to me with furrowed eyebrows. "I'm not actually sure."

"Actually? Asher, please speak proper English." Tobias's clipped steps entered the kitchen and he leaned against the island. "We hire cleaning staff, Love."

He was speaking to me, yet his attention focused on my shoulder. His expression resembled a thunder cloud.

"*Proper* English," Asher muttered with an accompanying scoff. Tobias tossed a robe at Bastien, then he handed me the other, still not looking at me. I pulled on the silky black material and tied the sash around my waist. Instead of dwelling on Tobias's avoidance, I turned my attention away from him.

The counters were bare, and the cabinet Asher left open

held plenty of wine glasses, and a box set of ceramic plates unopened.

Nothing was ever used.

But at least they had hand towels and a sink. I strode over to grab one of the clean and folded white squares and shook it out. On a whim, I pulled the bottom of the sink open and found a few bottles of cleaners.

I pulled the disinfectant out and walked over to the counter. Bastien was no longer sprawled across the island when I turned. He watched me with eagle eyes from his position against the far wall.

"What are you doing, I'll have the humans over to clean."

"My blood and—" Need, were on the counter. I cleared my throat and sprayed the blood on the edge of the dark granite. With quick efficient swipes, I cleaned all evidence of them biting me and eating me out.

Returning to the bottle under the sink, I stopped with the towel bunched in hand.

"Where's the trash?"

"Leave it in the sink," Asher said, adding a can of tomato to the water. He didn't turn to look at me, his lips were pursed with concentration.

I dropped it and took a seat at the island beside Ren who leaned on the edge with both elbows.

"We should move," Tobias said, focusing on Ren's hand brushing my hair behind my ear.

Irritation flashed through his gaze so quickly, I might have imagined it.

"If we move now, we won't have the opportunity to hunt the fucker that dared attack our Coven," Jax sniped, seemingly appearing out of thin air. Had he been around the entire time?

The angry vampire moved like a feline.

I put my elbow on the granite and leaned my chin on my palm as they continued their back and forth. Bastien stood behind me until his chest was flush against my back.

"We established that a vampire male is after the human. Just hand her over."

I perked to attention at that since my heart jumped at his comment. I had to have misheard him. Hand me over? My throat closed up and made it hard to swallow. I turned to Tobias, then Ren.

"Then you're announcing to everyone that we are weak," Tobias said. His fingers drummed against the island.

"She's ours." Ren's hand flexed around the back of my neck.

Jax scoffed.

"That human is not mine."

"I don't want to be his anyway," I pushed through gritted teeth, my face burning from embarrassment.

Jax narrowed his eyes at me and sneered.

"You have chosen to be a part of this Coven, which means we work together. Unless you are saying you want to defect." Tobias's comment seemed innocent enough but Jax stiffened like he'd snap in half.

"Not a bad idea. Your sired children are not as many as Asher's, so it won't be too much of a loss," Ren said, big arms returning to the granite.

Every single vampire stilled.

Sometimes they seemed more like enemies than a Coven that worked together. Or that could be how they always spoke to each other. After all, what did I know about vampires other than what I fabricated in my own little fictional world in an attempt to make sense of my shit experiences.

In my defense, when I chose to write romance novels about vampires, I never expected to encounter them again. Especially with how hard I tried to avoid the inhumane monsters.

"All for a pointless human?" Jax snapped.

I gritted my teeth, meeting his hate filled eyes. I wouldn't turn away from him. He couldn't do anything to me. His nostrils flared, obviously displeased that I challenged him instead of cowering.

Bastien grabbed my shoulder and hissed at Jax.

"Enough. Jaxon, you're not going anywhere. We are a Coven and we stay that way. Accept her." Asher set the ceramic bowl in front of me. "Eat," he prompted in a much softer tone.

The soup swayed in the bowl. Lentils, a simple enough dish, but he'd left them to cook for too short of a time. The little legumes hadn't swelled enough.

His hopeful expression didn't waver.

"Can I get a spoon?" I asked tentatively.

"Right! Apologies, Pet, it has been so long since I've been human." He quickly fetched me one.

I swirled the soup.

"Asher, I've contacted Talia and let her know what we need. I've also hired a human protective service to surround the place while we are vulnerable. We'll all have to move to the lowest floor until the issues are resolved."

They planned while I slurped . . . and bit back my grimace from the overly salted broth.

"How is it?"

Every time Asher cooked, he seemed excited about it and I didn't want to burst his bubble.

I held my breath and took another spoonful. The still hard granules were difficult to chew.

"Mmhmm." I put my thumb up and took a deep breath then quickly ate another bite.

"There are a few hours until sunrise. Talia will hire humans to bring furnishings for us." Tobias finally looked at me. "You should go rest for a while in Asher's bedroom. Take Bastien with you so he does not murder a human while they're working."

In two strides, he took the bowl from me and jerked his chin to the side, prompting my escape. I sighed with gratitude and nodded. Grabbing Bastien's arm, I pulled him after me to go upstairs.

Tobias seemed just as hyper aware of me as I was of him.

ASHER KEPT LOOKING at the kitchen exit long after the girl disappeared. Love-sick fool. A thought I'd never thought to have about Ash in general. And even less after turning. Emotions and vampires didn't mesh. We didn't fall for anyone, yet this slip of a girl had her hooks in my Coven. In a way Imogen never had. I shoved him to bring him back down from whatever cloud he floated on. He staggered, an offended look on his face. He brushed at his shirt like I'd left wrinkles. His attention focused on me, then slowly dropped to the bulge outlining the seam of my jeans.

"What do we have here." Smug bastard.

"Fuck off." I sneered.

"Or . . . and hear me out." Asher waved a finger down at my stiffy. "Fuck on." Asher and his stupid fucking antics.

I'd been on the verge of joining their feeding session. Too close.

Blood dripped down my arms under my shirt where I sliced my sharp claws into my inner forearm to stop myself.

"Look at how you're all doting on the little traitor." I filled my voice with as much disdain as I could. The traitorous little human should suffer. How dare she make me care for her only to turn around and stab me in the back.

It was her pussy that did me in.

Just that reason was why she confused me. Humans were nothing. The lowest on the food chain, how could I care for one?

I only craved her because she drank my blood, all I felt was the blood-bond. My scent was all over her, but it was beginning to fade, overpowered by Ren and Ash's scent. I gritted my teeth, the urge to feed her my nectar a suffocating urge. Desperation to not let my scent fade from her knotted my insides.

"Why do you act like you don't want her? Violently— cruelly?" Humor faded from my twin's gaze. His eyes narrowed. "I warned you to stay away from what was mine. But I still shared even when I didn't want to and you threw her away." Asher hissed.

"Was that how it was, Asher? You never cared if we all shared," Ren smirked. Sharing came as easily as feeding for all of us.

We both ignored Ren.

"How can you want a traitor?" I switched to our native language, so the interloper didn't interject with each sentence.

"Cheap," Ren snorted. "私でもできるよバカ." He tossed as he walked away.

"If she did, it does not change that she is ours."

"If?" I narrowed my eyes. "You were as sure as me that she had."

"I have my doubts."

"Her pussy is transformative." Sarcasm spilled from my voice.

Asher pursed his lips.

"It is." He raised an eyebrow. I hated how true that was. She refused to unlatch from my mind. They took over, overwhelming my waking thoughts. Fucking my hand while thinking of her had to be the most shame I'd experienced since I became a vampire.

My life as a human remained veiled behind a shroud. Making it seem elusive to grasp onto, but when they managed to formulate, the memories served as a reminder of greed. Something I'd been well acquainted with as a human.

She surfaced emotions that left a coat of distaste on my tongue. Feelings made me feel weak—feelings that I had not experienced since I was human. How could a human cause me to long for her presence? I hated her for it.

"Are you thinking of Imogen again?" Asher slitted his eyes.

Imogen. I loved her. I admired her. My loyalty belonged to her . . . why was a human causing me to buckle?

"Enough of your angst." Asher waved his hand like swatting my thoughts away. "Our female is here now. Imogen is ashes."

I sneered. He'd said variations of this to me over the years. It'd been a while since the last because I'd beat him bloody. Harder than we'd fought before, but he kept running his mouth.

"Have some respect for our Sire," I spat.

Asher waved his hand in the air again.

"What we need to do is make our Pet happy." His eyebrow twitched. "You know, she's probably worried about her cat's whereabouts. Or assumes he was killed in the fire."

I bared my teeth.

"Fuck off. No."

"Morph or I'll tell her you've been beating your meat to her every night."

A new to me colloquial term, but I understood what he meant.

"I ordered you to stop sneaking around invisible." I shoved him back. He brushed his shirt dramatically. "And stay off the internet. Your use of slang is giving me a headache."

She could not know how deeply she'd dug her human fingers into my soul. She could not know that if she simply asked for me, I would cave. Asher would doubtlessly ruin it by telling her if I didn't do as he said.

I shucked my clothing and tossed them at my twin. He hung them on the stool while I morphed. Heat stretched across my flesh on the heels of a shiver. My body shrunk until I stood on all fours.

"Perfect." He swooped and lifted me in his arms. I yowled, but he managed to take hold of me. "Making it believable and all that."

I flexed my claws into his arm, gouging blood free. Asher gritted his teeth.

"Oh, *Kitten*," Asher moaned emphatically in my ear. He was mocking me. The fucker did spy on me! I hissed. He took that as my assent and started walking. I kept my claws flexing in his arms, reveling in the blood dripping on the floor with each step.

He reached the second floor and turned right toward his bedroom. He rapped on the door once and popped it open.

She looked over from where she sat on the bed, glaring up at Ren. She was dressed in a long shirt that reached her knees. Bastien sprawled on the bed, watching them. Not maddened. Just watching her.

Her eyes dropped to me. She sprang up and a smile spread across her plump lips. Creases formed in the corner of her eyes with how hard she smiled.

She never looked at me like this.

"Binx," she cried, rushing forward. Relief leaked from her posture.

Asher lifted me by my torso and shook my limp body. My hind legs wobbled side to side.

She collected me to her warm chest. Her succulent aroma blanketed my senses.

A purr vibrated free.

No.

Hissing, I sank my claws into her arm. She gasped but didn't let go.

Her blood would send me into a frenzy, and I wouldn't be able to stop myself from fucking her, so I begrudgingly calmed in her arms.

Ren chortled from over her shoulder.

Her eyes flitted from him to Asher. I pricked her arms. Watch *me*.

"I'm so happy he's still alive! We need to get him kitty litter and . . ."

I fought the urge to nuzzle into her plump breasts.

TWENTY-ONE

catalina

I PREFERRED Ren wanting me dead. I ignored him as I cuddled Binx to my breasts.

Ren laughed again.

What did he find so funny? I scowled over at him.

"Will you hold me to your perky breasts like . . . the animal?"

His smirk caused some unsettling dips to my stomach, and I wet my lower lip.

"Why are you smirking? And no, Binx gets special treatment."

"Binx," Ren repeated and choked on a laugh.

What was up with this vampire?!

"Ren, come help us compel the humans," Asher shouted as he started walking out the door. He sounded irritated to the max. Something was going on, but I didn't have the energy to wonder about everything century old vampires squabbled over.

"Little putty tat," Ren said as he passed us. Binx's body stiffened in my arms and a frightening sound escaped him. It sounded like a demon.

"Binx," I chastised.

Ren's eyes glinted with humor as he left. It was nice seeing the dimples, but not when he laughed at my expense.

I went to shut the door with my toe as I balanced Binx in my arms. The knot in my throat hadn't loosened. I had missed the cat. I had thought he had perished in the fire since I hadn't seen him since then. Now he was the only remnant of everything I'd lost. Bastien seemed on edge, too; he kept looking at the cat and then pacing from one end of the room to the other. I would have to keep an eye on him so he didn't try to snap its neck from jealousy.

Settling on the bed, I placed him on my lap. "I'll have to get Asher to order you a collar."

He meowed like I'd just offended him.

I missed the sound of it. He always managed to sound grumpy. I pressed my nose into his neck and scratched his chest.

"God Binx. I'm glad you're okay," I breathed into his fur. Tears sprang to my eyes. "I don't know what to do." A purr started up in his chest. It comforted me.

Bastien knelt before me and touched my cheek gently. He lifted it off my face and into his mouth. Uh, okay.

Bastien hissed at the cat.

"No." I stuck my finger in Bastien's face. "No." I repeated.

He tilted his head, but finally backed up, returning to his pacing.

A damp layer coated my cheeks, and I brushed the back of my hand against the moisture.

I should probably take a shower after . . . the events on the counter. A pleasured flush swelled through my body. Clearing my throat, I hopped to my feet to dash toward the bathroom. Bastien watched me with his head tilted. He'd smell my arousal.

I picked up pace and slammed the door behind me, Binx in my arms. He wasn't normally allowed with me in the restroom, but I didn't want to lose sight of him in this mausoleum of a house. Nor to find him drained of blood when I finished bathing.

Sure, it was a little off-putting the way he looked at me whenever I showered, but I'd take his hyper focus now that he was back in my life.

I SHOT up in bed with a gasp. My eyes felt grainy and tired because I'd been in and out of sleep, and now I couldn't see a thing. My heart jumped. My leg hit a hard form and I lunged to pat the mattress, but it was not Binx.

Bastien. In the depths of a vampire's sleep. It was still morning, that's why it was so pitch dark in here. I squeezed the bedsheet with a trembling hand and scooted off. Closing my eyes, I inched toward the door, using my memory to make my way.

Faint light came from down the hall, washing the pitch black away. I sighed in relief and snapped the door shut. It was deathly quiet. I crept down the hall.

The bottom of Asher's long sweats dragged and I tightened the string as much as possible, but I still had to hold them to my waist. The big shirt fluttered around my arms.

It was absolutely silent. I padded down the steps as a light knock echoed on the door. I froze. Was another attacker here to end my life? I slowly approached to peek through the glass sliver bordering one side of the door.

A girl, dressed in a recognizable delivery service outfit.

Grabbing the door, I yanked it open so fast the woman

startled. Wait a minute. I had opened the door. I peeked over my shoulder. No one was running out to stop me.

"Um, hi, I left your packages there. There's a lot of them so I knocked."

I could escape. The window of leaving came much sooner than expected.

"Can you give me a ride?" The words burst free. But Binx . . . where was he? I gritted my teeth and focused on the driver. Carrying a cat would make being on the run difficult.

The girl's eyebrow furrowed, and she looked behind me at the expensive house. She scratched her head.

"Uhhh."

I took a deep breath and relaxed my shoulders and let a smile spread. I didn't have to fake a blush because my face burned from the adrenaline pumping through my veins.

"I just forgot all of my things and it'd be embarrassing waking him up." I shuffled from foot to foot. "You know how one-night-stands go."

Her eyes widened and understanding pinched her expression. She scanned me from head to foot. Taking in the oversized sweats, the messy puffed up hair, and sleep riddled expression. She looked down at her electronic wristwatch.

"My next delivery is toward downtown, but that's as far as I can take you."

I must look as freshly fucked as I felt.

"Perfect." I reigned in my nerves and took a deep breath, trying to act nonchalant.

I took one step out of the house. The sun fell onto my skin, but it was still chilly. I curled my toes into the rough cement, then took another step and froze.

From here, I could see the dent the dead woman's body had left in the flowers.

If I ran away . . . the other vampire would find me.

Panic squeezed my chest. That would be worse than this. I shuffled in place and cleared my throat.

"Wait," I said, rushed. Her eyebrows furrowed and she kept looking over my shoulder and into the lavish Manor. "Can I just borrow your phone to order a ride?"

She turned back with a frown, digging into the chest pocket of her blue work vest, and handed it over unlocked. I tapped on the login for my email. I sent a quick email to my lawyer, informing her of my passing as if I were a 'relative'. I was going to do it from the computer they got me, but the faster I did it the better. Even as my fingers flashed over the screen, I understood my decision would leave me with no choice. There was no turning back. A terrified thrill caused my hands to shake, but I saw no way out of my situation. It was best I disappeared in the 'human' world. She would inform everyone . . . my agent, my insurance agency . . . my brother. A knot formed in my throat.

I logged out and handed the phone back. My breaths came out in short gusts. Standing here, I'd worked myself up until my pulse fluttered like butterfly wings.

"Thanks and sorry for the change up." I held my breath, so my panic wouldn't be excruciatingly obvious to her.

My decision . . . I wouldn't turn back.

"No worries, the morning after is always super awkward. I get you." The worker slipped it back into her vest and she retreated toward the delivery van idling outside of the gates. The multitude of boxes on the floor stared at me mockingly. I didn't have the energy to bring them all in. I turned and closed the door on the bright sunlight, sealing my fate.

I'd chosen.

Each heartbeat tried to punch through my chest.

I'd never get to see Peter again.

The excruciating pain in my lungs tightened. It felt like I was having an asthma attack, but I hadn't had one ever since they'd fed me their healing blood. Whenever they fed me, it served as a balm on my weak lungs.

I crumpled to the floor and thumped my head on the door. This was safest for Peter.

A shaking sob left my lips and I hugged myself.

"You made the right choice to not run off."

I gasped, slamming my elbow on the door with how fast I jolted.

With a grunt, I bowed forward, palming my elbow.

A brunette stood over me in yoga pants and a nylon, form hugging shirt.

Hoisting myself off the floor, I straightened to find that she was extremely fucking tall. Two heads over my average five foot six and a half inches.

I searched her face. She didn't have the smooth porelessness I was used to seeing on vampires, and her chest moved up and down in rhythmic breaths.

"You're human."

"I am," she drawled in a thick southern accent. "I'm glad you chose to stay. Tackling you would have been embarrassing. I'd hate to get on your owners' bad side."

Owners?

I wanted to exclaim and ask what she was talking about but

it didn't seem the most important question to someone I'd never met.

"Who are you?"

"I'm Maddy, Talia's human."

She said it with such ease and pride. Talia, the female vampire that Asher sired?

"I've heard a bit about you. Human Pet to Crimson Coven."

"You've heard about me?" I poked at my chest as if it wasn't obvious.

She grunted and pulled open the front door and started dragging the packages into the house. She hugged the last box to her chest and kicked the door shut with her toe.

"You're the human they took to Crimson Nights. Talia is extremely curious about you, almost fixated and I have not seen her focus on something like that for a few decades. All vampires view us humans as less than them, there are a few here and there that are sympathetic like Talia, but the Crimson Coven?"

She grimaced as she hugged the last box then turned to walk down the hall leading to the kitchen. "They're hard core. The only one known to show empathy is the priest, but from what I hear, even he struggles with his apathy default setting."

"Oh."

I picked up my pace to keep up as she returned to the kitchen with even, wide steps.

"But you've not only gotten their attention, but you've also become their Pet." She looked over her shoulder and wiggled her eyebrows up and down. "And they don't want to kill you for betraying them? Crazy props to you."

"How do you know about that?" My lips felt numb. She spoke of it so easily, as if it hadn't affected my entire life.

She dropped the box on the granite counter where I'd been thoroughly licked yesterday.

"Word has spread. The gossip is gossiping since yesterday. If it's true, you're one lucky human." Instead of focusing on the offended anger, I reigned it in. She seemed to know what she was talking about.

"Is there a way to get them to release a Pet? With zero . . . killing?"

She froze from cutting a knife through the tape. Her eyes rounded on me and she scoffed.

"You should be grateful they've chosen you. There is no human they've ever taken as theirs. The only one woman they'd entangled themselves with that wasn't a quick fuck was the woman that 'will not be named' according to Talia."

"Imogen," I said grimly.

"I don't know her name. Talia said it was safer for me unless I wanted to meet a quick end." She shrugged. "Human to human, you need to be careful with how you speak to vampires, especially ones that have just taken you in. They value loyalty above all else. One hint that you've betrayed them and they'll come after you before you know what's going on." She snickered. "I've seen it, trust me, it doesn't look like a walk in the park. They're big on torture."

"Oh," I muttered, wrinkling my nose. The attacker's head falling off his body flashed in my memory.

"Anyway, if you need anything from now on, just let me know. I'll get you hooked up. I already ordered you some clothes. And get me a list of everything you enjoy eating." She grinned. "I have to thank you for that, I was selected because I was a chef before Talia chose me. Now I get to feed you."

"You're talking about it like it's some honor."

She popped the top of the box open and met my gaze.

"Are you kidding me? I'm servicing the Crimson Coven Sires. One of the most powerful vampire groups on the western side of the United States."

My lips parted.

"What makes them powerful?"

"You're that brand new?"

I tugged the island chair and plopped down.

"Girrrrl, they're a group of six incredibly powerful vampires who've collectively sired hundreds of vampires. All who are allied under them. They have an army at their disposal. From what I've heard, that woman brought them together and made them a powerful force. Her little experiment went as far as making other vampires attempt to form large Covens, but there have been very few successes."

She said six . . . so including Imogen before she left.

"To put it frankly, you are one well protected human. And just a heads up, you would have never crossed the gates with that delivery driver. The place is surrounded with guards. They compelled them to protect the manor and you, with their life." She snapped her fingers. "I also wouldn't leave without protection. You've been perceived by other vamps. Other Coven Sires are waiting for a reason for Crimson Coven to have a weakness. There's even a movement for it, so be careful when dealing with other vampires. They will come after you just to get at them."

I sat back, blown away in the worst way possible. "And they won't destabilize centuries of peace for one human woman, so your best bet is to just stay put and do what they ask you to."

That was why the other guys weren't sure who had Ren, so they'd had to tread with caution.

Dread settled in my belly.

catalina

AFTER SHOWERING, I idled in the living room and knocked out on the couch instead of staying upstairs and brooding in the dark bedroom. I'd been awake a while now and sunlight no longer beamed through the slit in the curtain.

Jax rested on the settee a few feet from me. I wiggled under the blanket and sniffed the sweetness clinging to the soft yarn.

"Are you keeping watch to make sure I don't steal from you guys again," I muttered, grumpy from the shuffling paper that disturbed my rest.

The newspapers in his hand rustled again.

I glared over at him.

"You know people don't read newspapers anymore." No comment from him. I huffed and yanked the blanket under my chin. "That's what phones are for." He finally looked up, but he hid the hate he usually blasted my way, then returned his attention to the documents in front of him.

I clicked my tongue and lifted off the couch, curling my feet under my ass.

"What, no hateful words to spit at me?"

"No need. You'll be dead soon enough."

I scoffed and shook my head. I didn't like him, but if I would live with these vampires, I didn't want to feel uncomfortable.

Nothing would happen with him, but I could be civil.

"Your petty comments are getting old, Jaxon Crimson. How about we agree to an impasse? Agree to disagree, we can't get along, so let's be civil." He slowly looked up with his eyes narrowed oh so slightly. He didn't like me full-naming him? Too bad.

"Over your dead corpse," he said, words heavily accented.

My jaw hung open. I had to wrap my head around his words. Unbelievable.

"You're not taking my olive branch?" I scoffed. "After everything you've done to me, you have no right to act like—"

I clicked my teeth together. It was useless to spout moral codes at him because he wouldn't care what I had to say, he was an asshole for one, and two, he didn't see me as more than a pathetic blood bag, so anything I said was useless to him.

All of the others gave me, 'sweet, adorable human' vibes when they communicated with me. Nothing I said was truly taken seriously, and him most especially.

Tears of frustration sprang to my eyes and I stiffly pushed off the couch. I padded to the front door with the slippers Maddy had dug out of one of the boxes.

"Where are you going?" Jax snapped.

"Fuck off," I mumbled and quickly made my escape. The hint of bravery didn't last long. I took a few steps down until the path veered to the right, opposite from where the body had been. A small cement bench sat within the mass of roses. I plopped my ass down on the cold stone.

Dashing my hand across my cheeks, I rubbed the tears off my face. Hopefully the jerk hadn't seen them.

I pulled my legs up to the edge of the bench and hugged them. There was something about wrapping my arms around myself that calmed everything. It was the same sort of reaction I had when I was hugged in general, and the only ones that unknowingly offered that comfort were a group of vampires who didn't take me seriously.

For someone that was never touched often, it was my fucking luck that it calmed me.

A meow reached my ears and I perked up. Binx suddenly hopped up next to me.

His head rubbed against my side and a purr started up in his chest. I sniffled again.

"There you are, Binx." I swallowed the ball of emotion that rose to the surface again. I'd been looking for him all around the house. My guess had been right, he'd managed to slip outside.

Binx meowed again and nudged against me harder. His little paws perched on my leg, and he sniffed toward my face. I moved my head away before he got too close. I dug my fingers into the top of his head and rested my chin on my knees, staring at the bed of bushes and flowers. From this vantage, I could see over the wrought iron spikes adorning the top of the brick wall surrounding Crimson Manor.

The closest house to them had been mine before they burned it to crisp, but I could see the faint lights a mile down the road. Overgrown dried grass surrounded the outside of the gates in both directions, such a difference from the opulence of their home.

Moonlight beamed across the front of their gated garden. The stone steps reflected the pale light, making them glint.

Sitting out here in the silence made everything feel a bit eerie. If I was someone who didn't know about vampires, I'd definitely imagine them living in a manor like this.

They really should work on keeping up appearances if their goal was to hide their existence.

"Catalina?" A crisp English accent floated to my ear. The cadence falling over me like a blanket.

I jumped.

Binx seemed just as startled as he slunk away in the opposite direction of Tobias's voice and disappeared into the flowers.

"Yeah." I cleared my throat and dashed my palms across my face.

"Jaxon upset you again."

It didn't sound like a question, but I still shook my head and waved my hand in the air like I could swat his words away.

Pressure culminated at the base of my nose so I closed my eyes before I started bawling and inhaled the flower's aroma.

Dried leaves crunched right in front of me and stopped. I could feel him standing in front of me, still as a statue. The wind rustled and my hair tickled my cheeks. I needed to get a hairband from Asher to put the mass of hair in a ponytail.

I finally opened my eyes. Tobias's features were shadowed and the moonlight outlined him.

Why was he standing here asking me questions? He hadn't looked at me since the club.

Belligerence bubbled to the surface and I popped off the seat. His gaze dropped to the top of Asher's unbuttoned silk shirt.

Without a bra and with the cool breeze, my nipples rubbed against the soft material. I tipped my chin up, trying to push through the hot embarrassment.

He wasn't the one that caused the hurt roiling in my belly, but I was still upset with him. Tobias focused his attention behind me and his cheek ticked. Having him avoid me didn't help my sensitive state.

My embarrassment won and I crossed my arms over my chest, curling into myself.

"I don't mean to offend you with the sight of me," I said through gritted teeth. His face blurred. I didn't want to be dressed like this—looking all disheveled and unkempt. I much preferred my outfits, my blow dryer, my face serums . . . I sighed. The only reason I hadn't gone absolutely nuts was because Asher had good taste in clothing and as loose as it was on me, the material was top notch.

I took one step past Tobias, my shoulder brushing against his bicep.

"I . . . have broken my vow of celibacy." He inhaled sharply. "But I find . . . I cannot stop myself from wanting you." His hands banded around my upper arms, squeezing tighter with each of my breaths. His gray eyes searched my face and settled on my lips. "Nothing has ever tempted me."

Tears stopped brimming my eyes, but the remnants spilled over and trickled down my cheeks.

Tobias hissed, cupping my face with both hands. He thumbed away the moisture on my face and his lips parted.

The tip of his nose tipped up slightly. The refined and regal nose fit for an aristocrat.

"I . . ." I licked my lips.

Tobias turned his head at an angle, gaze fastened on my lips. He closed in and caught my mouth, swallowing my words.

Our lips met in a clash of desire. One I hadn't expected

from him. His lips pillaged mine, licking and nipping with hunger that tightened every nerve in my body.

"Tobias," I said against his lips, muffled. "Are you sure?"

He molded his mouth to mine, making it impossible for me to say anything more. He remained bowed forward, making it easier for me to reach him. Tossing my arms around his shoulders, I sank into his touch, lapping and licking back with each ravenous kiss he pressed to my lips. Lust swelled and rampaged through my veins.

Tobias pressed his fingers into my waist and guided me a few steps. He could have tossed me about and I wouldn't have cared, but instead he sat on the stone bench.

With his guidance, I climbed on top of him, straddling his hips. The position lined up my pussy with his stiff cock. A groan wrenched from my throat.

Sliding my hands around his neck, the tips of my fingers buried into his silky hair. His face tipped up, and a strand fell across his forehead. The brown hair and gray eyes looked black in the shadows. I settled on his lap; a tingle worked its way up my spine. His eyelids fluttered and my attention dropped to the regal, strong bridge of his nose. The curve of his mouth remained soft.

I rolled my hips against his thickness.

Tobias groaned and he gripped my hips, grinding me down on him harder. A cry wrenched free.

"Mm, Catalina," he murmured and forced me down to his lips. With his height and me on his lap, it lined us up perfectly.

His tongue curled around mine while he continued grinding me on him. I let him maneuver me as he pleased.

Lust licked over every inch of my body. Spurring on the swell of pleasure. My clit throbbed painfully. His movements held an edge of desperation. God, he made me so weak in the knees.

I desperately tugged at the sweats.

"Take it off me," I breathed, and he tore the cotton from the seam, taking along my panties too.

I knew it was coming, but I still gasped at the suddenness. Cool air licked my thighs. I hadn't needed to ask twice. My bare pussy settled on the wool of his slacks. My smile melted away, overtaken by a moan. The rough texture elicited a shiver. The fabric felt good against my needy wet folds, but it still wasn't enough.

I delved under his sweater and wrapped my fingers around his waistband.

This explosion of lust had built from the moment I saved him. He'd been the first one of the Coven I'd encountered. I fumbled with the hook of the slacks, and Tobias leaned back, bracing his hands on the ledge of the bench. Finally getting it unhooked, the back of my hand grazed against his hard abdomen. He was just as built as the others, only a bit leaner. It didn't take away from his strength because he felt like a silk stone under my touch.

I tugged the zipper down and released his stiff member. I couldn't see the full magnitude of his shaft with the shadow cast by my body, but the outline of it looked intimidating. Pre-cum glinted at the top.

"Tell me you want me, Love." His breathy tone was enough to wrench free another gush of need until moisture dampened my thighs.

Spreading my hands on his belly, above his cock, I nodded jerkily. I smoothed my fingers across the happy trail starting at his belly button. His lips curled at one corner. It was the most predatory I'd seen him. Almost devious.

"I want you," I managed to push through my throat. I squirmed.

"Then take me."

I sucked in a breath, my heart beating overtime.

Pushing up with my thighs braced against his and my palms on his chest, I raised myself.

I lusted for him so much.

Poised over his dick, I hesitated in the face of his hunger. His sweater stretched tight over his shoulders, straining at the seams. His regal features stiffened, and his nose flared from his deep inhale. A crack echoed and I gawked at the crack in the bench originating at where he gripped it.

"Are you sure?" I didn't know how I managed to rip the words from my throat.

In answer, he grabbed my hips and slammed me down on his cock.

I screamed. Christ, he was so big. His cock deliciously stretched the walls of my channel. He groaned, his head falling back while he watched me with lowered eyelids. I stilled over him, letting my body open for him in this position. My pussy throbbed around his shaft, trying to take more of him.

He hissed between clenched teeth and his fangs flashed.

He was so wide I could feel him press against my clit in this position.

My lashes fluttered and I braced on his shoulders to move up on his shaft. I got maybe half way, before slamming back down. When fully seated, his tip shoved against my cervix. I whimpered.

Using my hands perched on his shoulders, and my knees

splayed against his thighs, I lifted myself up. The smooth, wet glide of his cock twitched. I bunched his sweater, swallowing another whine.

"Yes, such a precious Love," he breathed. "Take me just like that." I slammed down again, my movements clumsy. My eyelashes lowered with my next glide up until I stared at him through half-lidded eyes. As much as I wanted to close them, I enjoyed the expression on his face.

Each time I rose on him and fell, a muscle bunched in his cheek. And those little reactions gave me life.

Settling on him, I twisted my hips in a circle, embracing the feeling of him in me.

Tobias audibly clicked his teeth together, baring his fangs. The thick cock throbbed in my channel and warmth spread in my core. A soft groan ripped free from the cage of his teeth and his hips bucked, shoving his cock deep inside me. Desperation tinged his movements.

He grabbed my hips and guided me up and down, making the motion smooth and toe curling.

"Love." He groaned again, his frantic bucking stilling.

His release slicked my entrance, making everything exponentially wetter.

"Harder," I whispered.

He flexed his hand around my hips and after a grunt, rammed me harder. Giving me more of his strength.

Moans escaped my mouth. My thighs slapped against his, but my bouncing turned frantic.

My orgasm loomed over my body, but I tried to hold it at bay. I wanted more of this delicious sensation. I sank my teeth into my lower lip.

"Yes. Yes. Moan, darling, let out those sweet little sounds for me."

Fuck.

I cried out as my orgasm crested, cinching my eyes tightly shut. His hands stiffened on my hips and using his vampire strength he bounced me on his cock, gliding me up and down his silky shaft.

I couldn't have shut up if I wanted to. Nonsensical words spilled from my mouth. Another wave of cum splashed inside me from his twitching cock and he groaned.

The sound did naughty things to me.

Another orgasm chased the one I just had, making my legs twitch from the force. I crumpled forward in Tobias's arms. Every bit of energy I had drained out of me with my orgasms. His chest moved a few times under my cheek, so he was as tired as me. A sick satisfaction speared through my gut. I tired out a vampire.

His arms fell around my back, and I curled my fingers in his sweater. He felt so good inside me. He wasn't as hard as two orgasms ago, but he was still stiff.

I was fully immersed in the dark side and . . . I loved it.

"Never thought I'd see the day the Priest broke his vows."

I startled with a gasp and fell backwards.

TWENTY-THREE

catalina

TOBIAS CAUGHT me before I tipped over and fell into a rosebush filled with thorns. As soon as I was safe with my ass on the cold bench, I scrambled to grab the ripped pieces of the sweats and draped it over my lap, then smoothed my long shirt under my ass.

"Get out of here, Ren." Tobias's fangs flashed with his irritated order.

"But you were about to get all sweet with her—"

I pressed my thumb and pointer finger against my forehead, massaging in little circles.

"If you wouldn't have spoken we would have been able to see it."

"Asher's here, too?" I exclaimed. "Did we seriously have an audience?" I rounded my head toward Tobias.

"I was otherwise engaged," he said dryly, obviously offended at my accusation.

"I had to watch," Asher sniffed. "Our precious Priest lost his virginity."

My face heated. I mean, it was pretty clear from their

conversations and his behavior that he'd been abstaining, but putting it all out there . . .

Tobias sighed, and deftly tucked his cock back into his pants.

I crossed my arms across my breasts as the two of them approached, seeing another large form behind them.

"Bastien, too?"

He just looked happy to be there. Okay, 'happy' was a stretch since he never really had any emotion going on. His attention focused on me. He stepped behind the bench, pressing into my spine. His hand curled around the back of my neck.

"He seems to like watching, which is interesting since patience and Bastien didn't go hand in hand even before his mind went." Asher moved his hand in a roundabout way like he gave a visual representation of Bastien's mind wandering off. I could already see those indications of lack of patience in his instinctive reactions. They saw it as his illness, but I wasn't too sure he wasn't regaining some of his prior self before getting sick.

"Let me show you something." Tobias pinched my chin to bring my attention to him. Pale moon light caused his eyes to glint.

I slowly nodded.

"It's not ready," Asher snapped. His reluctance made me more curious.

Tobias ignored him and pressed a palm into my shoulder to guide me forward. The shirt fell to cover my ass, fortunately, and I set the ripped clothing on the bench. His movements and manner of speech often reminded me of some seventeenth century lord; very proper and gentlemanly, as if we hadn't just fucked away in the middle of flowers like a smutty scene out of a historical romance novel.

Whoa, I needed to get my hands on a computer to type the ideas down about a Regency Era vampire male lead.

A smile played on my lips. I hadn't yearned to write in so long.

The weight of his gaze settled on my face. I stifled my smirk, running my fingers through my hair and clearing my throat. Shuffling after the vamps, I rushed into the house. The chilly breeze raised the hair on my arms and made the sticky mess between my legs extra obvious.

"Wait, I'm going to scrub off quickly. I'll be right back." I called over my shoulder and ran up the staircase. I was dying to see what had them all worked up.

I DESCENDED THE STAIRS, washed and wearing a fresh pair of underwear. They were not in the large wardrobe before, so the undergarments I found were a new edition—all in my size.

In my hurry, I'd tugged on the same shirt. I liked being in their clothes and since they were such giants, they fit me like a comfy dress. Asher and Tobias looked up at me and stopped mid-conversation.

"Where are we going?" I stepped into the foyer. Bastien captured my hand, keeping it engulfed in his.

"Downstairs," Tobias answered without elaborating, stepping in front of me as we entered the hall.

Why was he being so secretive about it?

"Miss Herrera," Maddy called from the kitchen. She came

into view and I turned to her. Tobias hesitated at the basement entrance.

"Oh, God, why are you last-naming me?" I put my hands up. "Cat is good."

Maddy grinned.

Bastien suddenly moved in front of me and I clung to him; his stance was nowhere near welcoming. He exuded 'threat'. Maddy took multiple steps back, dropping her eyes as she inclined her head slightly to bare her neck. The visual was very submissive.

And I kind of didn't like it.

No. There was no 'kind of' about it. I didn't like it.

It screamed offering.

Like how those blood-whores behaved at the vampire clubs they'd taken me to. It was the same way they coached me to behave.

Tobias pressed on my shoulder and my mind started working again. I yanked Bastien, but when I couldn't budge him, I slipped away from Tobias and stepped in front of him.

Asher's chuckle echoed from the hall and I chose to ignore it instead of tossing him a searing glare like I craved. He always had this uncanny connection to knowing when I was jealous.

Tobias rapped his knuckles on the wall. I pushed my palms against Bastien's chest.

"Let's go." I shoved at him. His head turned down and he relaxed, finally allowing me to budge him. Tobias waited, arms crossed. Letting Bastien go, I followed him down the stairs. He was the only one left with us, everyone else had descended.

As soon as I stepped off the last step, the differences were glaring.

The couches remained in the middle, but soft, plush cream

carpet covered the floor. I left my slippers on the tile base so I wouldn't track in any dirt. Paintings graced the walls, and the pink cherry blossoms images added a pop of color. A suede L-shaped sofa stretched in the middle of the space and complemented the carpet with its tan color.

I'd asked them to make a better living space for Bastien, and they took me seriously. It felt good being listened to. Butterflies flooded my stomach.

"How did you guys get this done so fast?"

"Money gets you about anything you want." Asher leaned close. "And we have tons of it, Pet." His sweet breath sent a shiver up my spine. "That's not the best part." Asher swept his arm around my waist, pulling me forward. The door swung open into the bedroom Bastien had been held in. "Your bedroom."

My sight was assaulted with dark purples and varying shades of black.

The bed seemed tailor made to fit from one end of the corner of the wall to the other. It had to be two king sized mattresses put together. Purple bedding with black embroidered detailing outlined the edges of it.

The same cream carpet extended into the bedroom. A desk was pushed up against the corner to the left of the door and a laptop rested on the top of the chestnut surface. The feminine edge to the furnishings and decorations was obvious, but it wasn't my style. Even so, I was so grateful.

Jax quietly stepped after us. He hadn't looked at me since earlier. I didn't miss the fugitive glances he kept shooting at me.

"This is mine?"

Asher moved in front of me, head swiveling to one side and to the other as he took in the details.

"Yes," Tobias said.

The color coordination . . . kind of reminded me of something. I opened my mouth and closed it.

"Thank you—"

"I clearly remember telling you to stick to pale shades." Asher scowled.

"This is elegant," Ren added, shrugging his shoulders.

The color ran line in line with the dresses in the upstairs chest. My stomach swirled with discomfort.

I hated those colors quite vehemently. This room was in Imogen's style and that was the problem.

"I thought women liked all this?" Ren jutted his chin at Tobias. "He confirmed everything in the order, too."

"It's very nice, thank you—"

"You obviously don't like it," Jax interjected.

"—for the space. I appreciate it," I said louder, ignoring Jax.

"Let's get to the conversation, I have things to do," he continued, ignoring my words.

I clamped my lips together.

What did they need to talk about with me? A feeding schedule? I settled on the bed to see all of them. That way I wasn't swinging my head from one vampire to the other.

I lifted an eyebrow, waiting.

"I'll have the room changed," Asher said to me, settling next to me on the bed.

I crossed my arms. "What do you need to say?" My heart raced and even though I didn't want to show it, I was sure they could see the thudding pulse at my neck.

"This is our gift to you," Ren announced. I opened my mouth, closed it, then opened it again.

"What does this mean?"

"That you're officially the property of Crimson Coven. Humans in the vampire community must belong to a Coven." Belong . . . as much as I hated it, my stomach dipped. I'd never belonged anywhere.

"What's the difference compared with what we are now?"

"The difference is that now you are our official Pet." Ren grinned. He had the sensitivity of an iceberg. I blinked. 'Official Pet' sounded crazy. "And we're not going to murder you." And that was worse.

Tobias shook his head and pinched the bridge of his nose. He seemed to be the only one that understood the human implications.

"We want you comfortable if you are to be our long term human—"

"If you go around spouting nonsense of not belonging to us, we can't protect you. We wouldn't have a claim on you." Ren cut Tobias off.

"How long is 'long term'?" I feared asking it but it needed to be done even though I knew they would have no true answer. My life could end on a random Tuesday because one of them fed on me a little too much.

"As long as you desire," Asher said, hand smoothing up my back.

Lie.

Vampires only knew how to own and devour. How long would it be before he tired of me? A knot swelled in my throat. They'd turn on me eventually.

"You will be well cared for," Asher added, continuing to wax on about how they'd make sure everything was taken care of for me.

"No," I whispered, and shot to my feet.

I licked my lips and curled my nails into my palms.

"What do you mean, no?" Ren tilted his head. He was comically shocked. He didn't hear 'no' enough.

"Humans need time to process the inevitable, Ren. Bulldozing her will not help you," Asher said, condescending to me again.

"You mean you'll keep me until you think I betray you or . . . or, you feel I wronged you guys in some way."

"That will not happen." Asher tried to pacify me again.

"You'll turn your back on me—again." I shook my head, backing up.

My throat clogged up.

"Catalina," Asher chided.

"You guys didn't even believe me when I said I didn't try to run off with Imogen's ashes." They still didn't.

"I—"

"You didn't," I interrupted Asher. "I'm here for the foreseeable future, but don't act like you all suddenly care for me." I glared at Jax as I backed away. "Especially you."

For once, he didn't have some rude response. His jawline fluttered and his hardened gaze stared me down.

"Didn't you say you wanted protection?" Ren drawled, his shoulder pressing into the wall.

I swung my head to look at him. "By vampire law, if anyone tries to harm you we will be powerless if you state you do not belong to us. It will not go well for you. We literally won't have any claim over you."

I deflated. Oh.

I was tired of being so weak . . . so human. They were strong. They could protect.

All five vampires seemed so relaxed and without worry. If . . . I was like them, I wouldn't be at their whim.

Could I be a vampire?

Should I?

If I became a vampire, no one could hurt me again, and I could stay with them, as equals. Questions bubbled behind my lips, but I held them in.

"I need to think." Whirling to the door, I padded over the soft carpet and stormed upstairs. The dull thud rang out with each slap of my slippers against the metal.

Childish, but it made me feel good.

I clocked the propped metal door. Yeah, sure, I got my own room, but it wasn't lost on me that they could also lock me up down there.

Maddy watched from the busy counter, slicing the knife through potatoes with rhythmic movements.

"You're just on time for some lunch."

I smiled at her, close-mouthed and plopped on the chair, lacing my fingers on the counter I'd been fucked on yesterday. Fortunately, a heavy smell of cleaner hung in the air.

Saying it was lunch was weird, but my days were backward now, so I guess it would be considered 'lunch time' even though it was one in the morning.

Maddy's slicing slowed and she peeked at the door. She set the knife down and pushed her palms into the counter as she leaned forward on the island.

Her boobs pushed over the collar of her shirt. It really outlined her figure.

"Girl, give me some tips," she whispered.

I blinked. She must have noted the confusion on my face.

"To get in with the Crimson Coven Sires. It'd be so fucking

amazing. You know how fucking lucky you are?" She sighed and clapped her palms together. "I hear they're phenomenal in bed."

A sour taste spread on my tongue, and I struggled to smooth my expression so the grimace didn't take over.

I gripped my hands harder until it hurt. Jealousy was a nasty emotion. I hated that they brought it out of me.

Being 'theirs'. Was this what I looked forward to? And if they saw me as property, I'd just have to accept whatever they chose, even if it meant they were with others.

I forced the corner of my lips up. The thump of steps approached.

"Tell me later," she whispered.

"Sure." My mask almost slipped.

Maddy returned to the potatoes and placed them in the boiling water.

Asher settled next to me, his shirt billowing and allowing peeks at his chest. The Viking-like vampire undeniably drew attention. As shown by Maddy who shot him furtive looks from under her lashes.

She didn't even try to hide her lust.

I cleared my throat and rubbed my palms against my thighs.

Asher's legs spread, caging me with one thigh at my back and the other wedging into my knees.

Asher drummed his fingers on the counter.

He said nothing and I tried to ignore him as I stared at Maddy cooking and shot him looks, mainly because he hadn't stopped staring at me.

"What?" I finally said, exasperated.

"You're upset. How about I chase you down and pleasure you?"

"No." I scowled. "Are you trying to make *me* feel better or yourself?"

"You'll enjoy it." His voice lowered an octave.

God, he was sexy.

Based on the glaze over Maddy's eyes as she gawked, she thought so, too.

I snapped out of my lust.

"What if we watch a movie?"

"I love films."

I clamped my lips together. It wasn't the response I expected.

"Which would you like to see? A few months ago, I watched something about a young boy discovering he was a witch." He frowned. "I think it was a witch. It may have been a werewolf." I combed my brain for a movie with the plot. I raised an eyebrow.

"That wasn't a few years ago, Asher. It was a decade ago."

He blinked slowly, processing.

Another aspect to consider if I chose to be a vampire.

"Nevermind with the movie. How about you explain what you guys meant the other day when you mentioned Bastien was kept because he held value?"

Asher hummed and nodded, looking away for the first time.

"Of course, the curious girl wants to know everything." He cupped the side of my head with his large palm. I couldn't deny the flutters that erupted at his claim. "Bastien has sired many vampires, and their allegiance is to Crimson Coven."

Maddy's explanation added context to those words. So if they all sired many, collectively they were powerful, or at least exponentially more than individually.

"So, Imogen wanted to keep him because of his

contribution?" I couldn't hide the horror in my tone. I recalled the careless way they chained him up . . . the lack of clothing. "And you guys kept him in that state for years because of his usefulness?"

"Decades really, but it was worse when Imogen was around. Bastien came to disgust her."

I sucked in a breath.

I hated her more with each piece of information I learned.

The doorbell dinged.

Asher brushed my hair behind my ear.

"I will return." He smoothly strode away.

I sat, wrapping my head around the new information.

These were all things I must consider if I turned into a vampire. I didn't want to lose myself.

Maddy had been watching us the entire time, but I tried ignoring her eagle-like attention. Slipping off the stool, I trailed after Asher.

"She's not dead," Asher's voice echoed to me as I strode down the hall toward the living room. "Who are you to search for her?" A threat rang in his tone.

"She's . . . not dead?" The familiar voice reached into my gut and squeezed my stomach.

No, no, no, no. He couldn't be here. My worst nightmare bloomed to life before me.

catalina

I FROZE FOR ONE SECOND. Two. Then I burst forward, elbowing Asher out of the way.

Numbness spread to my fingertips.

No. He had to go. They couldn't see him. What would I do?

I was going to throw up.

"Peter." I couldn't feel my lips. "Wh-what are you doing here?"

"You're not dead?" His voice cracked. He clutched a phone in hand. "I got a call from your lawyer, and I was told to collect what may be left in the fire. They said you died." He shook his head, eyelashes damp. "I needed to charge my phone."

He rambled, shaking.

I moved forward, arm outstretched. Asher clutched my shirt and yanked me backwards.

"He's my brother, Asher." I elbowed free. I wrapped my hand around his forearm and pulled him inside. He didn't seem to focus on anything.

His features stayed washed out as he followed my tugging. I managed to get him sitting on the living room couch.

"What happened to your house?"

I sighed, rubbing my palms on his arms. He was freezing. How long had he been standing outside in front of the burned remnants of my place?

"Brother-in-law." Asher's grin widened, sprawling on the couch next to Peter.

"What are you doing?" I hissed and twisted his shirtsleeve.

He only winked.

This was all wrong. My brother spoke to the vampires when I worked my entire fucking life to keep him away from the danger chasing me.

Peter blinked repeatedly, sputtering.

I shook my head vehemently at Asher.

My hair fluttered from the sudden appearance of a vampire swooping in front of Peter.

"Who do we have here?" Ren said, leaning into Peter's face.

"Leave him alone," I spat out so fast I was surprised it came out in a cohesive string.

Ren didn't ever listen though, that was the problem. He gripped the back of my brother's neck, forcing a grunt from his mouth.

"Stop!" I lunged and gripped Ren's hair, managing to grab as much of the short strands as I could to yank him.

Ren hissed, but I didn't let go as I clung to him.

Peter let out an ear splitting scream, focusing on Ren's distended fangs.

"Please, let him go!" I begged, close to tears, but still holding on. "Please." I slammed my clenched fist into his shoulder.

Peter's mouth clamped shut and his eyes rounded on me and then Ren. His chest heaved, but he no longer screamed. Numbness spread to my fingertips. I wanted to grab Peter and run.

Ren tilted his head to peer into my face. He studied me. I didn't move my eyes from his, putting as much plea into my expression as I could.

His bicep flexed and there was a grunt as Peter's weight dropped to the floor, but I could only assume because I hadn't looked away from Ren.

"You should have said so sooner." A spine chilling grin tilted the corner of Ren's lips and he straightened with me still hanging onto him.

My toes scraped against the wrinkled carpet that had lifted on the wooden floor at my desperate lunge. I loosened my grip so my heels settled on the ground. My breaths puffed from my lips. How could I not be huffing and puffing with my life flashing before my eyes like that?

"Ren." Tobias's voice rang through the sound of my breathing. I whipped my head in his direction. There was an edge to his tone and his gaze was fixed on the vampire I held onto. Tobias shook his head just slightly and the bicep I gripped onto twitched. They exchanged some look I couldn't read and Tobias nodded oh so slightly.

I clenched my teeth, not liking the secretiveness, but it also went far in reminding me that they'd been together centuries and knew each other well. On top of that, Tobias read minds, so there had to be some sort of communication going on I wasn't privy to. Peter only had me to protect him, so I couldn't let my panic win. Taking a deep breath, I tried to focus on calming the tremble of my hands because dropping and curling into a ball wouldn't help anyone.

I could do that later once Peter was far from here.

At least my lungs weren't betraying me and giving out. It was the only perk of ingesting blood . . . well, not the only perk, but I'd let myself be a little delusional.

Ren's palm settled on my tight grip, and I dropped my hands quickly. I'd been tugging and grabbing at him like nothing. My face heated and I cleared my throat, but kept my mouth shut. I couldn't apologize for protecting Peter. But what surprised me was that Ren didn't look like he'd tear my head off, he just looked contemplative.

The usually combative vampire took a step back and retreated. "I'll handle Bastien."

I sucked in breath. I'd forgotten about him still in the kitchen. While Ren could reign in the crazy, Bastien would only react.

Peter huddled on the ground, his back against the couch. His eyes kept bouncing from me to Tobias, then in the direction Ren had disappeared, Asher going with him.

I clung to Tobias's sleeve. His gray eyes settled on me, cold and calculative. A vast difference to the lust and desire I'd experienced in the garden.

"Compel him to forget." I squeezed his arm. "Make him forget, please Tobias."

My words chipped the ice from his features and his shoulders visibly relaxed.

Frowning, he scratched his eyebrow. "Are you sure, Love?"

I nodded jerkily.

His hand cupped the back off my neck and he forced me to

look up at him. His attention dropped to my throat where my pulse went haywire.

"You are ours, he will be protected," he breathed in my ear. I wanted him protected and shielded from all vampires, even them.

They shouldn't have, but the words comforted me. I closed my eyes tight as he released me. "I will try, but, Cat, I cannot read his mind."

My limbs became stone.

"What are you doing?" Peter's fear riddled voice jolted me out of my daze. I whirled to find Tobias knelt before him.

"Look at me, child."

"Child?" Peter scoffed. A hint of temper glinted in his gaze.

"Would you prefer fetus? I'm centuries older than you." That shut Peter right up. Tobias' attempt at humor didn't hit the mark based on Peter's dropped mouth. "Forget everything up to the point of arriving here." His voice dropped a few octaves.

A few beats of silence passed with me holding my breath.

"What? No fucking way," Peter spat out.

I closed my eyes tight, trying to stifle the tears that sprang to life. Like me, he couldn't be compelled. Why was this happening to us?

Knowing about vampires was a death sentence. I'd lived because they kept me . . . I had a feeling the same wouldn't be applied to Peter.

The knot in my throat only grew, but I swallowed down my emotions.

I approached and pulled Peter's arm until he stood. He'd only grown taller in the years we'd been separated. Time flew by too fast and I hadn't had the chance to watch him grow up. He towered over me now. How had he turned into a man so quickly?

"Come with me."

He didn't argue with me as I pulled him toward the kitchen. His steps dragged.

"What is happening, Cat?" he murmured so low, it was almost a whisper. That told me he understood he had to be cautious. And it made me feel even worse. Had I been trying to protect him too much when he could have handled the truth?

I pressed my palm to the frantic pump inside my chest.

Keeping Peter away from vampires was my only goal in life. I'd stayed away from him. I'd separated us, just so he could live life without getting wrapped up in my running. So he could have a life.

Now he stood in a vampire's living room, talking to a vampire.

Why had this happened? I whirled, halfway to the kitchen.

"Why did you come?"

"Your lawyer called me." Peter's shoulders dropped. "I thought you were dead."

I deflated like a needle to a balloon.

His lips flattened into a line. The shadows underneath his eyes didn't look good and hollows dipped his cheeks. I grabbed his hand and squeezed it in both of mine. When had his hands gotten bigger than mine?

"I'm sorry, Peter." I licked my lips. "I should have protected you better."

"Vampires exist?" he whispered, clutching my sleeve. I didn't have the heart to let him know they could hear him.

I could only close my eyes tight and rub my temples.

He exhaled harshly.

"I knew you feared something, but I would have never imagined it was vampires." He scoffed.

"Wait, you knew . . ." I rolled my lips between my teeth. I tried hiding my emotions from him.

"How could I not know, Cat? You jumped at every little sound, you woke up screaming, you always acted like someone was right behind you. I knew you were hiding from someone."

I could only gawk up at him.

"And no, I'm not going back to school until I know you're okay."

My hands trembled at my sides.

"You're not safe here—"

He just shrugged. Who was this little brother of mine?

"I'm hungry. You got anything to eat?"

I scoffed and shook my head. I shoved his shoulder.

"Kitchen is that way." He stormed forward and I hurried to catch up to him.

"So, what? It took you ten seconds to accept the existence of fictional creatures?" I muttered behind him.

"Kind of hard to deny it." He sat at the island, elbows thudding on the counter.

"Maddy, can you make some food?"

She's already clocked him and her gaze bounced from me to him. We had very similar features, so it wouldn't be a stretch to guess we were siblings. We'd always been told we looked alike.

"Sure thing," she said. Porcelain clanged as she rifled to get a plate out. He didn't seem torn up about the existence of vampires and he really should be.

Peter fixed his gaze on his dead cell phone.

"Maddy, can you keep him here?"

All she did was give me a thumbs up. In the short amount

of time I'd known her, I'd come to realize that she got the clue fast. She'd make sure he stayed put while I dealt with my overwhelming emotions.

Off-kilter, stunned, discombobulated . . . they were all words to describe the madness rolling through my chest and the frantic thoughts overwhelming my brain weren't helping the matter.

It took only a few steps down the hallway for the ground to shift and I stumbled into the wall. My back slid down until I was in a half-slouch, propping myself up.

"Catalina." Tobias's whisper held a sharp edge to it. "Are you well?" He gripped my forearm and helped steady me on my feet.

"Where are all the guys?" I forced the words free from the back of my throat where my emotions had clogged.

"In your bedroom."

I grabbed onto him and pulled him to the metal door across from the kitchen, unable to bear looking at my brother lest he see the tears forming on my eyelashes.

catalina

BASTIEN SPRAWLED ON MY BED, arms behind his head. His eyes were closed like he was sleeping. The other three were in the living room area. Ren's shoulder rested on the wall near my bedroom door, and the twins sat on the couch, Jax's legs sprawled out and Asher crossed one ankle on a knee.

It looked like I interrupted their conversation.

I wanted to lean back against Tobias to get a bit of strength, but I straightened my spine.

Swallowing down my nerves, I took a few steps forward and placed my back to the wall so I could see all of them.

Taking a deep breath, I straightened my shoulders and dropped to my knees. Asher immediately stood.

"Please, leave Peter alone—"

"Cat—" Tobias's words were interrupted.

Jax was suddenly in front of me, lifting me from under my bicep with an aggressive yank.

I smacked into him from the momentum. My arms smushed between my breasts and his chest. I sputtered.

"Do not beg in such a way," he said vehemently.

I blinked, floored. Why was he reacting so violently? Him especially. I would imagine he'd like to see me humbled . . . humiliated.

A palm pressed to my spine and the scent of orange candies ticked my senses, yanking me out of my daze. I shoved away from Jax before he had a fit.

Jax's jaw worked, eyebrows pulled down over his blue, stormy gaze, and he crossed his arms.

"I . . ." I started, looking over my shoulder at Tobias. His expression stayed shuttered. If I'd known how angry they would react, then I would have never thought to ask for anything. "I'm sorry for asking for a favor." I paused, swallowing hard. I fucked up, but I would pay for it, not Peter—

"The only time you should be on your knees is when you're begging for my cock, Cat."

I whirled toward Ren so fast the room spun. I floundered for what to say, sputtering nonsensically.

"Do not ever do that again." Jax's voice rumbled with aggression. I was going to make myself throw up with how much I turned from one side of the room to the other.

"Love," Tobias gripped the back of my neck and squeezed gently to get my attention. "We will not harm him, but he cannot leave."

I gasped, struggling to swallow.

"P-please, guys. Please. I will do anything—" I choked out, halfway to the ground because my knees gave out. Tobias held me up and cradled the back of my head to meet his gaze. My chest heaved against his.

"It's almost sunrise, Catalina." He sighed, searching my face. "No harm will come to him. We can discuss it later."

My heart slammed against my rib cage, and I struggled to keep it together because all I wanted to do was freak out.

Large arms wrapped around me from behind, lashing my arms to my sides. I wiggled. Without breaking his hold, he pulled me back, making my feet hang off the ground. He exhaled against my neck and the sweet scent that clung to them all enveloped me. My frantic breathing stuttered and I dropped against the barrel chest. Although they were all large, Bastien's chest was the widest. Amazingly, my panic receded within the blanket of his cradle.

"Is he comforting her?" Ren said, stunned, no longer leaning against the wall.

I sighed and let my eyes slide closed to focus on breathing.

"He can tell you're agitated," Asher said, awed.

Why were they acting like this was big news? Bastien usually seemed pretty in tune with how I felt about things.

"Honestly, he seems the most responsive in my dreams."

I'd thought it was silent before, but this took it to a new level.

"He's been dream walking?" Tobias breathed. He took a small step toward me and stopped, tilting his head oh so slightly. Confusion flickered over his features.

"Yes?" I said hesitantly.

"That shouldn't be possible."

I gathered that based on their reaction.

"He hasn't dream walked since he was infected."

Oh, okay, it did sound serious. I lifted my head and wiggled in Bastien's arms, but he didn't let me go.

"What does this mean?"

"He started getting better a few years ago and then—" Tobias stopped and shook his head.

"What? You guys are scaring me."

"It leveled out until you entered our life. He reacts to you, Pet."

"Isn't that good?"

Jax scoffed. "Good? We have to figure out why before that's determined."

"Will you ever not be suspicious of me?" I griped.

"Honestly, Jaxon, enough!" Asher spat.

"We will have to continue this conversation tomorrow," Ren said and yanked up the bottom of his shirt and pulled it off. His hands hooked on his waistband but before I watched him fully disrobe, Bastien toted me into the bedroom and tossed me on the bed.

I grunted upon landing, the bed bouncing under my weight. I jostled on the mattress as he climbed next to me and pulled my back to his chest. Asher settled in next to me. He leaned over and pecked my forehead.

"Allowing you in the room with us is a trust. Do not betray it." I glared at Jax over Asher's shoulder, but he didn't see my disapproval because he was already outside the bedroom.

"But my broth—"

"Maddy will get him situated," Asher murmured, yanking me back down.

I wouldn't be able to sleep, so I would lay in the cradle of Asher and Bastien's arms until they fell into their slumber.

MECHANICALLY LOCKING the metal door behind me, I stared at my feet as I trudged to the seat and plopped on my ass.

I propped my elbows on the counter, digging my fingers into my hair.

"Are you okay?"

I followed the soft voice to a young girl who looked to be about thirteen. She lifted an eyebrow.

"Uh, yeah," I answered hesitantly. She smiled and leaned forward to return to sipping her hot chocolate.

Her chin propped on her fists.

"Sorry," Maddy said sheepishly. "This is Sidney, my spawn." She glared at her daughter. "She knows to introduce herself." She cleared her throat pointedly. She must have had her young, since Maddy seemed to be only a few years older than me.

I looked at her and then at Sidney who just rolled her eyes. Ah, she was hitting that moody stage. When Peter hit that age, he'd been insufferable.

"I asked Mr. Crimson if she could stay during sun-up and he said she was welcome to, so I keep her and then drop her off for bedtime at my mom's." Maddy's lips thinned.

There seemed to be a lot more to the story, but I didn't bother prying.

"No school?" I hesitantly asked Sidney.

"It's summer." She said it like it was obvious.

"Right," I mumbled. It kind of didn't feel that way since the weather remained gloomy. "Where's Peter?"

"I took him to the spare bedroom upstairs right after you disappeared with the . . . others." She peeked at her daughter and smiled.

"I was waiting for you to come back up." Peter appeared from around the hallway.

Sidney inhaled slightly and when I looked at her, she tracked my brother with her mouth pursed.

"Who's the kid?" he asked.

"Kid?" Sidney huffed with a little frown. She said it so low, I was sure Peter hadn't heard her disgruntlement.

"Maddy's daughter."

"Where did those v—"

I sliced my hand across my neck to cut him off. He got the clue and shut up. Sidney whirled to look at me as I brushed my hand through my hair as nonchalantly as possible. Based on her narrowing eyes, I wasn't as successful as I thought.

". . . very large guys go?"

"Nowhere you need to worry about." My tone didn't need to be as sharp as it was, but I didn't want him to get any ideas. Peter sank into the seat beside Sidney, who hadn't taken her gaze off him. If she were a cartoon, there'd be hearts for eyes.

Peter didn't like the answer, but he looked at the company in the kitchen and obviously bit back his irritation.

"You had your daughter young?" I said the first thing that popped into my head.

"Not at all, I had her at thirty-two," Maddy winked at me. That would mean she's forty-five-ish. Her smooth skin didn't show any age, but I was sure she was human. Sidney tapped her fingers on the granite, shooting furtive glances at Peter.

"And the kid is what? Fourteen, fifteen?" Peter scoffed, head turning from the mom to the girl. He went into a slew of questions and shock. I could understand it, she had some great genes. I wouldn't have guessed her age.

"I'm not a kid," Sidney repeated, too low to be heard over Peter's shocked rambling.

"Peter, are you ready for me to take you to the airport?" I asked as soon as there was a lull in conversation.

"What? I'm not leaving," he scowled.

I clenched my teeth, straightening to swivel my torso toward him.

"Yes, you are." I feared my attempt to keep my tone level didn't work.

"Sidney, let's go see some, uh, thing over here." Sidney rolled her eyes and trailed after her mom.

I waited a beat and scooted close to Peter.

"Take the money I left in my will," I ordered. "Don't tell anyone I'm alive."

"I don't want your money!" he exclaimed. A vine wrapped around my neck and tightened with his every word.

"Let's put a pin in the conversation," I said, trying to stifle the bite to my tone. He set his expression mulishly. He wouldn't let this go and we'd argue in circles.

"We can't talk about this later."

"Sure we can, after you go back to school to finish off your year, we can discuss it."

Peter scoffed, glaring.

"I'm eighteen, Catty, you can't force me to leave." I opened and closed my mouth, unable to spit any words out. "I have an assignment to finish." He stormed off, leaving me staring after him.

I dropped my face in my hands; I wanted him away from all the uncertainty. It was best for him to get out of here before anything went wrong, and something was bound to go terribly wrong.

I had no chance of protecting him unless I was as strong as my opponents . . . If I were a vampire . . .

If you can't beat them, join them.

Then I could protect Peter from anyone that tried to touch him.

It wasn't completely selfless, though. Deep, deep in my gut, excitement bloomed. To no longer be helpless.

The thought of becoming a vampire intrigued me a little more than I wanted to admit.

catalina

I'D GONE UPSTAIRS to sleep and woken an hour before sunset then come back down to settle in the living room. Peter sat on the settee with his computer in his lap while I'd sprawled across the long couch, wracking my brain on how to get Peter out of here with the minimum amount of drama. It wasn't like he hadn't built a life for himself over there. Only his worry for me kept him here.

His fingers rapidly swept across the keyboard.

The quick slap of footsteps thudded down the hall. A harried Maddy rounded into the foyer.

"Hurry up, Sid," she shouted. An apron still hung around her neck, swaying with her ragged breaths.

"Everything okay?"

"I lost track of time." She brushed her messy strands back. Strain tightened the corners of her mouth. "I need to drop Sidney off at my parents. Hopefully, I'll be back before they rise." She chewed on her lower lip, shiftily looking at the screen of her phone.

The lowering sunlight reflected golden light from the

window sill. If her attempt was to get back before they rose, I didn't think she'd make it. Peter continued tapping away at his computer, hyper-focused.

"Peter can take her." Anything to keep him out of the way.

"Are you sure?" Maddy scratched her arm, not really looking at me as she swept a finger over her phone screen.

He shot me a narrowed eyed look from the corner of his eyes. His lips parted, but I scowled at him. He sighed and stood. Sidney ran up, smoothing her hand down her hair and her eyes rounded on Maddy handing Peter her car keys.

"You're doing me a huge favor." Maddy continued her thankful babble. Sidney's lips parted and a flush crawled down her neck as she shot furtive glances at Peter. "Sidney can direct you there."

"Let's go, kid." He was too busy sending me a look to notice her lips purse at his command.

Yet, she didn't say anything and followed him out the door with her head slightly lowered. I couldn't see any bit of her spunk which seemed to have dissolved under the flush overtaking her face.

As soon as the front door slammed shut, I closed the distance between Maddy and I.

"If you have any other errands to run. Have him do it."

"Oh, I couldn't—" Awareness dawned on her face and she slowly nodded. "Will do, I need some things from the store, I'll have him pass by for me."

Good, by the time he gets back I wanted him too tired to stay up and get more involved with the vampires than he was.

I smiled at her, putting as much gratitude behind it as I could. I headed down the hall to get to the first level. The metal door hissed shut, encasing me in silence.

I approached the vampire laying stiff on the couch, he was the only one that hadn't stayed in the bedroom. Like a magnet, my fingers hovered over his face. He wouldn't know . . . his silky cheek was cool to the touch. He had such long eyelashes, I'd never noticed because he was always glaring at me, but they fanned out, golden and glinting in the low light of the living room.

I liked him better like this, sleeping and soft. He was rather beautiful. Even though he was Asher's twin, there were hair strands slightly darker interwoven with his eyebrow.

I dragged my fingertips to the edge of his never smiling mouth. The only time I'd seen it curl up was when he made some sly, sarcastic comment.

His eyes flung open, and I gasped, yanking my hand back. From one moment, he'd been utterly still—stone-like, to the next, his gaze glinted with awareness. He said nothing, which was stranger than him speaking. I brushed my hair behind my ear, retreating through the bedroom door with quick steps.

Asher was sprawled out, arm flopped across Ren's torso while his hand hovered near his face. Bastien lay face down, arms under his head and long white hair spilling over the edge of the bed.

Giving me a space of my own, their reactions to Peter showing up . . . none of it was expected and I was too weak to not be moved by it. And the possibility of having such protection? It buckled my knees.

Who knew not living in fear felt so good?

The rustle of clothing dragged my attention to Tobias. He'd been sitting at my desk chair to the side, and I hadn't seen him. He smoothly stood and approached me. I tilted my head up to keep eye contact.

His finger swept across my lower lip and I tamped down my smile. I'd been standing here, grinning like an idiot as I stared at them. I offered no comment and cleared my throat.

Ren's eyes popped open and he jerked his head, causing Asher's hand to plop on his chest. He flicked the arm off him. Asher groaned and rolled to his side, invading Bastien's space, who didn't appreciate it based on him rolling off the bed and hitting the ground. He sprang to his feet with a hiss.

Tobias resting his palm on my lower back cut off my muffled snicker.

"We'll be attending a gathering tomorrow night," he murmured. I was less focused on the words than on the way his breath fluttered hair around my ear. A shiver coasted down my spine. I stopped my hand halfway to his chest and curled my fingers into my palm, dropping it to my side. Their effect on me should be normal to me by now, but I feared I'd ever get used to it.

"You're welcome to touch me," he said huskily, grabbing hold of my wrist, rubbing it to smooth my hand onto his chest. The soft fabric tickled my palm. I sank my teeth into my lower lip, shyly looking up at him. I swayed closer to him, like he had some sort of gravitational pull.

A palm cupped the side of my neck and I twisted to see who gripped me. Bastien's nose grazed my temple, his big body crowding me and forcing me closer to Tobias.

"Oh please continue," Asher said huskily from where he sprawled on his back with his hands behind his head. His gaze burned with heat and a bulge lifted the front of his linen pants, obvious, intimidating, hypnotizing.

It felt different being with them . . . butterflies encased by my ribcage wouldn't stop flapping their wings.

My brain chose that moment to switch on and process his comment.

"Where are we going tomorrow?" The usual tension in my chest expanded. Eighty percent of the time I'd stepped out into the city, something went wrong. I wasn't looking forward to another event.

"We're going to Calliope's," Ren said from his sitting position at the end of the bed. He was in the process of pulling on his tan boots.

"Why?" I gasped. "Didn't you think she's the one trying to kill you guys?"

Ren waved his hand around. "And?"

I could only blink at the oddity of these males. I let myself get carried away way too much. They weren't human. I should get it tattooed on my hand.

"What, you're not excited to meet up with your friend?" Jax drawled, smirking. I clocked the jab. I squeezed my lips together until they flattened.

"He's joking," Asher said.

I wanted to retort but it was pointless, so I ripped my attention off Jax, not giving him a reaction. My goal was to ignore him. He could be a lamp for all I cared.

"We'll answer any questions on the way to the shopping center."

"You mean, you'll answer," Jax interjected. If I wasn't mistaken, a hint of petulance was woven into his tone.

"Shopping?" I asked, again ignoring Jax, focusing on the twin that never failed to answer my questions.

"Yes and after, you will have a visit from another Coven's Pet who can put your behavior into perspective."

My behavior? I scowled.

"That's exactly it, you can't scowl at your master, human." Ren approached, his eyes searching my face.

"Master?" I blustered, at a loss for words. Heat flooded my cheeks. Outrage and shock trapping words within me.

Asher reached into his pants, and he very obviously gripped his cock. He shuddered and moved his girth into the waistband so the stiffy no longer bounced.

Ren continued, getting in my face. My eyes widened until he was a finger's length away from touching his nose to mine. "You must keep yourself to a standard appropriate as a belonging of Crimson Coven."

Asher elbowed him back.

"What he means is, your behavior will be a reflection of us. If there is weakness, it will be exploited." Asher cupped the back of my neck, getting so close I almost went cross eyed. What was with them stepping all up in my face? It reminded me of when Peter was young and he wanted me to give him my undivided attention. "So when around other vampires, you must behave in a way we do not expect you to behave in the comfort of our homes."

"What does my behavior have to do with going shopping?"

"Well, Pet, you need something suitable to wear since you complain about wearing anything in storage," Asher said with a smug grin. I couldn't disagree. All their 'storage' consisted of what belonged to Imogen. "Your first show by our side must be done in style."

I harrumphed, not liking the spiel. "And how exactly are we going? Everything is closed."

"A Coven Sire we know owns a shopping center," he said, his nose practically touching mine. I wasn't sure if he was trying to overwhelm me into just going along with whatever they said, but it was working.

"A Sire that runs an escort service and now one that owns a mall. Vampires have their fingers in a lot of pies."

"We mold ourselves into society. It'd be stupid of us not to evolve and build wealth," Jax said. "Money equals power."

Asher straightened and I clawed myself out of the cobwebs he conjured whenever he neared. And a small part of me, the smallest, teeniest bit, craved going shopping. Such a silly desire considering the dramatic shift my life had taken . . . but I couldn't change anything. And I'd decided to accept this new life. Tentatively accept it.

"Fine, when are we leaving?"

"Now," Tobias said, withdrawing his palm from my back. The absence left a cold spot on my spine.

"We'll have to chain Bastien up again." Every follicle in my body fought against that sentence. I nudged past Asher to swing my glare at Ren.

"No."

"No?" he repeated, eyebrows raised. "She's failing at her role."

"He shouldn't be chained up, he hasn't done anything. And it's not like there aren't four of you that could stop him from doing anything. Plus, didn't you say they're opening the store, that means there won't be any humans, so he should be safe to come with us—"

Asher smirked, placing his finger across my lips. "Take a breath."

"We shall bring him, Love."

Well, that was easy. There was no bluster from Jax, either.

I narrowed my eyes suspiciously. They were giving into

what I wanted so quickly. They had been giving in with suspicious ease.

"I can't go out like this," I huffed, raking my hand over my clothing.

"Your new clothing should be in my wardrobe. Maddy unpacked and organized them there since we hadn't completed your room," Asher murmured in my ear.

"You had clothes for me the entire time?" I scowled, plucking at the overlarge top draped over me.

"I don't see the problem." Asher dragged his gaze over my form and settled on my breasts. I could feel my nipples stiffen under his gaze. I crossed my arms over my chest and shook my head, then turned on my heel.

catalina

THEY PULLED into a parking garage and headed toward one of those gates where the plastic barrier swung up when you pressed a button. Ren had been on his cell phone for the last few minutes, listening to whatever the buzzing voice said on the other end. The others seemed to hear the conversation based on the glances they offered each other.

The curiosity ate me up, but I kept my mouth shut.

"Did you find them?" he snapped and swiveled his head to look at me squished between Bastien and Tobias.

"You need to go handle it," Tobias said.

"*We* need to go handle it." Ren ended the call.

Tobias's jaw twitched.

The garage wove onto a ramp that turned into an upward spiral spanning floors; I lost count how many, until Jaxon pulled the SUV into the parking spot in front of a glass wall.

"You two go, and take Bastien, Asher and I can handle taking her shopping." The way Jax offered, his tone bland, made me want to claw his hair out. He'd become different recently, less hostile, and I didn't trust it.

I glared at the back of his head.

He rolled to the front of a large glass entrance. Fluorescent overhead lights glinted off the surface, but I couldn't see anything inside until doors swung open. A woman stood with her hands clasped before her in a neat skirt suit, the gray hem reached below her knees. Her hair was neatly pulled back into a high bun.

I tucked one of the loose strands that fell out of my half ponytail behind my ear. I'd brushed the hell out of it, but only made the frizz worse. While I was here, I was getting my anti-frizz product. Tobias opened the door and smoothly exited, then reached back with his hand outstretched. I hesitated only for a moment and took his hand to exit the car. Bastien followed me out, causing the car to jostle a bit from his mass moving across the seats. His fingers curled on the outside of the car as he pulled himself out causing the metal to dip a bit. My eyes bugged out, but no one blinked an eye at the damage.

"Hello, Mr. Crimson," a commanding female voice said, and heels clicked in approach. The woman calmly and smoothly stopped in front of Tobias. She had the same ethereal aura to her as all the other vampires I'd encountered. "I'm Taylor and I'll be your escort through the necessary departments. I will ensure this is a successful visit for our esteemed guests."

"Alistair won't be making a showing?"

"My Sire sends his regards and said he will visit Crimson Nights to have a drink."

"Who's Alistair?" I shook Tobias's arm.

"He's a Coven Sire. He owns this shopping center." Tobias smoothed his large palm down the side of my head. "Catalina, we will return for you when you are done." The woman's gaze flicked to me, but didn't seem phased in any other way. "If you will lead them."

"Absolutely." Her gaze lifted over my shoulder. Her blue eyes slightly widened and she gasped.

Bastien could not care less for the attention, he stiffened, narrowing red eyes at her. I caught his hand, scooching close so my shoulder pressed into his torso. His threatening sneer faded. Tobias cleared his throat and she snapped out of the gawking.

"Go with Jaxon," Tobias said to me then gripped Bastien's arm and shook until he released me, but he did not budge otherwise.

"A little help, Love," he drawled.

I grabbed Bastien's arm and guided him back to the car. He easily acquiesced to my manhandling.

"Go with them." Bastien's eyebrows furrowed, but he settled down.

"I'll see you soon, Cat," Ren called from the front of the car. My heart skipped a beat. And I muttered some muffled version of okay. I closed the door and stared at Taylor expectantly. For the briefest moment, confusion flashed over her features.

"Ah, yes, if you follow me." Taylor clicked forward on her expensive heels. Were those mother-effing Louboutin's? I was so jealous.

A throat clearing dragged my attention up. Jax raised an eyebrow from where he waited a few feet away with his arms crossed. Hurrying to his side, I laced my hands in front of me and didn't look at him. Entering through the open glass door, a few lounge chairs artfully littered the carpeted room, but no one sat. A girl nervously shifted her eyes side to side as she shuffled on her feet. Her wide-eyed attention was on Asher slouching near the door.

"It took you long enough," Asher announced, straightening.

"This way, please." Taylor waved a hand at the opened elevator. "You, human, hurry," she snapped at the girl still standing by the door, frozen in whatever thought held her in its grip. She jolted and scampered forward. I'd never seen someone actually scamper, but that was the only descriptor that satisfyingly encapsulated her flurry of movement.

Human . . .

The girl didn't even merit a name? I crowded next to Jax, but made sure to have enough distance so we didn't touch. Asher leaned his shoulders against the fabric coating the elevator, one foot crossed over the other. The doors smoothly slid shut.

"Did you open all the shops?" Taylor's vibe rubbed me the wrong way. The dismissive way she looked at the girl was frankly fucked up.

"Yes," 'the human' whispered.

Taylor swung her gaze toward me and I smoothed my glare. I'd reached new levels of comfort, here I was, glaring at a vampire without fearing for my life. Jax pressed his palm into my shoulder, raising an eyebrow at the woman. My eyes widened in the reflection of the gold-plated elevator doors as Taylor looked away.

The corner of my lips twitched up slightly.

Jax could have been a statue with his lack of expression. Asher on the other hand, had this Cheshire grin he did nothing to hide. Smugness radiated from him. I was too busy trying not to nervously clench my hands to say anything.

The elevator dinged open. "After you, Mr. Crimson." Taylor swept her hand forward.

"Gladly," Asher took hold of my hand and tugged me into the brightly lit mall. His long strides made it hard for me to keep up.

"Asher." He peeked back and grinned. "Not all of us were graced with crazy, long legs," I huffed, taking a bit to catch my breath. Usually, the wave of pressure passed quickly.

I put my hand to my chest. This was the first time it felt this tight in a while. Drinking their blood correlated with how well I felt.

"Let's go in here." A squeal escaped with how quickly he pulled me to the left.

My other arm was snatched midair and I was pulled the opposite direction. I gasped at the force against my joints.

"You're tugging her around like a ragdoll, Asher. *Ta hand om hennes kropp*," Jax snapped.

I gawked. Asher narrowed his eyes. He didn't get angry often, but when he did, his irritation couldn't be missed. I whipped my head from one to the other. His eyes briefly flashed red. Okay, time to break it up.

I jerked both arms away and rubbed the wrist Jax had held. His grip had tightened painfully. "I can walk by myself." I put both hands up and shuffled into the brightly lit clothing store.

In every direction I looked there was some name brand, but I didn't want to be obvious about wanting to leave, so I looked at the closest rack. One of the dresses caught my attention. A black number with straps; simple and elegant. A lace slit hugged the hip areas.

The silk fell through my fingertips. Such buttery consistency would kill my bank account. I let it slide out of my fingers. Not like I owned one anymore since I was classified as a dead person. I could accept everything insofar since they literally set everything I owned to flames, leaving me with nothing, but this price tag was excessive. I cleared my throat and made a show of continuing to rifle through the rack. Nothing was in a frugal price range.

A hanger screeched. Asher plucked the dress from the rack and a store clerk hurried to grab it from his hands.

"What are you doing?"

"You liked it."

"It's unnecessary," I retorted.

"Humor me. You'll be modeling it."

"But—"

"There won't be any budging him, Cat, you're just going to make him bitch more," Jax drawled from a few feet ahead of me, arms crossed.

I puffed my cheeks out. Fine, but I'd look for some clothing that I wouldn't feel guilty about selecting. Moving through the racks, I quickly found that would be an impossibility. My mouth watered with every graze of soft, expensive fabric. Pieces that I'd seen in recent collections.

Everything I even peeked at was snatched up by Asher. The poor human girl had started a pile in the fitting room. I scowled back at him, then changed tactics, moving to the men's section.

Jax followed close by. His attention had been focused on me the entire time, curiously watching me shuffle through everything so far. "What are we doing here?"

"To get clothes for Bastien." His eyebrows raised but he made no comment.

I pushed back the hanger to look at the polo shirt.

Asher folded his arms on the display, his chin on his fist. "He wouldn't like that one."

"What would he like?" I raised an eyebrow.

"Believe it or not, but before he lost the plot, he was more of a 1920's suit sort of guy." The only image I could conjure of the style was of hats with a dark strap at the base.

"The 20s were glorious," Taylor murmured, her eyes taking on a faraway look. "Such order." She sighed.

Okaaaay.

"We have a selection over here that may suit that taste."

I stopped in front of a mannequin wearing one of the outfits that were much different to the current style. It had a higher waist and wide lapels, the pattern looked retro vintage in its dark blue color with lines a shade darker running through.

I grabbed hold of one of them and approached Jax. I crooked my finger down and his nostrils flared but he bowed so I could lift the coat to his shoulders. Bastien's shoulders were much broader than this.

"Put it on?" Jax blinked and his palm settled over mine.

"Hate to interrupt the soulful looks, but I know his sizing," Asher interjected from his spot leaning on the stand. I yanked my hand out from Jax's touch and cleared my throat.

The girl stood to the side, head slightly lowered.

"Here." I offered a smile. She dipped her head and grabbed it from me. I didn't want to get her in trouble, so I didn't push anything. Asher grazed his hand over the surface, eyebrows raised as I approached with a warm face. The hesitation with Jax was a mere lapse in judgment.

"Do you think he'd like this?" I lifted a long dark blue tie. Asher's lips twitched at the corner and he tapped the bowties.

My brain did not compute. I eyed him suspiciously, but

plucked one in the same color. The girl was there to grab it for me. Bastien was a bow tie guy? I couldn't compute the big, feral male wearing this outfit.

"Let's get to the fun part," he straightened and strode to me to hook his arm around my back, guiding me into a private side room. A white semi-circle couch faced a section with a curtain in front of it.

The girl hurried inside to pull the curtain back. "I hung everything here for you."

"Thank you." I wrinkled my nose. "I don't want to refer to you as human. What's your name?"

"No worries," she put her hands up, peeking at the exit. "Human is fine. Please call if you need anything."

She rushed off with me gawking after her. Okay then.

"Start trying things on, Pet." He patted my ass, sending me into action. I frowned at him and jerked the curtain shut. I made sure both sides were sealed tight then started removing my clothing. I grabbed the first dress in line. The one to catch my eye when I initially walked into the establishment. I removed everything but my underwear even though this wasn't made to be worn with them.

The silk fell over my skin with a caress. I smoothed my hands down my sides, turning to look at my reflection. It hugged my waist perfectly, the lace at the sides showing my skin down to the hem. Two thin straps rested on my shoulders, and the neckline was squared, leaving much of my skin on display. My long, almost waist-length hair fell around my bare shoulders. I wrapped it in my hand and held it up to see how it would look. Turning my head side to side, a smile bloomed on my lips.

"You're taking too long." The words joined the rasp of the

curtain being swooshed open. I widened my eyes at my reflection. Asher stood behind me, his intimidating stature looming well above my head.

His lips parted and he dragged his gaze down, devouring me with his eyes.

"Have mercy," he breathed.

TWENTY-EIGHT

ren

BODIES AND BLOOD littered the dance floor. Throats had been torn open and limbs littered the establishment. I nudged a limp body with my foot and approached the long stretch of bar wrapping down the furthest left wall. Good thing we had left Bastien in the car.

I lifted the flute filled with red liquid and sipped. The taste paled to Cat. A gasp brought my attention to the human male standing a few feet away. He turned green.

"There's a finger in there." His voice shook.

I peeked down at the severed finger resting at the base of the glass.

"It's fresh," I shrugged and downed the rest of it, thumped it on the bar surface, leaving the digit swirling inside.

"There was zero indication of the incoming attack?"

"None." Talia's lower lip trembled. "They behaved like they were compelled; the humans attacked every vampire they saw."

Like what happened to us. "The vampire hunters are back, they got Roberto," Talia wailed, pointing at a pile of dust.

This massacre was not executed by hunters. Long ago, when

they still existed, I'd seen enough of them, and this was never their MO. Whoever we were dealing with wanted to make it seem like they had returned. The attack was targeted to us, especially after the attack at the house. It had been the same method, too.

I scoffed in disgust, did the filthy vampire have no imagination?

This vampire male trying to make a claim on Catalina was desperate for her. I sneered. War was what he would get.

Tobias met my gaze and his head slightly inclined. Great, we were in agreement.

"Get this cleaned and shut down for the night," Tobias said. I turned on my heel and left.

"You," I barked at the woman sweeping up broken glass. "Get me the security footage."

"Yes, Mr. Crimson," she said. Her shirt was ripped near the stomach, the jagged edges of the tear fluttering as she left.

Tobias walked up next to me.

"You believe it is him attacking us?"

"No, he is challenging us."

Realistically, it could be anyone. We'd faced similar situations in the beginning of the formation of Crimson Coven. We also didn't have the best track record after offending many vampires, but this? This was waving a red flag in front of a bull.

"She is not to be unaccompanied or out of our sights," I said and didn't need to look at him for his agreement. He was as protective of her as I was.

TWENTY-NINE

I WHIRLED AWAY from the mirror to look up at Asher. I adored the way he looked at me. With such overwhelming need. Oxygen sucked out of my lungs. Everything became enhanced until his beautiful face was my only focus. His eyes flashed red, and then he was flush behind me. The red irises faded, replaced with his blue eyes.

"Aren't you a delectable piece of art?" His murmur tickled my cheek. "This . . ." His fingertips grazed the see-through lace along my sides. Even with the thin layer between his fingertips and my hip, his touch caused goose bumps to raise along my body. Asher slowly walked around me, dragging his touch along my belly. I instinctively sucked in. His proximity, his touch—it was all too much. His loose, billowing shirt skimmed along my arm as he walked behind me. I stared at the plain wall, panting. My body blazed with lust. Asher leaned down and his nose nuzzled the side of my neck.

A groan wrenched free, and I slumped against his wide chest. He banded his arm around my belly, pulling me flush against him. God, he always made me feel so tiny.

His hard length nudged my spine, and I arched to get closer to his thick, pierced cock.

"I want you," I breathed. He chuckled against my ear. Ohhhh. I melted against him, wiggling my hips.

A hand wrapped around the curtain and Jaxon appeared. He scanned us with those piercing eyes.

"Brother, isn't she gorgeous?" Instead of speaking, he stepped forward, stepping in front of me. One breath, then another until finally his thumb grazed my lower lip. I exhaled hard. Jax's features rippled and his jaw line twitched.

A hiss exploded from Jax, and he knelt at my feet. I caught a look at his red irises before his eyes closed and he pressed his forehead against my belly, inhaling hard. Scenting me.

I licked my lips.

All I could see was his wide shoulders and his head bowed forward. His touch grazed up my calf until he settled at my thigh.

"Don't ruin the dress," I whispered. Jax gently lifted the dress inch by inch until I was only in my panties. Asher took over and continued pulling it up until my breasts bounced free. In a smooth motion, he tugged it off me and it pooled on the stool attached to the wide mirror.

Asher's arms snaked around me again, his palms traveling up my bare body and cupping my breasts. He thumbed my sensitive nipple. I shuddered, becoming weaker with every touch.

Jax's fangs had popped free at some point. I focused on the sharp teeth. He gripped my hips, the tips of his fingers digging into my ass. With a snap, my panties were gone and I was bare. He buried his nose against my mound, and he inhaled hard. A moan vibrated against my sex.

"Jax," I whispered. His fingers flexed and red flashed through his irises. He settled his mouth over the hood of my clit and his tongue lashed across the sensitive nub. I jerked back against Asher, my hands instinctively reaching out to grab Jax's short hair. My fingers sank into the silky strands barely long enough to take hold of. He stiffened and as if in answer, Asher's arms flexed like he was preparing to yank me away from him.

It was too late for me though, his mouth against my sensitive flesh caused me to tilt my hips higher to force his mouth against me. The tension leaked away from his shoulders and his tongue flicked out, rolling around the bundle of nerves.

A whine rose in my throat and he moved his tongue faster—vampire fast.

Asher's head dipped to press his lips against my ear. He lifted my arms and hooked them around his neck.

Jax nibbled on my clit. I gasped.

"Arch like the little kitten you are," Jax murmured against my pussy huskily. My breasts rose and fell in frantic pumps. Jax dropped to taste me. He angled his head to the side and sank his fang into my clit. I screamed, yanking at Asher's hair.

Fangs punctured the side of my neck. I groaned, arching my breasts up. Jax kept hold of my writhing hips and he sucked blood from the wound he'd pierced on my clit. Bursts of light shattered behind my eyelids and the orgasm slammed into me with wrenching violence. I made noises I didn't even know I could make. All the while, Jax continued sucking from my clit. My core clenched, needing something to grasp. Fingers suddenly speared into my channel. I grunted with each thrust of his fingers.

"Yes, please, Jax," I panted. "More. More."

Asher chuckled against my throat and licked his bites, eliciting another shiver to life.

Jax's golden head moved as his tongue swiped the blood and my need clean.

I whimpered and Asher removed one of his arms from around me. The zip of his pants echoed, and his warm cock prodded my spine. The cool bead of his Jacob's ladder piercing rubbed my skin.

His chest moved and something crinkled—like a packet. Asher slid fingers between the cleft of my ass and smoothed them over my entrance, leaving behind a wet consistency.

"Is that . . . lube?"

His chuckle sounded husky.

"Mhm, I know how you tense up, it should make it feel better." His voice deepened with need.

"Well, aren't you prepared," I said drolly and then stopped talking as his silky shaft nudged between my ass. His cock piercings rubbed against me delightfully.

Then lower . . . and lower until his tip pressed into the entrance.

I stiffened with fear at the prod of his cock.

"Shhh, *Älskade*, I have you." His soothing words settled over me like a balm, my fear fading. He pushed the tip in. My ass gave way, and I sucked in a breath. Jax rose to his feet, his mouth wet. His cock was hard in his jeans. I reached for the thickness, caressing it from the outside. He groaned and his hips jolted toward my touch. He made quick work of his jeans, and his thickness bobbed a few inches from me. I wrapped my hand around the steel shaft.

He shuddered and crowded me against his brother.

Asher fit another inch inside me in a smooth glide. The

ridges of his Jacob's ladder piercing rubbed my entrance, but the lube made it easy to take him. His hands wrapped under my thighs and he braced me as he lifted me. Oh God, he was right about the lube, it felt so good. My upper body fell back. I was utterly at their mercy.

Asher presented me to Jax. His eyes reddened and he slid into my core with a smooth glide. My wet pussy allowed his invasion. At the same instance, Asher inched the rest of himself into my ass.

I grunted at the fullness.

Jax's eyes returned to normal. His features strained. He seemed to be working through something. I lifted one of my arms away from Asher and touched his cheek lightly. He exhaled and leaned into my touch. He glided out and slammed back in.

Me tensing forced Asher to grunt. His hand wrapped around my chin, and he forced my head to the side so I faced the mirror where I had a full view of us.

"Watch us fuck you."

My nude body was sandwiched between their large bodies. Jax rammed into me again, jostling my breasts. Asher ground inside my ass. He was so deep it verged on hurting. I whimpered —I was a noodle between them. I could not gather any strength. Jax slid out and rutted into me again. I couldn't look away from the concentration on his face. For such a stoic male, his lips softened endearingly as he slammed into me. His pace picked up with the static of electricity traveling up my shaking legs. My cries became louder and louder.

Jax clasped my cheeks, staring into my eyes as he pumped in and out of me. His eyebrows were furrowed and tight. He slammed into me again and again. I couldn't keep my head up any longer, and the fire blazing up and down my spine exploded. I jerked between them, desperately pulling at Asher's hair. My pussy clamped onto Jax, forcing his release free. He pinned me against Asher, setting his forehead against mine as his cock throbbed inside me.

Asher groaned in my ear and his arms around my sides and his hands cupping my breasts stiffened. Fullness expanded my lower half as they filled me with their cum. To the point that it felt like some leaked out.

We panted in a mass of limbs. It was a good thing they were holding me up because I did not have a working bone in my body.

"Take hold of her," Asher said. Jax's arm snaked around my back, the other hooked under my knees, and pulled me to his chest, nestling me close. I drooped against him while Asher disappeared.

I didn't have the energy to glare at him or fight his gentle hold. Asher returned with a long hoodie and some underwear.

Jax set me on my feet and when I swayed, he wrapped his arm around my waist. Asher tossed him the sweater and knelt to take one of my feet. My flats had slipped off in the flurry of sex. He poked my feet into the underwear, jerking them up. I smacked at his hands and pulled them up the rest of the way.

Jax shoved the hoodie over my head, and I wiggled my arms into the holes. The hem fell to my knees. Jax swept me back up into his arms.

The 'human girl' peeked around the corner and seeing that everything was PG, walked in the rest of the way.

"I have everything packed up as well as the dress you liked. It is ready to be loaded into your vehicle." Her face was flushed, her eyes were wide, and she was breathing hard. How embarrassing, she probably heard us going at it.

"Perfect." Asher plucked the pooled dress off the floor. "We'll take this one, too." He tossed it over his shoulder. I closed my eyes, lulling in Jaxon's arms as he held me with more care than I anticipated. The sway remained steady, and I mentally mapped the return to the front.

"What did you two do to her?" Tobias snapped. I jostled in Jax's cradle as another pair curled under my torso. Jax's grip didn't loosen, and a frowning Tobias acquiesced.

When we arrived at the van, the hatch was slowly closing, packages neatly piled inside. Tobias scooted into the passenger seat and Jax slipped me into the middle seat next to Asher.

Bastien sat all the way in the back. Watchful and silent.

"While we were gone, I picked up your gifts, Catalina," Tobias said, and he lifted two fingers. A thick card was nestled between them.

"Is that a credit card?" I frowned.

"Your credit card. Unlimited. For your ordering pleasure," Asher purred in my ear. "You will be taken care of."

I pushed my hands out like a barrier between us, shaking my head.

"Just take it," Jaxon ordered, snatching the credit card. I just stared at the card, struggling to process.

"There are perks to being ours, Love," Tobias said gently.

"I . . ." I coughed, eyeing the platinum card Jax waved out to me.

"Catalina, take the card."

"Well, if you insist," I muttered and took it.

Who was I kidding, I loved spending money. I loved things. If I hadn't been so careful about making sure tuition was paid for Peter, then I'd be a menace. Also, they destroyed all my things.

I enjoyed this whole 'being taken care of' thing. I nuzzled close to Asher, ignoring Jax's effort to hold me closer.

"I would have given you a black card a long time ago if I knew it made you this touchy," Asher drawled.

ASHER

She finally made my brother buckle. A feat none had done before, even Imogen. I smiled smugly. He'd never fucked anyone while facing them.

Catalina had him in the palm of her hand.

He hadn't stopped caressing her arm. As for Catalina, she had much longer to go before she allowed him the gentleness she allowed the rest of us. She had not forgiven, and it was clear she held a grudge, but I had to give it to Jaxon, he continued caressing her despite her leaning away from his touch.

Jax did not know it now, but she would provide what we'd been missing for so long. What he *believed* he had with Imogen.

Imogen had been cruel.

Vampires were known for their lack of morality, but the level she reached was needless, especially toward those that she claimed belonged to her.

One time he'd pissed her off, she'd tied him to a table facedown. He'd bowed his head to her. I tried to stop it, but he'd been angry at my attempt. Her reaction was worse. She'd taken a razor to his body and sliced little incisions all over his back, opening fresh wounds. Over and over again until a pool of blood lay under the table. She'd almost drained him like this. He had lost consciousness, and I'd had to be the one to clean him off.

She promised to do it again if I ever stepped out of line.

She'd known this was the very thing humans did to him before he'd become a vampire. He still bore scars from the event since he received them before he was turned, and she feasted on his weakness.

I watched him watch our human. Vehement yearning splashed on his face.

Catalina would offer him the soft touches and gentle kisses he desperately craved. Something he had never experienced. He needed it even if he did not know it.

A buzz filled the vehicle. Tobias fished the cell phone out.

"You know, for someone who hates electronics, you've been on the phone quite a lot."

Tobias glared at me over his shoulder.

"You have been indisposed to do your part," he said dryly and looked down at the screen. True, I was usually the one that took charge with anything having to do with relations to other Covens.

"The human is heading to the house."

"Is Alistair coming with her?" Ren asked.

"I requested the human come alone."

I agreed with Tobias. Alistair was still the Sire to his Coven. A powerful one. We needed to tread carefully even if we were on friendly terms. As friendly as vampires could be.

"This is the person you guys want me to learn from?" Catalina perked up. At Tobias's nod, she clasped her hands together. "Are there any rules I have to follow with her?" Her slightly bitter tone wasn't lost on me. I grinned and cupped her jaw until my palm settled under it.

"You are the cutest." I gave her a squeeze, so her plump lips puckered. "Sometimes I have this overwhelming urge to squeeze you until you pop."

"Are you serious? You have 'cute aggression' toward me? Like one would feel toward an actual pet?" She scoffed.

I understood about eighty percent of that, so I just smiled.

"You are not a dog, silly." I gently scratched her nose.

She sighed.

THIRTY

THE OTHER SIRE'S PET waited for me on the top floor of Crimson Manor. The same space hosting Imogen's old stuff. I walked inside, Maddy at my heels. Thank God she'd come with me. A woman with a high ponytail watched me with cool eyes. Her shoulders moved with her steady breaths, and her posture remained straight as an arrow. To the point that it looked like it hurt. I sank into the couch. Maddy settled in next to me.

The woman arrived just in time for Peter to head to the bedroom he was staying in. A good thing since I didn't want him to overhear the conversation about 'vampire etiquette'. All of which sounded intimidating, but . . . the woman did not seem happy. Why was she sitting so straight? It looked like it hurt.

I kept my lips sealed, waiting for the woman staring me down to speak.

"Erm." Maddy coughed into her fist. "Well then, this is Catalina Herrera—"

"I am aware," the girl said. She seemed supernaturally still, but I could tell she was human. Even if her blinks seemed to be few and far between. She was dressed in a short silky number that draped across her skin. Her neck was fully exposed, quick to access.

"I belong to Blackthorn Coven," she slightly inclined her head, finally speaking. My exhale did nothing to hide my relief.

"Hello," I responded hesitantly.

Her lips thinned. I'd evidently displeased her. Uhm.

"That is not appropriate."

I wasn't sure how I should respond to this.

"That's why you're here Petunia, to explain things," Maddy said, her voice low. Petunia returned her piercing gaze to me.

"You are blessed to have been taken in by a powerful Coven. Because of this, you are held to a high standard. What you do improperly will be seen as a mar on their reputation."

That sounded intimidating and honestly, unreasonable.

"Even as human?"

She scoffed. "Even more as a human. We are a class beneath vampires. It is obvious. If they do not have their human in hand, it shows their weakness." Um, okaaaay.

"And you are okay with being less than vampires?"

"We are not here to debate the topic," she said sharply.

I straightened my spine. Before I could say anything back, she twisted to face Maddy.

"I thought since she was already their Pet, that she was in agreement with the ideologies."

"She's new to all this. It's not her fault. They've allowed her to behave as she wishes."

I could only blink. They've allowed me?

Oh no, I wasn't liking this. A few tense seconds passed of them glaring at each other.

"If you want to leave. I can tell—"

"No," she said rushed, her eye almost twitching. Her attention turned back to me.

"When introducing yourself, you would say, I belong to Crimson Coven or to the Crimson Coven Sires. You must make it known who your master is, but only if the opportunity presents itself. Otherwise, stay quiet. Never stand beside your vampire, one step behind is customary, never speak first. And when you address someone, ensure you do not look into their eyes, it's poor form. Lastly, it is custom to offer your neck to all vampire Coven Sires at a gathering—"

"Offer my neck?" I parroted. I clutched my throat. A twitch assaulted her cheek.

She stood in a smooth motion. Her gaze seemed to spit fire at me.

I licked my lips and refocused on the angry woman staring me down. Everything I said seemed to be wrong in her eyes.

"You will eventually be replaced. You are not an appropriate candidate for your position." Why did she talk about it like it was some job? She turned on her heel, leaving me in silence as she stormed out.

"What just happened?" I scowled. But honestly, good, she was a bitch.

Maddy chased after her, leaving me here in silence. A few minutes passed and she still hadn't returned. I was beginning to doubt she would. I hoisted myself off the couch and slowly approached the dresses. Something shiny glinted, catching my eye. A rectangular item covered in fabric leaning against the wall. The gold corner of the frame reflected the light from the chandelier. I tugged the rest of the satin fabric until it glided off, exposing it.

A portrait of Imogen. The corners of her mouth turned up slightly. Her regal features, thin and sharp. She wore one of those dresses with bright colors, unnecessary jewels, and tulle.

Reality bulldozed over me. I stared at the beautifully painted portrait. This was who they valued and saw as an equal.

Could I ever be seen anywhere close to the same? I sighed and rubbed my tired eyes.

If this 'Pet' meeting wasn't happening, then I should visit Peter. He'd been avoiding me. I knew it was because he didn't want to hear my spiel, but it had to be done.

I trudged down the hallway and down to the second floor, my steps heavy and thudding. This conversation would not be easy.

I knocked on the last door in the hall, technically the third floor if taking the basement into account.

"It's me," I called through the wooden door. Nothing. I pressed my ear against the surface. I couldn't hear anything, which made sense since the rooms were sound proofed. I turned the doorknob and poked my head in.

He sat on the bed, his computer on his lap, very much not asleep. I shut the door behind me, approaching until the end of the bed frame hit my knees.

"I didn't answer the door for a reason," he said. He finished typing whatever he was doing and then looked up expectantly.

"You're right, I've been treating you like a kid." I sighed and closed my eyes. "Vampires aren't good, Peter." Moisture gathered on my eyelashes and I did my best to stamp down my tears. "You remember when I disappeared?"

He nodded, setting his computer aside. I perched on the edge of the bed, next to him.

"A vampire captured me. He—" I swallowed hard. "It wasn't pleasant before I managed to escape." I paused and wet my lips. "I never meant to get involved with vampires again, Peter, but it's like I'm cursed." I squeezed his hand. "I can't get away, but you can."

His expression crumpled and I saw that little boy I found alone and hungry in our apartment. The one that thought I'd left him to die. My heart broke all over again.

"I knew you went through something, but . . . I didn't think," he paused, sucking in a deep breath between his teeth.

"You've got a life, you have friends, a future. It's too late for me. Stop being stubborn and go back to the life you know you love."

"Is that supposed to be a dig at me?" he snapped defensively. "I know, I should have visited you more. I should have asked you how you were. I should have helped you—"

"Peter." Tears welled in my eyes. "Stop. The way you can help me is by taking care of yourself. Return to your life. Be happy. Have a family." My voice cracked. I puffed my cheeks out and let out a breath. He stared at the hand I held, gaze unfocused. Another few moments passed.

"Fine." His swallow was audible.

That one word rolled a wave of relief through my nervous system and my shoulders sank and I bowed my head to hide my tears.

"Thank you," I said in a watery tone.

"Don't." His lips twisted. My heart squeezed. Now that he'd agreed to go, I had to get him on a flight out of here, asap.

The sun was still out. There would be a few hours to go until they woke up.

"Collect your things."

He moved to the duffle on the floor and tossed it on the bed. His gaze became unfocused as he shoved his sweater in and then his computer.

"I've seen the guards. Sid told me they patrol the area while those vampires are sleeping."

I opened and closed my mouth. Fuck, how had I forgotten about them?

"I will get Maddy to distract them."

"What if you run with me—"

"No," I interrupted, shaking my head vehemently. Crimson Coven would hunt me down. And with the money at their disposal, it wouldn't take them long to catch me. "At least if I stay, they won't come after you."

He pressed both palms against his temples. "And you think that makes me feel any better?" His voice cracked.

"I'm sorry," I whispered because what else could I say?

"I will leave on my own. They haven't tried to stop me ever since they questioned me when I left to take Sidney home. I'll catch a cab." His stiff tone caused my wretched heart to fall.

"Live your life, Peter. Just like you were before you found out about my death."

"This is stupid." He said it low, but with enough volume.

I took a step back, lowering my head as I backed up to the door.

He approached and hesitated. Then he put his hand on my head.

Tears gathered on my eyelashes.

"I'll leave, but I won't act like I don't know you're alive. Call me. Same time as usual."

I exhaled in a shudder.

Making him leave was the correct thing to do. He needed away from vampires. I rubbed my eyes. I wish I didn't have to be so breakable . . . so human.

THIRTY-ONE

JAX CLEARED his throat from where he stood at the entrance of the living room. "I heard you chased away the Blackthorn female." Color me stunned. He didn't normally initiate conversation. I looked at him and then away, returning to rubbing my stomach. It'd been hurting all day. The nerves from seeing Imogen's portrait, the conversation with Peter, him actually leaving, and waiting for the other shoe to drop when they discovered he left, all of it settled on me like weighted bags.

It took me a moment to collect my thoughts. I popped up from where I leaned my hip against the couch.

"She was a tad extreme," I said carefully. Jax walked toward me, not stopping until he was arms distance away.

"I figured you wouldn't do well at a vampire function, but they won't listen to me," he shook his head slightly. I pursed my lips, and he put one hand up. "It's not a comment meant to offend you. Just an observation."

Contemplation laced his words, but his eyes wouldn't move away from my body. He rubbed his thumb and pointer finger against his closed eyes, hiding the flash of red.

"It's a little too late to be saying that now, since we're leaving in a few hours," I drawled, crossing my arms. I'd showered and done my hair already. I was waiting until we were closer to go-time before I finished my make-up and slipped into that beautiful dress the twins fucked me in.

His lips quirked up at the corners. "I'm all for not going. If you'd like to let the others know, I wouldn't be opposed to it." I shook my head, put off by how close he was getting to me. "I'm going in there as a Pet—what are you doing?" Jax's thumb stopped rubbing against my cheek. He blinked as if coming out of a trance and he scowled.

"Your cheeks flushed . . ." he cleared his throat, spearing his fingers through the top of his short blond hair, slicking it back.

I pressed the back of my hand against my cheek. It suddenly felt too hot in my new matching matcha-colored silk pajamas.

"Oh." What else could I say? I stepped back. His focus made me nervous. He was the quickest to anger. If I spat the truth out to him about Peter, then I could release this suffocating weight on my shoulders. Also, he would stop looking at me like that. He needed to go back to his glaring. "I had my brother leave." I set my jaw in a stubborn tilt, daring him to come at me. Jax's lips twitched.

What was his problem? He'd never reacted this way. I expected an explosion of accusations flying at me. This though? It caused somersaulting in my stomach.

"You guys look cozy," Asher said, smugness coating his tone. I jumped back, putting space between me and Jax, but I kept shooting him furtive peeks from the corner of my eyes. Angry twin grunted.

I opened and closed my mouth, at a loss for words.

Jax hummed, not taking his attention away from me. I had

no idea how to even place meaning to that, but this was Jax. A more mercurial vampire I'd never met. "She did as we expected and had her brother leave."

"It took her much longer than I thought it would."

My head ping ponged between both of them.

"Y-you knew?"

Asher raised his eyebrow with a droll expression on his features.

"Pet, you can't be serious. We have centuries on you."

I rolled my lips inside my mouth. I'd underestimated the situation. Clearing my throat, I clasped my hands in front of me.

"Are you guys going to go after him?" I forced the question out. My throat felt like it was closing.

Asher closed in on me and clasped my chin.

"Relax, no one will go after your brother." My sight blurred. "No tears." Asher tsked.

"Why is she leaking from her eyes again?" Ren's voice bounced off the walls.

"Why?" I repeated. I couldn't wrap my head around the why.

"She's touched." Asher grinned.

"Catalina is of sane mind, there is no need for name-calling," Tobias said haughtily as he walked in and adjusted his sweater vest.

"Not that type of 'touched,' Priest." I'd never seen Jax smirk without it having a malicious or bitter edge. He seemed different, calmer, relaxed. "You must never mention anything about your brother. Especially about him knowing of vampires. We can be called before a council if anyone discovers we know of an unclaimed human knowing about our existence."

They weren't going to hurt me? Or chase Peter down? I expected to be on my knees begging for their mercy. Not whatever this was.

"There's a council?" It sounded daunting. "I didn't know you guys had a ruling body."

"No, no, Pet, vampire Covens are self-ruling. There is only one thing that unites us to seek order: The existence of vampires remaining a secret. Under no circumstances are we allowed to expose ourselves and if there is an accusation, a council is created to vote on the—"

"Don't worry yourself with the pesky bureaucracies of vampires, Cat, we will protect you," Ren said with a grin. Those words comforted me more than I wanted them to.

"Where's Bastien?" I wove around Jax and Tobias to peek down the hall.

"I locked him in the basement," Tobias said.

"But why—"

"I didn't chain him up, I simply locked the door. Understand, Catalina, no one knows about the state he is in."

I scowled at him.

"Whatever," I mumbled. I hated the idea of him alone, but I also understood. Their secrets were theirs, and I couldn't be spreading them. "Okay, are we doing this?"

"Are you prepared? Do you have any questions?" Asher asked. "Remember, you must behave deferentially."

"Yes, yes, I got it. I can't have an opinion and I'm less than you guys, right?" I huffed, crossing my arms.

Asher grimaced.

"Yes," Ren said, deadpan.

"Moron," Asher muttered, shaking his head. I rolled my lips between my teeth to stop my laugh.

"Well, I only have to get dressed and put some make-up on and then I'll be ready." I started to cross the carpet.

The ache in my stomach abated and pressure expanded. There was a sudden wetness. Did I pee?

Fuck, no I didn't pee.

It was a very familiar gush.

Tobias, who stood the closest, frowned and he lifted his chin just slightly, and inhaled. Fuck, fuck, fuck, why did he choose now to use his super nose?

"What is that delicious smell?"

A horrifying thought I never thought would ever come became reality. They could smell my period.

This was a sign to make my exit.

"I'll be right back," I smiled and inched away slowly, squeezing my thighs together like my life depended on it. Asher stiffened next, his eyes widening. Tobias's comment had them all inhaling. I gritted my teeth and took another step.

"Cat," Ren said, his voice almost shaking. Suddenly, he loomed over me.

I screamed and bounced back.

"Stop doing that . . ." I trailed off. Hunger flickered over his features. Oh, fuck. He inhaled audibly. My mouth dried right up. In a flash, he had me on the ground, his large body hovering over me. I clawed my fingernails into the carpet, dragging myself backwards.

"Ren?" I breathed. Red flooded his eyes. His fingers slipped into the band of my clothes, and he yanked. My panties snapped along with the new shorts. The cool air brushed against my pussy. "Ren!" I shouted. His head lowered while simultaneously forcing my legs wide open. My shout turned into a garbled choked gasp. His tongue speared into my channel. "I-I'm bleeding." His tongue flicked against me again. I whimpered.

They descended upon me like wolves. Appearing with such speed they stole my breath. Asher and Jax ran so fast they collided with a loud thud. Their eyes were full on red. They turned and hissed at each other. Tobias appeared on my other side, and suddenly sank his fangs into my exposed belly.

My shocked inhale dragged the twin's attention to me, and they stopped their grappling. Soon Jax was hovering over my pussy, shoving his face next to Ren. They jockeyed for space until they both won, remaining between my wide-spread legs. Jax's tongue joined Ren's. An orgasm rampaged through my veins. I writhed under their tongues and teeth. Whimpering, whining, crying with each throb. Ren suddenly sank his teeth into my pussy, piercing my clit and the crevice to the side. I stopped breathing, as stars erupted behind my eyelids.

I floated on a cloud. Higher and higher.

Another hand wrapped around my knee, widening my already opened legs.

Asher slid his arm under Jax and slid two fingers inside my pussy, forcing their way into my channel with Ren and Jax's thrusting tongues. He withdrew them with red staining the tips. He popped them into his mouth. His eyes closed and he hummed.

Another release crashed into me. I sobbed. Moving my head back and forth.

Tobias sank his teeth in again. Suck after suck sent shockwaves of electricity through my clit. My head was beginning to feel light.

Tobias yanked himself away and stilled. He kept his head lowered; eyes squeezed shut. I reached out to touch him, but he was too far. My hand thumped on the ground. He finally raised his head and his eyes were no longer bright red.

"You're taking too much," Tobias croaked, yanking at Ren's shoulder. "You're going to kill her."

All three simultaneously ripped their fangs free of my flesh.

I lay weakly, struggling to keep my eyes open.

"We took too much," Asher whispered. His face blurred.

"Fuck," Jax added.

Skin pressed against my mouth.

"Swallow, Pet." Asher sounded painfully gentle. "Come now."

I swallowed the delicious taste of his blood. Once then twice.

"Tobias, give her your blood." The arm pulled away from my grip, replaced by another.

"She won't replenish the blood fast enough." Horror touched Jax's voice.

Tobias clasped my jaw and gently pulled away. He pressed a kiss to my forehead. "I will return." With that, he was gone.

Ren pulled me into his arms, cradling me on his lap.

"I prepared in case one of us lost control." Tobias walked back in and tossed a kit toward Jax. He caught it and tore it open.

Relief flitted over his features.

He was at my side, kneeling. His mouth was red with my blood. If I had any blood in me, I would be blushing right now. I closed my eyes instead. Wanting to escape. I should just float away . . .

"Hold her arm out." At Jax's order I peeked through slitted eyes. Ren jostled me on his lap and his large hand wrapped around my wrist, extending my arm. "Hold this up." Jax tossed

Asher a bag with blood. He held it high. A tube was attached to it.

Jax flicked the tip of a needle. His thumb pressed into my inner elbow and he poised the needle. I squeezed my eyes shut, flinching at the pinch.

Asher had said something about Jax having to deal with a lot of medical situations when he was a human.

I stirred.

"Stay still for a while, Kitten," Jax said gruffly. He chuckled. "Almost drained of blood and she's scowling at me."

My mind wandered as the seconds turned to minutes. Between the infusion and them feeding me their blood. My brain started to clear. Like cobwebs slipping away.

"How long will she smell off?"

"You almost drained me and that's what you're worried about?" I glared up at Ren. He grinned down at me.

"It isn't a crime to prefer your scent."

I scoffed.

"I'm too tired to feel embarrassed about what's about to come out of my mouth." Ren raised an eyebrow. I licked my lips, preparing to spit out the rest of the sentence out. "Period blood isn't the same as the blood that runs in my veins. Why did you guys get all psycho over it?"

Jax opened his mouth and then closed it. He looked dumbfounded. "You're correct, it is not the same," Tobias said. I dragged my eyes up to where he hovered nearby, watching the blood drip down the long tube. "It's you, Love. Your scent. Everything about you." His nose flared.

"The taste between them is different." Asher chimed in. He wiggled the blood bag he held up. "Mm, think of something fermented. The taste is different, but still delicious."

I studied his dazed expression. And if period blood wasn't the same, then their . . .

"The red in your cum is not the same, right. Because news flash, I'm positive you lot, or most of you," I side-eyed Tobias, "have had a blow job in the past. So, you've been spreading your bonding-juice if it is." I thinned my lips. I actively worked not to think about things I couldn't change, namely their sexual past, because it was bound to upset me.

Asher chortled, his head falling back. "Bonding-juice." He wiped an invisible tear from his eye. "Correct, it's not the same."

That was a relief. A cramp seized my stomach, and I grimaced.

"I better not find one of you guys fishing a tampon out of the trash and using it like a damn tea bag," I mumbled, closing my eyes again.

An infusion, a shower, redoing my routine, and a tampon later, and I was ready to go.

I crossed the foyer to the front door Jax held open for me, my heels clicking against the floor. He met my eyes instead of avoiding them as he usually did.

"You seem too upbeat, are you guys going to sacrifice me?" I muttered. He said nothing but the corner of his lips twitched. I stepped onto the cement front step. The dim front light turned on, illuminating the door.

A crow cawed and flapped its wings, taking off in a flurry of movement.

My gaze focused on the spider web hanging right in front of

my nose. I screamed, climbing the closest male to me with a speed I didn't know I had. The hair on the back of my neck stood.

"You're pulling my hair," Jax hissed, hooking his arm under my flailing legs.

"What is it? What is it?" Asher rushed out. "Another body?"

"A spider," I hissed, my stomach dipped at the reminder of the dead body.

Asher raised an eyebrow at the grip I had in his brother's hair. "Such a fearful little human. Worry not, you now have five vampires to protect you from any and all dangers."

I liked the sound of that too much and my body did, too, and it *had* been liking the safety they'd coated me with. I no longer went out and peeked over my shoulder at every moment like I used to. Even though them owning me was the exact opposite, it was freeing.

My chest heaved, a hint of tightness pressurizing my lungs. The asthma attacks had all but faded after I'd had so much of their blood at Crimson Nights. This was the first it'd shown up since then. I hadn't missed it.

I cleared my throat. "You can put me down."

Jax released a huff of air, his sweet breath rustling the fringes of my loose hair. Instead of putting me down, he descended the stairs with my legs swaying. The straight line of his jaw hovered near my face and the column of his throat looked smooth to the touch. He'd been sweet to me before he thought I betrayed them. All I'd been getting from him was glib comments and attitude until recently. I didn't trust this. He maneuvered me at an angle to avoid the roses and thorns entwined with the gate.

He stopped at the base. The moon cast a glow over the lonely street.

Lights twinkled far off, closer to the city.

"What are we waiting for?"

"Ren is bringing the SUV around."

"Where do you guys park all the cars?" I'd seen about four different cars.

"There's a garage connected to the back of the house."

I'd assumed something of the sort unless they could conjure cars out of thin air with magic.

"Do you guys use magic?" I blinked up at him. He wasn't the most verbal with me, maybe I should ask Asher or Tobias—

"No, vampires do not use magic."

"Are you laughing at me?" I scowled. "It's not a stupid question, you guys are able to compel and read minds."

"Reading minds is only Tobias."

"Oh . . . right."

"It's his ability, Asher's is invisibility—"

"I didn't stop to think that you all have something different." Mostly because I hadn't had the chance to consider vampire abilities with everything going on. "What's yours?"

He suddenly looked uncomfortable. "Ren's pulling up."

At least he didn't straight out tell me to mind my own business. I caught a peek at Asher over his shoulder. He'd been hovering behind us the entire time, but he was quiet and grinning like a madman. Jax jostled me into one arm and pulled the back door open. He settled me on the seat, the leather creaking under my weight.

"Why are you being so nice to me?" I asked, squinting up at him.

Asher's arm curled around my hip, and he scooted me close

to him toward the other side of the cushion. Jax settled inside and closed the door. I was smushed between the twins again.

"He's done fighting his desire for you. You forget, Pet, he believes his loyalty should be to Imogen. He's been fighting that side of himself." Asher didn't bother lowering his voice. I rounded to look at Jax, waiting for his explosion at the mention of *her*. Except . . . he didn't.

"I'm not here to fight a memory. That's losing a battle," I said it loudly and lifted my chin, eyeing him warningly.

"No one is asking you to compete with anything." Jax's response floored me. And left me speechless.

"When we get to Calliope's event," Asher murmured near my ear. "I need you to have patience."

"That's not suspicious at all." A long sigh exploded from his lips.

"Trust us."

"Fine." I peeked at Jax. "But that one, no, I'm not trusting him."

Jax flinched, and I was not a bit remorseful.

catalina

WE ARRIVED at Calliope's quickly because of Ren's hectic driving. Fairy lights had been strung around the two columns framing the front door and they glittered with each step through the pathway cutting through Calliope's front lawn. The backdrop of her mansion consisted of tall pine trees swaying with the chilly breeze.

"Remember to behave accordingly," Tobias murmured into my hair and pressed his lips to my temple. He brushed my hair over my shoulder. I'd elected to straighten it and so his movement made the tips flutter against my butt.

All the rules mushed in my head, but I understood the gist. Behaving accordingly consisted of keeping my mouth shut and my head down.

Hopefully Petunia wouldn't be in attendance, she was obnoxious.

I lowered my head and took a few steps back until I trailed behind the vampires.

"It's a stupid custom," Asher hissed. I peeked up to find his blue gaze fixed on me.

"You never complained about it." Ren cupped the back of his neck and forced him to face forward. Ren winked over his shoulder at me.

They had other humans? My stomach dipped. They were ancient, of course, of course . . . The cement steps glittered with each step forward as the little stones embedded within glinted. My heart shouldn't be hurting from the comment. My jealousy frustrated me to no end, but I couldn't help how I felt.

I kept my head lowered, following close at Jax's heels, the one who hung back. It wasn't lost on me that he'd slowed so I could catch up, but he still stood a bit in front of me. This vampire world wasn't something I wanted or could change. The hierarchy they lived under seemed an overkill, but I understood it. Nature had a food chain.

My heel caught on the groove of the stair, and I hobbled forward. That was what I got for not paying attention.

I slapped my palm on Asher's back. The soft fabric of his linen shirt dipped, and his muscle twitched under my touch. He looked over his shoulder at me with a sly grin.

"There's no need to paw my clothes off, Pet." My hold on his shirt tugged it down so the collar skewed to the side, exposing the seductive line of his muscled shoulder.

"Ren," Calliope chirped, illuminated by the light spilling out of her mansion. I yanked my hand away and backed up. His chuckle followed me. He enjoyed my embarrassment. I lifted my foot and stretched my ankle side to side. I'd twisted it with my lack of attention. Walking in heels was as easy as breathing for me, so it better not fail me now.

"Calliope," Ren responded. She raised on her toes to kiss his cheek. What in the world? They weren't behaving like one of them had trapped the other for close to a month. Questions bubbled behind my lips, but I clamped them shut.

The clink of glasses and the chatter of people inside spilled out of the home. Ren moved out of the way, allowing me a clear view of the female vampire. Calliope wore a sleek body suit.

Upon entering, every guest surrounding the open foyer looked at Crimson Coven. They posed a striking group. All were tall and each attractive in different ways. Tobias looked every part an aristocrat, Asher and Jaxon looked like striking, intimidating Vikings, and Ren's wide shoulders and relaxed stature gave him a threatening, unpredictable air.

The vibe felt more upscale than I'd anticipated. I was talking ball gowns. It felt like I'd walked into a Halloween party with a Marie Antoinette theme.

"Enjoy yourselves, Crimson Sires. We have a show and a game later." She waved her hand in a flourish. "Let me introduce you to the Burrow Sire. He's in town for the weekend." Calliope hooked her arm through Ren's and . . . he followed, weaving through throngs of people. Curiouser and curiouser. Did sharing a Sire bind them in some way?

"Follow Ren," Tobias's tone held none of the warmth he always directed at me. He spoke toward me as if I were inconsequential. I slinked after Ren as he strode toward the table hosting various champagne glasses full of red liquid. A vampire woman stood behind the bar. A nose ring glinted in the dull lighting coming from the rounded sconces.

"Freya," Ren said, raising an eyebrow and motioning at the bar. "Calliope *still* punishing you for fucking me?"

My gaze flew to the back of his head.

Freya sneered. Her braids were wrapped in a tight bun with a few framing her face. Her lips twitched. "I had a little too much to drink that night, Ren." She tsked. "Don't cause me any more trouble. You know how sensitive my baby girl is." She leaned over the top of the bar toward a glaring Calliope to pinch her chin. She'd let Ren's arm go at some point. "Now here." She thumped a wine glass on the counter. Amazingly, it didn't shatter.

"It's fresh, but if you prefer straight from the vein there are feeding stations in the upstairs family room if you're not craving the same old blood." She directed that last bit at me, dismissively scanning my face. Her lips twitched into a faint smirk.

Feeding stations? Smooth your expression, I chanted to myself. A laugh a little too loud dragged my head toward where Asher was speaking to a lithe beautiful woman who was hanging onto Asher's every word. As if sensing my attention, Asher turned and met my gaze, his lips twitched down the barest inch and he blocked my sight of the woman, giving me his back. So, this was what they meant when they said 'trust me'. More detail would have been appreciated. A couple glided by, blocking Asher from my view completely. My lips thinned. No sign of Tobias or Jax in the crush of mingling bodies either.

A long coat brushed against my leg.

While my attention had been elsewhere, a male vampire had approached. He rivaled Ren's height. The bottom of the tweed coat fluttered at his knees. He stood to my left while I hovered behind Ren who had yet to turn around. Freya slinked away and Ren finally turned.

"Ren Crimson, your absence was noted at the club last month." The smile across his lips seemed smarmy. I wanted to cringe back from his proximity, but that wouldn't be very 'Pet' of me. His hollowed cheeks gave him a gaunt look that didn't take away from his attractiveness.

"Charles," Ren said, smirking. "We're all bound to get distracted by pussy once in a while." The words rolled off his tongue with such ease. I rocked my weight from one foot to the other. My toes were starting to get numb.

"Indeed, we are," he purred and my skin crawled. "Is this the said pussy?" I looked up at the attention and his smile widened like a creep. I valiantly tried not to cringe and stuffed down my urge to huddle behind Ren.

"Say hello," Ren ordered, placing a palm at my spine, forcing me forward.

Instead of saying anything, I turned my head slightly to the side to offer my neck. I focused on the flared collar of his black buttoned dress shirt. He stepped close enough that I could smell the faint sweetness to his breath, but it was overwhelming, to the point that nausea twisted my gut.

Charles's fingertips grazed my throat. I couldn't stop the tremble of my hands. My pulse jumped. Dead eyes stared at me.

"I'll be honored to sample your human." His head lowered and I held my breath. It shouldn't be too bad, just like when the guys bit me. It'd feel good. I licked my lips, relaxing my shoulders.

Ren slapped Charles's touch away and yanked me back by the back of my neck. I grabbed onto his long leather jacket, so I didn't topple to my ass.

"I said, 'say hello,' not offer yourself to him." He showed me too much fang. I swallowed with effort and dropped my eyes, working to steady myself on my toes. His grip on my neck turned painful.

Charles stiffened; his hands still held out from where he'd been about to pull me toward his mouth.

"Well," Charles raised both eyebrows. "I suppose . . . not?" He chortled. Ren's arm banded around my waist, his large fingers settling on my waist none too gently. A puff of air escaped my lips. Ren was pissed.

"It is not like we have not exchanged blood-whores in the past." Charles made another reach for me, but I curled tighter to Ren.

"Not this one." Ren's jawline bunched and he seemed increasingly irate despite the curl of his lips. I thought we were supposed to be blending in? They nailed into me that I must behave as their blood-whore.

Whatever challenge he sensed, Charles visibly thrived on it. Glee filled his odd, almost black eyes.

"Are you denying me a taste of a human?" Charles tilted his head. In the snap of a rubber band, he no longer seemed to find humor in this. He seemed ready to strike at Ren—a cobra about to attack. We were supposed to be blending in.

"Stop." I hung onto Ren. Fear rode me hard and my breathing elevated.

"Is a human . . . speaking?" Had I messed up? No shit, I messed up. I wanted to apologize, but I knew it would only make things worse, so I lowered my eyes.

"Seems like she is. Come now, don't tell me your human doesn't try to defend you?" Asher dragged his words out in a mocking manner. He glided up with a smirk, blocking my view with his wide back. "You know how possessive Ren is. Wait a few days and he'll lose interest." I gritted my molars so hard my jaw hurt.

Ren's hand at my waist flexed. I peeked up at him. His eyes were narrowed, but his expression was stiff.

"You will not punish her insolence?"

Asher scoffed, "We enjoy humans with a bit of fight."

"You may have your human do as you wish, but she will not disrespect the customs."

"Charles, you crotchety twat, what has you blithering?" a rakishly handsome vampire with a golden skin tone queried. "Are you trying to feud with Crimson Coven?" He smirked. "Your Sire may not take too kindly to that."

Charles's lips thinned.

"Alistair," Asher said, genuinely pleased, and clapped his shoulder.

"I'll take my leave." Charles huffed and left with his coat rustling behind him. He did seem like a twat.

"And who is this human?" Alistair's intense gaze settled on me. His hair was slicked back, but strands curled artfully at his forehead as if they could not be tamed with the rest of the waves. His name rang a bell . . . the vampire that owned the mall and Petunia. He seemed way more laid back than I expected. A different glazed-eyed woman stood behind him; she looked up at him adoringly. He hooked his arm around her shoulder. "Quite a beauty," he said, tipping his head toward me.

"Don't you have business to run or women to plunder? You hardly ever show up to these social events," Asher said.

Alistair studied me carefully, analytic eyes roving over me. Curiously. Like a human inspecting a bug. I felt bare to him.

"Avoidance is not like you, Asher." Alistair stared into my eyes. "What are you to them?" The low, almost musical tone of his voice told me he was trying to compel me.

"Their Pet." I forced my voice to remain even.

Ren shouldered between us and gripped the front of Alistair's fancy frilled shirt. Alistair only stared at him, serious and unmoving.

"Now now, I invited you all in good faith." Calliope strutted up with a cheshire grin across her lips. "And for a bit of entertainment." She winked at me. "Now I must take my leave. Catalina, pleasure to see you."

"I can't say the same." The comment came without thought and I pursed my lips. Alistair threw his head back, releasing a deep belly laugh. Ren had tensed, but it was nowhere close to how wound up I was.

Calliope walked away, her tinkling laugh fading.

Ren clicked his tongue looking pissed, then he disappeared.

"Head off to mingle with others, love." Alistair's arm slipped off the woman and patted her ass. Irritation flashed over her features before she stifled it and walked away. "Asher, let me take her for a turn." Alistair invaded my space.

"No." Anger spilled into Asher's tone. I side-eyed him. Wasn't he supposed to keep his cool? The other vamp seemed even more intrigued.

A loud rhythmic clapping echoed. One, two, three, in quick succession caused the cacophony to simmer to a murmur.

I followed the direction all the vampires faced. To the far wall across where a slightly raised platform had been set up—a stage. Vampires were so dramatic.

Calliope clapped her hands again, standing on the rising.

"Fuck—" Asher hissed, looking over the crowd at something I was too short to see. "Don't move from here. Stay with Ren."

"But." I wheezed. Ren had left . . . I couldn't tell Asher because he disappeared through the thickening crowd. I needed to get out of here before I became too compressed. I twisted, and a female vampire brushed past me. Her little arm nudge caused me to stumble. I struggled to catch myself. Then more bodies pressed into all my sides as they jockeyed to be at the front of the line. I panted, turning in circles, trying to find one of my vampires. I'd even take Jax at this point.

"Watch it human," a vampire hissed, poking my shoulder. To an outsider it would have looked like it wouldn't do damage, but his strength sent me stumbling back against a chest.

"Got you." Alistair grinned down at me. I hurried to pull away from him. "Ah, ah, if you go running off, you don't know who will catch you."

I swallowed hard, turning from side to side. I couldn't see my vampires. Tears welled in my eyes and panic settled in.

A sharp scream froze me in place. A smattering of applause exploded through the room. Freya dragged a man onto the stage. He fought against her grip, uselessly—so human.

"Let me go, let me go," the man screamed.

"What's going on?"

Alistair lifted the flute of blood to his lips and took a sip. Red stained his lips.

"A vampire broke law."

"Law?"

"Exposure," he murmured, leaning too close for comfort. His gaze caught mine. His nose slightly flared. "You . . . You can't be compelled."

I gritted my teeth, holding his gaze and blinking as innocently as I could.

"Compelled? What do you mean?" My effort to sound nonchalant didn't work out.

The corner of his lips twitched. "Interesting. Very interesting."

Acting ignorant wasn't working. I swung my head side to side, but none of my vampires were in sight. Shit. Fuck.

"It's really not," I said, forced.

He leaned close and his nose flared again. Shit, he was sniffing me now?

"Your scent . . ." he hummed and closed his eyes. A few seconds passed. He opened them. His eyes had dilated.

"Would you like to switch to my Coven?" His fangs flashed. "I'm sure I can come to an agreement with the Crimson Sires."

"No, thank you." The words came out sounding like a jumble.

He took another step closer.

"If you change your mind." He handed me a black card. His name was embossed in gold font across the front and on the back was a number. I gawked, limply holding the card.

I couldn't address the madness of the statement because cheering swelled. Whirling around, I shoved the card into my bra. Vampires huddled closer, making it difficult for me to see.

asher

JAX WOVE THROUGH THE CROWD, through the hall, and toward the staircase. I hurried to catch up, but had to keep a reasonable pace to not call attention to myself. I could have turned invisible, but too many eyes were on me already. It would make more sense for me to head to the feeding stations upstairs. The onlookers wouldn't know I was attempting to catch up to Jax before he let his temper shove its dick down our throat.

He was hot on Charles's heels, chasing him down. I could only fucking imagine what Charles had been running his mouth about to set Jax off.

I reached the base of the stairs and zoomed up. Jax hadn't grabbed Charles yet. Just in fucking time. Picking up speed I grabbed his shoulder and pulled him back. He rounded with a hiss, and I flicked his forehead.

He shut up.

"We don't want to start a fucking feud, Jaxon," I hissed. "You kill or maim the fucker, he's going to go crying to his Sire, and once that happens, one of our allies turns their back on us."

"You should have heard the repulsive—"

"Don't even tell me." I put my hand up. "Think of Pet."

"I was thinking of her."

I narrowed my eyes. "What did he say about her?"

"About who?" Ren appeared at my side, gaze flickering from me to Jax.

"You're not with Catalina?" I stared at Ren, horrified.

"I left you with her." Ren's eyes slitted.

I groaned. I felt like I hung onto my control by a thread. We were foolish creatures, struggling to keep our temper more than our human.

"Keep this one out of trouble." I poked Ren. "Look at what kind of responsible pussy you're turning me into." I sneered at my brother and turned on my heel.

If Catalina's safety didn't depend on our behavior, I would have been wreaking all the havoc. Now look at me, behaving like fucking Tobias.

No one could know the grip she had on us, and for that, she needed to stay out of touching range from other vampires. Charles made a comment about her earlier and I'd been close to losing it on him.

I arrived at the base of the stairs in time to watch Calliope detach a human male's hand.

Fuck. Her gentle soul would struggle seeing that.

Look at me, I was getting better at considering human feelings. I smiled, satisfied with myself and went hunting for my female.

I WAS GOING to throw up. Calliope ripped the human's hand off like it was a piece of paper. My stomach heaved and I swallowed repeatedly, hoping the urge to vomit my guts out would disappear.

Throwing up in front of everyone was likely to get me the attention the guys didn't want on me.

I was so desperate for support, I even turned to look at Alistair, but his attention was fixated on the scene, a creepy little smile on his lips.

I rubbed my palms against my sides, rubbing the dampness on the lace.

"The human has betrayed us." She paused and flicked her finger. Two large males dragged a woman onto the stage. Her fangs flashed as she grappled between them. "And one of our own, my Progeny, has had a hand in it. Because of her stupidity."

"Sire, please have mercy," she begged.

"Silence." Calliope slapped the female so hard I clasped my own cheek. She turned to look at the silent crowd. Smiles littered the fascinated faces as they watched the 'show'. "Let this serve as a reminder. Humans with knowledge of us must be controlled until the time comes to discard them."

I struggled to breath. When, not if.

Calliope's gaze settled on me and my stomach dropped. How had she found me so easily through the thick crowd? My God, I wanted to run.

Without taking her gaze off me, she yanked the crying human male closer and rammed her nails into his throat. Blood spurted over her arm, splashing her body as he choked and struggled.

A scream almost pushed free, but a hand clasped over my mouth. Or what felt like a hand. There was nothing I could see touching me. My heart raced, painfully pounding in my chest.

A second touch clasped my side. I tried to turn around.

"Settle," Asher breathed against my ear. So incredibly low. I stopped trying to move and embraced his hug. A sob of relief built in my chest, but I swallowed it down.

Asher's hands grazed down my sides. The soothing caresses calmed my rampant heart, until he cupped my boobs.

"Asher," I hissed between clenched teeth.

Teeth sank into my earlobe. I stifled my groan.

"—news anchor writing an exposé on us," Calliope spat. "As the head of my Coven, I will use this as a warning."

My burgeoning lust abated and the sick feeling in my stomach returned with a vengeance. Even Asher tensed against my back. If humans found out about vampires, it would be madness.

"You endangered us all." Calliope addressed the vampire kneeling before her. She held her hand out and Freya placed a metallic stake in her palm.

"Now you will bear the consequences. You are lucky we no longer live in the times when vampire hunters existed." Calliope's lips peeled back.

Without hesitation, she shoved the tip into the vampire's chest. She began decaying. Bit by bit, her body fell apart and into a pile of ash.

Calliope returned to look at the limp human male still being held up. He'd died at some point and he no longer gushed blood in spurts. Now it just leaked, causing a huge puddle at his feet. She shoved her fingers into his chest, opening a cavity in the depths. She yanked the heart out.

A scream built in the back of my throat, but before it could burst free Asher's palm covered my mouth again, muffling my scream. Elated shouts rang throughout the crowd as I was dragged backwards. I clawed at the back of the hand, blinded by the tears sheening my eyes.

"Shhh, *Älskade*." I went limp against him, sobbing against his palm. My surroundings blurred. Both from tears and the speed he'd picked up. A door slammed shut and he turned me in his arms. I wrapped my arms around his midsection, burying my face into his chest.

The image of the ligaments and bones snapping wouldn't leave.

"What did you do?" Jax said, his accent thickened.

"Calliope ripped a human heart out on her stage." Asher sighed.

Teeth audibly clicked.

"Can you make her stop?" Jax said gruffly, his hand smoothing down the side of my head.

"Why couldn't she just compel him to forget? Why?" I cried. "I thought a council was called to vote when there was something like that." I would be surprised if he understood what the hell came out of my mouth. Jax continued rubbing the back of my head in soothing little circles.

"Because it did not need to be escalated. Calliope was that vampire's Sire; she has chosen to handle it in-house," Ren's voice interjected.

"We should have anticipated a move like this from her." Asher's arm fastened tighter around me with his words.

"Hand her to me," Ren demanded. "Cat." His voice rumbled and he pinched my chin, lifting my face high to look at him. He blurred behind my tears. "Nothing will happen to you."

Tears continued to drip down my chin.

"She seems catatonic," Asher said gruffly.

Jax muttered in his language. He didn't sound happy.

"Catalina," he snapped. I couldn't move even if I wanted to. He shouldered Ren out of the way, stepping within my sight. Instead of saying anything. He ripped his t-shirt off and unbuttoned his slacks. Sex was usually the answer, but right now I couldn't stop thinking about gushing bloo—

Jax's muscles rippled and shifted and changed. Fur sprouted and from one moment to the next, Binx sat on a pile of clothes.

I gaped. This—the—I shook my head.

I held my palm to my chest.

I'd asked him earlier what his ability was and he'd seemed to want to avoid it. He changed into a cat. . . a cat that had spent quite a lot of time with me. Time I'd been very vulnerable in.

I could only blink.

"H-he." I couldn't get any damn words out.

"Now you broke her." Ren frowned.

"Your mouth is hanging open, Pet." Asher closed my mouth.

"You're Binx?"

Ren laughed. Jax, in cat form, hissed at him. His body started rippling until Jax stood a few feet away.

"Binx," he grumbled. "You couldn't have chosen a less stupid fucking name."

I scoffed, offended. Binx was a fine name!

"I should be the angry one, you watched, no, spied on me!" Awareness dawned. "Oh my God, you've watched me shower!"

"Don't get too worked up." He scowled. "You tried to put a collar on me."

"And you scratched me for my efforts," I retorted. His lips pursed.

"What is going on in here?"

I whirled to look at Tobias in the large opening.

"Him." I pointed at Jax accusingly. His teeth clicked together. Now that I wasn't blinded by tears, I saw we were in an entertainment area of sorts. With all the 'man-cave' fixings. A pool table, a large, oversized television, recliners . . .

I marched over to Tobias. "You knew that he was Binx. All of you did." I huffed, shaking my head. "Did you guys enjoy making a fool out of me?"

I thinned my lips.

Tobias took hold of my shoulders and rubbed his palms down my bare biceps. The smooth rub of skin lifted goose bumps.

"We can address your dissatisfaction at a later time, Love. We have an issue." He looked over my shoulder at the rest of them. "There will be a game. Each Coven present is to provide a human."

I could hear a pin drop. Something was wrong, but I didn't understand . . . a game? And they had to provide a human to play it?

They'd only brought me.

I didn't bother asking what had them so on edge. If it was a game and they were vampires, I was sure it had a lot of death involved.

My throat seized like someone had wrapped their hand around my throat.

"We have to get her out of here," Jax snapped.

"If we leave now," Tobias started and paused. He ran his hand through his hair.

"She will be even more of a target."

I jumped and immediately cringed into Tobias at Calliope's approach.

THIRTY-FIVE

catalina

"EAVESDROPPING, CAL?" Ren snapped and his hand wrapped around her throat. Blood formed under his fingernails. She gasped, her nails digging into his arm, leaving deep red lines behind.

"You're in my house. What did you expect?" She wheezed.

"For you to be smart about how much more you could push me." Ren smiled, but his eyes held no humor. I'd been on the receiving end of that look, and I didn't wish it on anyone. Okay, maybe Calliope was one that did deserve it.

"I had to," she choked out. "Tell you that I had some information." The last part sounded jumbled.

"Mmm, information you say." Ren smirked. "What do we think?" Was he talking to himself? I gawked, my hands sliding off Tobias's chest.

"Let's hear her out," Tobias murmured. Jax just grunted.

"I say we kill her," Asher announced.

Ren snorted and let her go. She dropped to her feet.

"This is my attempt to make peace with you, Ren. Don't retaliate for . . ." she cleared her throat.

"Keeping me locked up past our agreed timeframe?" Ren raised an eyebrow. "Bringing us here? Your little show from earlier?"

"You agreed to it!"

"But I didn't agree to be starved," he hissed. Calliope flinched.

"I have information. That's why I came looking for you lot."

"Spill it," Ren said, the deadly look in his eye not fading.

"But then we're even." Calliope slowly rose to her feet. Ren only stared.

Calliope sighed. "You've become just like our Sire." She scratched her forehead. "There's been talk at Saphire."

"What's new," Asher said, inspecting his nails. Was he nudging dried blood from underneath them? I wrinkled my nose. "Everyone loves talking about us."

"About her." Calliope twitched her head toward me. "Questions about who she is. Where she's from—"

"Of course there are questions. She's the first human we haven't killed within a few hours," Jax said oh so casually.

I gasped.

"Worry not, Pet. None of them mattered." He smirked. "You should have seen the one that pissed Ren off for asking him to whisper sweet nothings in Japanese and he 'accidently' snapped her neck." Asher's air quotes didn't make me feel good.

"You could chalk it up to how you guys have kept her, but there have been whispers about Wrenhaven talking to other Sires."

"We've had no issues with them." Tobias crossed his arms, stepping forward so we were side to side. "They have jurisdiction in half of Oregon."

"They want to expand."

Tobias scratched his chin.

"That's why I invited Charles Foxbrooke and the Burrow Sire." She lowered her voice and looked behind her. The noisiness from downstairs continued. "I heard they've been approached by Wrenhaven."

Heaviness accumulated in my stomach. This all sounded too dangerous. If they were digging around about me . . . what if they discovered Peter's existence? I swayed.

Jax's arm curled around my waist. I clutched onto him, leaning all my weight against him. I wanted to ask but I would save it until we were safe and away from all vampires.

"You're not fooling anyone. You're playing both sides," Ren drawled. Her eyes flicked to the side and she acted like she hadn't heard him.

"That goes against the treaty." Jax's chest vibrated under my ear.

"They are not planning to go against anything. They want to catch one of you in a mistake, a slip up, some way in order to call a council." She focused on me. "And they think this girl is the way to get to you." I pressed tighter against Jax. His palm pressed into my spine.

"Such sweet devotion." She sighed with a mocking smile. "Your human truly looooves you, doesn't she?" Her focus turned to me. "They won't keep you long term. You should have taken my offer." She clicked her teeth disappointedly.

"Ah. Yes, your offer. You want the ring so desperately you've orchestrated a plant in our house?" Jax scoffed.

Calliope scowled, obviously confused.

"No," she said slowly. "When I found out she was staying with you, I hunted her down to threaten her."

"Threaten her with what?" Asher said, tensing like he'd been hit.

"Your safety." She waved her hand, encapsulating all the men with one motion. She sighed. "She did not take the bait."

"She was protecting us," Tobias said, head tilted as he focused on Calliope. She sighed and glared at the mind-reader.

"Leave them alone," she cried out in a high-pitched voice. I scowled.

"I don't sound like that," I said through gritted teeth. Calliope rolled her eyes.

"You wanted to protect us?" Jax asked. His voice lowered with huskiness, with emotion.

"I would have never betrayed you guys. I said it." Over and over. I almost added, but it seemed redundant.

"Calliope," Ren said conversationally. He was then next to her, yanking her head back so her throat strained. "I'm going to rip your head off."

She squalled. "I can be an asset. And I could have spread news far and wide that you have a human that is not able to be compelled, but I didn't because I'm on your side, Ren."

I should tell them about Alistair knowing, but this was definitely a bad time.

He scoffed and sucker punched her right in the mouth. Blood squirted from her lip and she yelped, clasping her face. Jax held me tighter than he'd ever held me before. His expression rippled and tensed. I could almost see cogs turning in his head.

"We should leave before the chase begins."

"If you leave now, they will turn on you—"

"You've said enough." Ren sneered. She clamped her mouth shut.

"Calliope," Freya called, echoing from down the hall. "They're waiting for you."

"Please, Ren, let me go." He only stared. "I will tell you anything I overhear about what's going on. It's only a matter of time until they try to get me to join them."

On my third breath, he let her go.

Calliope disappeared by my next blink.

Asher was suddenly in front of me, clasping my face between both palms.

"Yohr sqwuaging ma face."

"I should have never doubted you, *Älskade*." His eyebrows furrowed and his lips twisted. "You may drain me or tie me to a bed post. Or not let me come for a year—"

"No." I tried yanking away.

Confusion flitted over his expression. "Do you require Jaxon's apology, as well?" Asher turned to his twin who still pressed against my side and jerked his head down at me.

"Whatever apologies you have. Stuff them. They're not enough."

"Not . . . enough?" Asher's frown deepened.

Was I speaking some fictional language he couldn't understand? I scowled and yanked away from Asher's grip so hard I would have hurt myself if he hadn't let go.

"We can talk later. Let's get this stupid game over with. I want to get back to Crimson Manor and soak in the bathtub."

I looked at Tobias. He looked too serious.

"Tobias, she said it was not enough. I don't understand." Asher blinked, running his hand through his hair. "What do those human mindset book thingies tell you?"

"They're studies, Asher. We have caused her stress and

suffering. She does not owe us her forgiveness—according to what I've read."

"But I want it." A small wrinkle formed at the bridge of Asher's nose. "Jax, too, even though he looks like he has a pole stuffed up his ass right now."

I peeked at Jax under my eyelashes. Jax stared at me expressionless, too expressionless, but his palm had slid around my side and pressed to my belly.

Asher's description was too accurate.

"None of you believed me," I said and wiggled my jaw. "Let me go." I elbowed Jax in the chest until he finally released me.

I fixed my dress back in place.

"Am I going to be expected to play this game like this?" I waved a hand down at my dress and heels.

"You will not be participating." Jax crossed his arms.

"You guys can't have more of a target on you. You were all right. You need to treat me like your blood-whore. They can't be wondering more about me. They can't—"

"Catalina, breathe." Tobias cupped my jaw. My chest tightened painfully.

"What if they find out about Peter?" I whispered so low it was practically only the movement of my lips. "No. I'd rather die." I lifted my chin, setting it stubbornly. "I can do it," I said and licked my lips. "I am doing it," I repeated, stubbornly.

"You don't even know what it is," Jax snapped. "Chased through the forest, with nothing to guide your way. The losing Coven Sires execute their Pet or blood-whore, whichever they choose to enter."

I struggled with pushing out my sentence. "So, we don't lose."

"The winners fuck in front of everyone."

I froze with my mouth open.

"Oh." I wilted.

A thick knot formed in my throat. Exhibitionism wasn't my thing. My face was already burning bright red. I stared at the carpet.

"Breathe," Tobias clasped my shoulder.

"I volunteer myself—"

"No. It can't be you, Asher. You fuck her like you can't control yourself. Half the fucking people here have seen you screwing, and they will be able to determine the difference. Tobias is out, too. I must speak with the Burrow's Sire." Ren looked at Jax.

"No," I croaked.

Jax sighed and rubbed his head. "I will take care of her."

A burst of laughter escaped. Shock, fear, and adrenaline melded into a big ball in my gut.

My mind needed to get busy asap.

"And I thought Asher flirting with all the women was bad." A burst of laughter escaped and I clamped my lips shut.

Asher's lips twitched, but he didn't smirk. Probably knew I'd lose it on him right now.

"Catalina, I was investigating."

I huffed and turned away. Tobias had disappeared at some point.

"You looked very cozy *investigating*."

He chuckled and I whipped my head in his direction. His face was smooth again. I huffed. Tobias re-entered the entertainment room.

"Let's go. All the contestants have been chosen. The chase is about to start." Tobias turned to leave again. Ren filed out next and I moved slowly forward, watching my feet.

My nerves were going to do me in. At least the task was a running one. I was good at running away even if my lungs struggled sometimes. I sank my teeth into my lower lip.

"You will be protected at all times. Jax will not let anything happen to you. None of us will. You are ours." Asher watched me steadily. He was trying to make me feel better. At least that much I could acknowledge.

"Thank you," I muttered.

"No worries," Asher swung his arm over my shoulder. "You can suck my cock later to show me your gratitude." He winked.

I sighed, shaking my head.

THIRTY-SIX

"WE NEED to talk about that fucking Coven." I thumped my knuckles on the linen cloth rhythmically.

"We will discuss when there is no potential about being overheard." Tobias kept the serene mask on his face. Move against my Coven? They would pay. Each and every one of their Coven members would fall with my sword. I would not stop until they were eradicated.

I'd done it to other lineages before. I would do so again.

"I don't like that grin on Ren's face." Asher pursed his lips and shook his head. "Nevermind. I like it. He's plotting someone's demise. Can I help this time?"

I twitched an eyebrow at Asher. "You've never showed interest in my hunting excursions."

"This time they've messed with something they shouldn't have," Asher said with derision. Meaning Cat. The beautiful human girl I could not ignore. The one I craved—dangerously.

I grunted. If he could keep up with me, sure. We could bond over their blood and guts and bring their entrails and ashes to the human's feet.

I liked how that sounded.

Calliope began her spiel as she began to announce the humans and their Sires. Her death was imminent. She had pushed me too far. If there weren't witnesses, I would have sliced her head off today.

"Do not. They are watching us," Tobias said out of nowhere.

Per Asher's pout, he'd been about to go invisible and follow Cat into the woods. Tobias was correct. Vampires watched us with focus, ready to report any untoward behavior to their Sires.

Jax approached. He'd changed into a black t-shirt and joggers. Asher clapped him on the shoulder with an affable smile. He leaned close.

"You better find her. Bring her back to me, alive," Asher hissed into his twin's ear. Jaxon, for once, didn't try to smack him. He only nodded once.

Interesting. This one human joined us more than Imogen ever did. I crossed my arms and observed. She'd become my weakness.

I threw my head back and laughed.

"What's so funny?" Asher grumbled. I continued to laugh at the ridiculous fact that a human woman had brought me to my knees.

catalina

I RUBBED MY ARMS FRANTICALLY, trying to gain friction to warm me up. It was too cold for this. I shuffled on my bare feet. Asher was supposed to be keeping the heels and dress safe. Turned out, no I wasn't running around through the middle of the forest in platform heels. I'd been handed a simple forest green A-line dress and told that shoes were not allowed. But there was one thing to be grateful for: the first days of my period weren't heavy, so I removed my tampon.

"Quickly, quickly, blood bag." Freya shooed me toward the group of humans congregated on the pavilion. I climbed up and the other people waiting around, six of us in total, looked as cold as me, but they seemed less bothered by it. They stood in a straight line, facing outward with their backs to me. Once I climbed onto the platform and shuffled next to a male dressed in the same A-line dress, I saw why. The lawn was decorated with fairy lights wound around the surrounding trees that created a sort of circular clearing. Scattered throughout were tall rectangular tables with white cloths draped over them.

Calliope stood at the base below the pavilion on the other side where I'd arrived.

"And our last human has arrived. Crimson Coven Sire's precious Pet." A smattering of applause echoed into the deep dark surroundings. Past the fairy lights, everything looked so ominous and dark. I licked my lips nervously.

Playthings. Entertainment. That was all humans were to vamps. And this game was stupid. I had to run through the dark forest, shoeless, and be chased by other vampires trying to kill me? Great.

Do not trust the other humans. And don't be last. Asher warned me before he strode away.

I peeked to the side. A total of five girls and one guy. The others looked just as determined as I felt to win. I breathed out slow and steady. I couldn't believe I was having to put my trust in Jax, the one I least trusted.

He would likely take the opportunity to off me himself.

Calliope faced us on the platform. With a sly, smarmy grin, she said, "Run." I needed nothing more. I pounded down the steps, angling toward the edge of the forest. A tall, lean woman surpassed us all, the man right on her heels. They crossed the boundary of the forest, disappearing into the thick foliage.

I gritted my teeth, pushing my legs harder. I could do this!

A sudden pull against the back of my dress banded the neckline to my throat. Choking, I slowed and whoever grabbed my dress kicked the back of my knee, making them buckle. I hit the ground with a thud that vibrated through my bones.

Now on all fours, I watched the rest of the girls dash past me.

Fuck. Fuck. Fuck!

I was last; exactly what Asher said not to do. Clawing my

fingers into the grass until dirt caked the bottom of my nails, I dragged myself forward. A few steps further and leaves slapped my arms, scratching my skin.

Ignoring all of it was my only choice. I pushed forward. Running as hard as humanly possible. My feet ached, but I couldn't afford to slow. I only had a moment to get as deep into the forest as I could. My chest pumped up and down, and the slightest pain banded my lungs. I hadn't been able to run this hard since The Pale One took me. I smacked a branch out of my way and dipped through an unmarked path veering to the right.

A loud horn exploded through the forest. Treetops rustled and birds exploded from them in a flurry.

As soon as you hear the horn, hide. Don't keep going forward, go left as soon as you're in the forest. Another tidbit Asher offered. He didn't have to tell me twice.

I wove to the left and hunkered lower, trying to find a hiding spot as I crept through. While at the same time slowing my panting breaths. Pressing on my chest, I focused on bringing down the volume of my panting. Adrenaline pumped through my veins. It was so dark out here . . .

I shivered. I hated this with a passion. My skin crawled and all I wanted to do was disappear. But this was about Peter's survival. I would win because I needed to keep protecting him. Once I was gone, Crimson Coven could get rid of him.

A branch snapping cracked through the silent forest, echoing from all around.

An unfamiliar man hovered at the main path, well within view of the moonlight beaming down and turning his skin pale.

He slowed and he inhaled hard, smelling me? I gritted my teeth, fear riding me hard. Something tickled my arm. I lifted it closer to see a thin line of blood.

A scratch. I covered it with my mouth, licking the injury. Thank God, it didn't keep bleeding. Upon lowering my arm, my elbow smacked a branch, rattling the leaves.

I froze.

The vampire whipped his head in the direction I hid. A scream rang out and he whirled toward the sound.

Bats exploded out of a nearby tree. The vampire disappeared. I contained the sob that begged to escape.

I continued trekking to the left as I was directed. Rhythmic smacking brought me to a halt. A vampire had his pants around his ankles, knees in the dirt as he fucked a woman. His head was tipped back, neck straining. Her dress was around her neck, and he gripped the end of it, forcing her into a bent curve.

Bites and blood littered her body. Was she even alive?

I heaved and crept by while he kept fucking her. Once I was far enough, I allowed myself to breathe normally.

Hurry, Jax.

Trees rustled and a shadow moved within the trees. I squinted. Alistair.

I ducked behind a wide trunk, pressing my back to the bark, and holding my breath. Walk on by. Please, plea—

"I wouldn't hide here."

A scream ripped from my throat. Terrified and loud. Too loud. He winced. "I wouldn't scream either," he drawled. I cringed against the tree.

The corner of his lips twitched.

"I'd hide there." He tipped his chin toward a thick bush. I could only blink at him. Was he playing with me? His lips full on spread into a fang-y grin. He winked and disappeared. I exhaled and slumped against the tree.

The spot he'd told me to hide in looked inconspicuous.

And If I kept walking, I was bound to run into another vampire.

I dashed into the dense bushes, hunkering down into a crouch and hugging my knees. Closing my eyes, I focused on breathing and listening.

A brief moment passed and then the sound of a whispered 'hello' echoed. I peeked through the brush.

The human male inched by. Sweeping his gaze from left to right. No way. I was staying right here. Even if he meant no harm, why was he walking around calling out. Too fishy.

I settled back in, closing my eyes and breathing slow. A snap of a branch forced my eyes open in time to see a hand plunge into the bush. The man grabbed my hair in a rough tug, dragging me from my hiding spot.

Screaming, I kicked at his calves, but he would not let go of my braid. From my peripheral, a rock came flying at me. Agony splintered through my temple, and I cried out.

He slammed a rock into my head.

I whimpered, clasping my jaw. The hit was so hard it radiated down. He tossed me down and I fell in an unceremonious pile.

"Why?" I croaked.

"I will win." So emotionless.

I dug my fingers into the dirt, about to toss it into his face so I could take off running.

Then, a large fucking tiger with coloring I'd never seen before pounced on his back. Those large claws slashed into the back of his neck, severing it in one swipe.

I gawked.

Jax turned into his human form. He stood over the body with a sneer on his face.

I closed my eyes. It was fifty-fifty. He would kill me, or save me, and I had nothing to hope for either way.

Jax placed his bleeding wrist to my lips. My eyes flew open, and I stared into his shadowed, blue lapis-colored eyes. My tongue flicked out to collect the offering. I gripped his wrist, pressing his flesh to my lips. I swallowed down another mouthful.

Jax pulled away at the third drink.

I made a sound of complaint.

"I can't have you drunk off blood."

Already the pain in my head felt better.

"Thank you," I croaked. He hadn't killed me . . . and he'd given me his blood.

"Are you okay, Kitten?"

The soft question sprang tears to my eyes and my lip wobbled. I lowered my head to hide the vulnerability.

He gripped my jaw and forced my chin to face him. My eyes fell on his concerned one.

"Jax," I sobbed and tossed myself in his arms. He stiffened and then his hand smoothed down my spine.

"Shh," he murmured, continuing to pet me. "Kitten, we have to get out of here."

I swiped the back of my hand across the dampness on my face.

"Okay," I whispered.

"Climb onto my back." He crouched. I stared down at the bare wide shoulders. Something moved within the brush to my right. I tossed myself on him, clinging like a monkey. He ran through the forest with ease. The loose strands of hair that had escaped my braid fluttered at my temples.

Jax slowed.

"What are you doing?" I whispered—no, croaked.

He turned his head. In a jerk to the side, he focused on a tree a few feet away. A slight form burst from the tree, running the opposite direction. He continued to stalk her until his fist went right through her chest. Blood gushed from the wound and spurted from her front. Jax had punched a hole right through her chest. In the same swift, no nonsense move, he yanked his arm out. Her flesh made the oddest suctioning sound and there were snaps of bones as he removed his arm. She fell facedown, still and with a hole in her back. Jax flicked his hand, and her blood splattered around. He swiped his hand over his thigh, removing the red layer on his palm.

My stomach heaved.

"Why?" I croaked.

It seemed so unnecessarily cruel.

"She should not have injured you."

What . . .

She'd been the one to trip me.

catalina

WHEN WE BROKE into the clearing, it was much different than when we'd left it. It was a full-on orgy.

I gasped and Jax squeezed my knee. The fairy-lights wound around the trees had been switched to red, lending to the sexual-filled ambiance. People fucked up-right, on tables, on the grass.

Was that—yes, it was. Calliope had Freya splayed on a table, her legs spread open as she feasted on her sex.

Were my vampires . . . I scanned, bouncing from one fucking couple to the other, fearing so much it was embarrassing. Asher and Ren remained in the clearing, sitting on a pale couch with their legs splayed, but completely dressed. A group of three fucked on the ground in front of them, but their gazes were fastened on Jax's approach. Relief lowered my shoulders from around my ears.

Jax's grip on my thighs loosened and he tugged me toward his front. His face was fixed into a grim, almost angry expression. All the prior concern utterly gone. He climbed onto the platform all us humans had been lined up on. Plush white blankets adorned the floor.

In a flurry of motion, Jax had me on all fours, facing the floor. I clenched the blankets and they wrinkled under my grip.

Nerves tightened my throat until it made it hard to breathe. I could feel eyes on me.

His teeth sank into my shoulder. A yelp crawled free, more from shock than anything else. Jax dragged blood from me. The tug reached to my clit and flared lust to life. I gasped.

He licked the bites to close them as he removed his lips. His shaft, hard and twitching, rested against the crevice of my ass.

A couple watched my face with their arms linked. My chest became tight. I wanted to run—

He bit me again and his arm pressed to my side as he reached under me and delved into my dress. His fingers pressed against my clit, erasing the eyes from my mind. He rolled the bud of nerves between two fingers gently.

A blaze of lust traveled through my pussy, and I quivered with need. My hips wiggled up against his cock in offering.

Since Jax was already nude, he only needed to bare my pussy. He guided his cock to my entrance. The tip prodded at my needy core, slipping inside with ease.

My sex pulsed, seeming to draw him in.

He plunged deep inside until his thighs slapped against mine. I jolted forward with a gasp, but he took hold of my shoulder, keeping me from moving too much. He thrust again and again.

Pounding into me so hard it verged on anger. The rhythmic slap of his flesh hitting mine only served to inflame my need. I couldn't stop my whimpers and moans. I craved moving against him, taking him harder, but he kept me still.

The orgasm smacked into me. My channel fluttered around him, trying to grip him and never let go.

I whimpered, my head falling forward, but Jax didn't stop pounding into me. My orgasm tapered off, leaving behind sensitivity.

Jax's chest pressed into my back and his sweet breath fluttered the hair framing my face. He grazed his nose against my neck. At this angle, he reached deeper into my pussy, and his shaft rubbed against my clit. I cried out, grinding back.

He hissed out a breath. Fucking me with dizzying speed. Nonsensical words spilled from my mouth. My thighs shook with strain, but I couldn't stop arching back into him.

My second orgasm sucked my breath away. Leaving behind electricity. I squeezed my eyes shut and bit my lip. My pussy squeezed him so tight he grunted. His cock spasmed inside me and juts of cum warmed my channel. Jax smoothed his palm along my back.

My arms grew weak, and I lowered to my forearms, panting.

"She's a noisy one." The random comment reached me, bringing me back to reality. To all the eyes on us.

Jax's palm constricted at my hip, squeezing me. Comforting me.

"Jax—"

"Silence," he snapped.

His thumb rubbed my arm. Gentle and a contradiction to his words.

As he'd always treated me with his words. Aggressive was Jax's default, but his touch was always careful. And I realized just how much considering the ease in which he'd punched a hole in the girl's chest.

Him being my cat . . . the gradual change in his behavior with me.

Binx was around from the beginning. Following me, cuddling me, comforting me. And that entire time it had been Jax.

JAX

HER CUNT WAS MINE. I thrust my cock deep into her pussy once more. She squeezed me again, wringing the last of my cum. My balls drew up tight. She drained the fuck out of me. I exhaled through my gritted teeth. I had to force a careful mask over my face. Uncaring, angry—as I'd always been.

Catalina slumped forward, her face nearing the ground until her spine arched beautifully. I ran my palm up her back, grazing, touching, claiming. She groaned and her pussy fluttered around my cock, prodding him to revive.

I was obsessed with this woman.

A low groan caught my attention to a male vampire palming his cock.

He was one of Alistair's Progeny. I cataloged his face. Alistair was bound to want something, and I would exchange it for the life of this male.

It wasn't hard to look pissed off.

All those fucking eyes. They watched me fuck her and lose myself in her. They craved what was not theirs. I clasped her to me, my cock slipping out of her pussy and she gasped as my cum leaked out of her.

I turned her in my arms and her palms pressed into my chest as she leaned into me trustingly. It felt like something constricted in my chest. I scowled and stared down at her upturned face.

I made sure not to let a drop of her blood fall. None other than my Coven would taste this woman. She belonged to us and only us. Until she no longer existed.

As lust faded, awareness spilled through her eyes and her brown eyes flicked nervously.

I nestled her face into the crook of my neck. Her panting tapered off in increments. The sick bastard from the Foxbrooke Coven approached.

He would request his turn.

No.

A snarl rumbled in my chest. Asher intercepted the male, but it wouldn't be long before he was on his way toward me.

I pulled her away from my chest, my fingers flexing on her fragile arms. She stared at me trustingly. Words of comfort hovered on my lips.

I could not stand watching her suffer at others' hands. And I could not offer her my blood or hold her the way I'd please. Too many observed us with eagle eyes.

I pressed my thumb into her throat. It would not dissuade him, but it would give me a reason to take her away from here. Her eyebrows furrowed and she gripped my wrists, her tugging turned more desperate with each attempt she made at freedom.

"No, Jax," she whispered, fear and betrayal soaking her tone. Her eyes filled with tears. She believed I was about to kill her. Truly believed it.

I gritted my teeth, sneering.

Her doe eyes became frightened as they began to close.

She thrashed in my arms. Clawing at my arms, gouging me. My Kitten became still—safe. In time for Charles to get away from Asher's chatter.

I tossed her over my shoulder. Her limp body flopping. As inconspicuously as I could, I tugged her stupid dress down to cover her pert ass. An ass that should have only been seen by us. I gritted my teeth.

I kept my gaze focused in front of me. If I saw any expressions gazing with lust, I would lose it and begin slaughtering, starting a feud between us and the Covens of all the vampires present.

Bad fucking idea with the enemies circling Crimson Coven.

THIRTY-NINE

SLEEP FADED IN INCREMENTS, aided by the low voices murmuring close by. I was extra warm and toasty.

"Even though we can't turn her, we can extend her life by having her stay with us. You saw the Ashvale Sire's Pet. She kept him for two centuries before the human disintegrated," Ren said.

"Two centuries . . ." Asher hummed.

"Is a tease," Jax snapped. "If we find a cure for blood madness, then maybe . . ." Jax trailed off.

I smiled, absorbing the conversation. They wouldn't know how pleased their words made me.

A scoff and then Tobias said, "There is no cure. We've already searched."

My throat ached a bit. I frowned. Jax choked me! I thought it would be the last of me. My eyes flew open.

"Her pulse changed." Tobias rubbed my jawline with his thumb.

"Give me a moment with her," Jax said and his voice

reverberated. I stiffened, jackknifing into a sitting position and scrambling back, dragging myself back until I hit the headboard. Where was I? Simple room, a plain, flat wooden headboard—Jax's bedroom. I'd rarely been in here.

Jax snagged my ankle and dragged me toward him. I screamed and smacked at his chest.

"Asher," I cried out. "Tobias." I peeled my eyes over his shoulder, but they were gone and the door was shut. He dragged me to the middle of the bed.

"Shh, Kitten, I'm not going to hurt you." He wrestled my arms together, binding me with one hand. I panted, thrashing. My chest heaved to the point that it was beginning to hurt.

I struggled to get away, but I couldn't move an inch.

With his free hand, he clasped my face. He lowered slowly and pressed his lips to mine. I sucked in a breath, and he slid his tongue into my mouth. He flicked it against mine, coaxing me into a kiss. He was a really good kisser . . .

"No," I gasped and yanked my head to the side.

"I fucking want you."

"I dislike you." I panted between words.

"I . . ." he paused and scowled. "I shouldn't have . . ." he trailed off again. His eyebrows furrowed. "I am sorry."

I went silent, studying his expression. I narrowed my eyes.

"Can you even feel apologetic?"

He hesitated.

"No."

"Then why are you apologizing?"

"Tobias said humans respond well to apologies."

The honesty. I snorted and shook my head.

"What I do know." He paused. "I do not want you upset. I

want you to seek me out. I do not want you to be disgusted by me. I want you to look at me how you look at my twin." He took a breath, which told me more than anything how worked up he was.

"Look at me as you look at Asher."

"You will never be Asher," I snapped, aiming to hurt him.

He drew back slightly and something curiously looking like hurt flashed in his lapis eyes. It was replaced by anger.

"I'm going to fuck you," he finally spat out.

I gasped, and his stubbornness flared my anger to the surface. He kept doing this angry bit and I was so tired of him.

"I'm going to fuck you," I snapped right back and wrapped my arm around his neck, using him to drag myself up to kiss him hard. His hands became limp and gave me enough leeway to pull from his grip. I sank my fingers into his short hair, gripping the back of his head.

His fang nicked my lip. The taste of my blood slipped onto my tongue. I moaned, tipping my chin up and sliding my tongue deep into his mouth.

Hooking my leg on his hip, I arched to feel his hard cock through his joggers.

He moaned against my mouth.

I urged him to his back.

Jax let me. He let me.

Elation spurred my actions. I settled on top of him, my pussy flush with his cock. I was naked and my hair was no longer in a braid. It flowed around my shoulders as it did after a shower. They must have bathed me.

It should have frightened me, but it made me feel taken care of.

And I really liked that feeling. His cock throbbed under me. I yanked his joggers down and he bobbed free. The tip glistened with precum, the slightly red moisture making my mouth water.

I licked my lips and pushed up on my knees. In a smooth motion, I sank down on his shaft.

Jax gasped, his eyes widening on mine. I lifted and lowered on him, grinding and riding him. He moaned, his fingers digging into my thighs, but the pinch only made my movements harsher. I loved his loss of control. I craved it.

His lips parted, eyes slitting until they were a thin line.

"Catalina," he groaned, thrusting up with furious abandon. I bounced on his cock, my breasts swayed with the rhythm. "I need you."

In a swift motion, he had me on my back again, not detaching from my pussy.

He dipped his head and sank his teeth into my neck. After one suck, he pulled them out and lowered them to my breast. He bit the swell of my breast. I groaned, arching my neck and moving my head side to side. He moved to my nipple and bit me again. My pussy seized around his cock and my release swelled until I crested over the edge. I cried out, coming hard.

Punctures littered my body. His marks. I ran my hands against the hard muscled shoulders, rubbing against the silky skin.

"Fuck," he groaned. "Fuck. Kitten."

I bowed my spine, meeting each and every thrust with desperation. His loss of control drove me crazy.

He gripped my chin and turned my head to the side. Tobias caught my eye. I was so lost in Jax that I didn't note him entering. He sat on the chair with his legs splayed and his cock in hand. The smooth, wet tip glistened.

Jax sank his teeth into the side of my neck, striking with fervor. My eyelashes fluttered shut. My orgasm slammed into me and my core gripped him in pulsating throbs.

"Jax. Jaxon. Jaxon." I cried out, half whimpering.

He relentlessly pounded into me, giving me zero mercy.

catalina

I LAY ON THE COUCH, my head cushioned in Ren's lap with a book in hand. Turned out, one of the doors led to a floor to ceiling library, so I'd had plenty to comb through before I settled on the first edition of Pride and Prejudice. I looked up from the book. Ren stared down at me with contemplative focus.

Asher lay behind me, his arm wrapped around my midsection, his head was also on Ren's lap as he held my back flush to his chest.

"Does it bother you?" Nothing but curiosity filled Ren's tone. Was he still talking about the conversation we had earlier?

"Because you were a criminal as a human?"

He hummed his assent. I pursed my lips. I'd abstained from asking further questions because 'ignorance was bliss' and all that. But he seemed almost confused by my lack of reaction. "What did you do?"

"Theft and murder." His brown eyes scanned my face.

"He had a signature kill, too." Asher's fingernail scratched across my throat. I jerked my chin down to block his access to my throat.

"Asher," I complained. He chuckled and retreated. When I returned my attention to Ren, he still stared at me.

"This does not shock you." It wasn't a question.

"That you were just as chaotic as a human? Not so much." What was shocking was his curiosity about how I felt about it.

"You're in a house of criminals and degenerates," Asher murmured in my ear. His hand delved under my long sleeve pajama top. I snorted, wiggling madly against him. His cock stiffened against my ass.

Asher groaned.

"I want your beautiful, tight cunt, *Älskade*." He nipped the shell of my ear. "Ren, would you like to fuck our pretty little human's ass?"

Ren's thigh tensed under my head.

I sank my teeth into my lower lip. My stomach clenched with anticipation.

"Does that require an answer?" he drawled.

"Go retrieve the lube in my bedroom."

Ren's hand cupped the back of my neck, and he propped me up as he slid his leg free. He gently set my head back down. Next thing I heard was him storming up the staircase.

Asher rolled me on top of him. I grinned down at his too beautiful face.

Then the doorbell rang.

"I'll get it," I shouted, sliding off Asher. His hard cock nudged my belly.

"Hurry, Pet." He groaned, cupping his dick. I rushed through the foyer and my socks slipped on the wood floor. I caught myself on the door handle and yanked it open.

The ground dropped from under me. I froze with utter shock as a whoosh of disbelief crippled me.

I couldn't—this wasn't—

catalina

FOR THE SECOND time in the span of a few weeks, my world shifted under my feet. This woman . . . I'd seen her before . . . in the image upstairs.

I thought Peter showing up at the door was the worst that could happen, but I was dead wrong.

The ground fell out from under me, and I wanted to vomit everything I'd eaten.

Imogen shivered, hugging herself. Dirt and blood stained rags draped over her slender form. Her hair framed her lean face in dirty clumps. This . . . was Imogen, but how? She'd died. She wasn't supposed to be here.

How was she here? My pulse skyrocketed.

No way, it couldn't be her. She'd died. I backed away from the door, shaking my head.

Imogen's skin was pale and washed out. In the painting upstairs, she hadn't been given much color, but she hadn't had the shadows beneath her eyes and in the dip of her cheekbones.

I'd never seen an emaciated vampire other than The Pale One, but he was closer to skeletal.

"Who . . ."

Asher stopped in place. I swung my head to her and then back to the frozen vampire. He was more stunned than me. She stumbled forward.

A dry sob wracked her body, and she dropped in an unceremonious pile in the middle of the foyer. I stood. Silent, watching, unable to breathe.

"Did you get the door?" Tobias's voice echoed down the hall as he approached from the kitchen. He scanned what he'd walked into and stuttered to a halt. My attention rose to the steps descending the stairs. Jax stopped halfway down the stairs. His gaze bounced to me and then to Imogen and then back again. He gripped the banister.

Tobias was the first to move.

"Imogen," he murmured, crouching where she huddled. "What happened to you?"

"He had me." Her fangs flashed with her words. "I don't know why he let me go so suddenly. I-I." A shiver coasted down her spine. "That fucking bastard hurt me."

My stomach soured. In sympathy . . . in confusion. She had been held hostage and tortured this entire time? She never died. I clenched my hands at my sides.

Ren's expression twitched the barest bit.

"Who had you, Imogen?" The threat in his voice made my stomach ache.

"Wrenhaven." She curled into her stomach, grimacing. "I am so hungry." She whimpered.

I felt eyes on me. Hers . . . and her vampire males. I was going to vomit.

"You want . . . me . . .?" None of them said anything.

Tobias's jawline twitched as he stared down at his sister. "I'll feed her," I finally croaked, approaching.

I hugged my torso because it felt like I would fall apart if I didn't. My chest hurt.

I slowly approached. She didn't look good. Her scraggly unkept hair hung into her face and dirt smudged her clothing.

Red welts bled at her wrists.

A smidge of sympathy rose to the surface. On an entirely separate note, despite my jealousy, she was injured and I didn't have it in me to turn away despite the visceral need to run the other direction.

I dropped to my knees and sat my ass on my calves. Asher had an expression I'd never seen on him before. He reminded me of Jax. The relaxed version of him was nowhere to be seen.

The one thing that could have sent my entire life into a tailspin sat before me, weakly shivering.

Her pupils were so dilated, her eyes looked black. I pulled back my sleeve and her eyes fastened on the pulse at my wrist. She struck suddenly, wrenching a gasp from my throat. Agony. Blistering agony traveled through my wrist. Like my bones were being ground together in her hand.

I sank my teeth into my tongue, so I didn't burst into tears. She sucked painfully hard. Another deep drag that tugged my breath from my lungs. And then another. I'd been fed on too much recently . . . I couldn't contain my gasp as she sank her teeth in again, opening the wound wider.

Tobias grabbed her jaw and sank his thumb into her cheek. She finally released with a hiss.

I yanked back and my sleeve fell over the bites.

"Go!" Tobias shouted at me.

Jumping to my feet with my head lowered so they wouldn't see the tears in my eyes, I rushed up stairs before I gave into the urge to cry and cling to them. This damn foyer was turning into a curse. Every atom of my make up pulsed with the tattoo of their names.

"Jax and Asher." I froze half-way up the stairs. A few more steps up and I could let loose.

I lifted my chin high and calmly walked up the rest of the way to the second floor. As soon as I turned the corner, tears welled, blinding me as I ran to Asher's bedroom.

A rupture had split through my chest, and it begged for release.

My shoulder smashed into something hard.

"Catalina?" Ren asked, catching my bicep.

God no. I didn't want witnesses to my piss poor insecurity. I had good reason for it. For God's sake, they had a picture of her and all her dresses still stored in the house, of course that hurt. It also didn't help making me feel less crappy.

And one that was not as good as the original.

"Let go," I choked out through my tight throat.

"Ren!" Tobias shouted. Ren's grip flexed.

"Go, Imogen is waiting for you down there," I spat, tears winning. His hand went limp enough for me to slip free and into Asher's room. I kicked the door shut and leaned against it.

God, I was a fucking mess and my wrist wounds hurt.

I couldn't bring myself to go to the basement room they'd set up for me. The colors of the bedroom were exactly how she liked.

I . . . I had been a placeholder.

bastien

CONSCIOUSNESS FADED IN AND OUT. In a moment where the madness released me, the barest moment, I understood my surroundings. The plush bed that creaked when I sat upon it.

A simple undershirt hugged my chest. Why were my arms bare? I scowled as I plucked the ribbed fabric. Asher called this a 'wife-beater'? Preposterous.

He'd yanked the clothes on me even after I tried fighting him against it . . . I squinted toward the living room. What was I thinking about?

I stood and the chains rattled with my movement.

Memories flickered across my thoughts like a photo book, but after the brief flashes, they faded.

Where was I?

The words . . . what was I thinking about? I gripped the chain binding me. My hand stung, agonizing blistering, heat burned my hand. I would . . . I wanted . . . what did I want?

I paced.

Blood. Blood. Blood.
Craving. Thirst. Frenzy.
Her blood. My human.

thank you for reading!

Catalina's story concludes in Feeding Frenzy.

Visit my website for more book information and be sure to join my reader group and follow my social media platforms to keep up with my releases.

acknowledgments

LeeAnne, thank you! I've met so many people in this book world and I am so glad it has brought you into my life.

Undying Thirst ARC team, I appreciate you guys so much. For real, you guys are amazing and I am so blessed.

Thank you to my entire family and to Aaron for supporting my dreams.

Como siempre, gracias a mi mamá y mi papá.

Allie obsessively reads books featuring sexy, possessive heroes and headstrong heroines. So, it's no wonder characters just like that bustle to escape her imagination.

When she's not working away at her keyboard, she can be found in bed with a good book or bingeing Netflix.